SHATTERED SOULS

FOR FIG

PHILOMEL BOOKS
A division of Penguin Young Readers Group.
Published by The Penguin Group. Penguin Group (USA) Inc., 375 Hudson Street, New York, NY 10014, U.S.A. Penguin Group (Canada), 90 Eglinton Avenue East, Suite 700, Toronto, Ontario M4P 2Y3, Canada (a division of Pearson Penguin Canada Inc.). Penguin Books Ltd, 80 Strand, London WC2R 0RL, England. Penguin Ireland, 25 St. Stephen's Green, Dublin 2, Ireland (a division of Penguin Books Ltd). Penguin Group (Australia), 250 Camberwell Road, Camberwell, Victoria 3124, Australia (a division of Pearson Australia Group Pty Ltd). Penguin Books India Pvt Ltd, 11 Community Centre, Panchsheel Park, New Delhi—110 017, India. Penguin Group (NZ), 67 Apollo Drive, Rosedale, Auckland 0632, New Zealand (a division of Pearson New Zealand Ltd). Penguin Books (South Africa) (Pty) Ltd, 24 Sturdee Avenue, Rosebank, Johannesburg 2196, South Africa. Penguin Books Ltd, Registered Offices: 80 Strand, London WC2R 0RL, England.

Published simultaneously in Canada. Printed in the United States of America.

Edited by Jill Santopolo. Design by Amy Wu. Text set in 11.5 point Garamond MT.

Library of Congress Cataloging-in-Publication Data
Lindsey, Mary 1963– Shattered souls / by Mary Lindsey. p. cm.
Summary: When a Texas high school student starts hearing voices, she assumes she is schizophrenic like her father, but instead she finds out that she is a "Speaker" who can communicate with the dead in order to help their troubled souls find resolution.
[1. Ghosts—Fiction. 2. Future life—Fiction. 3. Supernatural—Fiction. 4. Interpersonal relations—Fiction. 5 Galveston (Tex.)—History—20th century—Fiction.] I. Title.
PZ7.L6613Sh 2011 [Fic]—dc22 2010044251

ISBN 978-0-399-25622-6
1 3 5 7 9 10 8 6 4 2

Shattered Souls

MARY LINDSEY

PHILOMEL BOOKS
An Imprint of Penguin Group (USA) Inc

ACKNOWLEDGMENTS

I couldn't have asked for a more professional or supportive group to guide me through my first publishing experience than the amazing folks at Philomel—especially Jill Santopolo, who pulled out her editorial defibrillator paddles and shocked additional life into my story. Thanks (also) to Julia Johnson, Ana Deboo, and Cindy Howle for helping to get my novel in gear with their keen observations and smart copyedits. I also owe a special shout-out to the Penguin art department for creating the most beautiful cover I've ever seen.

This book never would have happened without Wonder Agent Ammi-Joan Paquette. I appreciate your unwavering optimism and confidence in me and your rare ability to deliver the killing blows as skillfully as the roses.

Thank you to my QueryTracker family, especially Patrick McDonald, brainstormer extraordinaire and ever-present shoulder-to-cry-on; to H. L. Dyer, M.D., Carolyn Kaufman, Psy.D., and my sweet "sis" Suzette Saxton for reading and critiquing countless versions of this story; to my lovely, patient friend Jennifer Hunt, who endured many miles and hours with Lenzi, Alden and me (are you sick of us yet?); to Lynn Lorenz for the lightning-quick, sometimes middle-of-the-night emergency rescues; to Stephanie Pickett for loving me no matter how obnoxious I got; and to Suzanne Semans and the studio girls, who provided more encouragement and enthusiasm than a pep squad.

Most of all, I want to express my gratitude to my family, who endured all manner of inconvenience while I struck out in a new direction. Robert, you kept me laughing. Emily, you kept me going. Hannah, you kept me real. Laine, you kept me happy—you always have. I love you guys.

True love is like ghosts, which everybody talks about and few have seen.

—François, duc de La Rochefoucauld, 1613–1680

ONE

The voice of a small child called out from somewhere behind me. *"Please. I need your help."*

I twisted around, heart pounding in my ears, and stared at the empty row of bathroom stalls.

I couldn't be like him. I refused.

Flipping on the sink faucet, I splashed water on my face and took some deep breaths to calm down. This was my imagination, nothing more.

The water dripping down my neck made me shiver. I yanked out a few paper towels and dabbed myself dry, then tossed them in the trash bin. Shaking, I rubbed my arms.

Why was it so cold in here? The bathroom had become a freezer—I could see my breath. Puffing little clouds, I turned around to check the long bank of stalls again.

Nothing.

"It's your imagination, Lenzi," I whispered, trying to calm my heart.

"Help me," the voice of the child begged between sobs.

"This is not real," I chanted. "I'm not hearing anything."

"Please, please," the voice cried.

Maybe there *was* someone there?

I walked slowly down the length of the bathroom toward the crying, which was coming from the handicap-accessible stall at the end. It was like I was in one of those slasher films where the characters can't resist finding the source of the scary sounds. Only, in the movies, this kind of thing always happens in the dark with no one around. The girls' bathroom was flooded with light, and I could hear students outside in the hallway.

I gently pushed the stall door open, but no one was there. I stepped inside. Maybe someone was crouching behind the door.

The second I let go, the door slammed shut behind me with a metallic bang.

"I need your help," the same small voice cried, now from right next to me.

I flinched so hard I smacked my head on the steel stall divider. Fear masked the pain from the lump rising on the back of my skull. There was no one there. I was hearing things, just like he did.

I had to get out. Now!

I yanked the door handle to escape. It wouldn't budge. My

fingers fumbled with the lock, but it was stuck. Gripping the handle, I tugged hard.

"Oh, my God!" I yelled. "Let me out!"

The main door to the bathroom rattled like someone was pulling on it, and I heard shouting out in the hallway. It was Ms. Mueller, who taught eleventh-grade history. Her voice cut through my terror.

"Miss Anderson! How did the door to this restroom get locked?"

Too freaked out to even answer, I slapped the stall door with my hands. "Get me out of here!" The temperature dropped again, and my teeth chattered.

"Help me, please," the child whispered in my ear.

I screamed.

"Miss Anderson! Open this door!" Ms. Mueller shouted from the hallway.

"Let me out of here! Please help me." I dropped to my hands and knees and wiggled under the stall door, clambering to get away from the voice. I jumped to my feet and bolted toward the exit. I jerked the handle of the door to the hallway, but it didn't open. I yanked again. Nothing. I twisted with all my strength on the knob—still nothing.

"I need your help."

"Please," I whispered. "Please go away and leave me alone." I slid down the door and curled into a ball, shivering. Clamping my eyes shut, I prayed it was a waking dream that would end any second. That I wasn't crazy. That I wasn't hallucinating like he did.

A faint sniffling came from the far end of the bathroom, as if the child were weeping. I could barely hear it over the chattering of my teeth. For a moment, I wanted to reach out, offer some comfort. Instead, I unfurled and sat up. "Go away!"

"Help me."

"I can't help you. I *won't* help you." I shook my head, hands over my ears to block out the sound. "You're not real."

The weeping stopped.

I sat in the frozen silence. Listening. Praying.

"Not real," I whispered.

The temperature returned to normal.

Bang, bang.

Ms. Mueller was whacking on the door again. "Unlock the door this minute," she demanded.

I pushed myself up and wrapped my fingers around the door handle, almost afraid to try it. If it didn't open this time, I was going to start screaming again, and I didn't think I'd be able to stop.

After a deep, shaky breath, I turned the knob. It released, and the door swung open easily. Trembling, I took several steps back. I closed my eyes against Ms. Mueller's glare and the curious looks from my classmates. The kind of looks I'd seen so many times as a child. The looks people gave my dad when he had episodes. The looks reserved for crazy people. People like me.

• • •

"You're lucky you didn't get detention, Lenzi," Mom said on the way out of the counselor's office. "Running out of class without permission and locking yourself in the bathroom. That's not like you. Has something happened?"

All the way to the car I wanted to tell her—I really did, but I couldn't do it; it would break her heart, just like it was breaking mine. My chest ached when I thought of what she'd been through and what she might have to go through again.

Sliding into the car, I rolled a hair band off my wrist and pulled my hair back in a ponytail. "I didn't lock the door. It just got stuck or something."

Mom pulled her sunglasses case out of her purse. "The counselor said you were screaming."

Tightening the hair band one more twist, I grimaced when my fingers brushed the lump on the back of my head. "Yeah, it scared me when the door wouldn't open."

She shoved the glasses case back in her purse and turned in her seat to face me. "Do you want to talk to somebody, Lenzi? Dr. Alexander said you could see her anytime."

Not this again. I leaned over, pretending to search for something in the outside pocket of my backpack. Right now I wasn't up to an argument. Imagined or not, the episode in the bathroom with the invisible bogeyman—no, bogey*baby*—had taken all the fight out of me. I was going crazy.

I snapped the seat belt, leaned my seat back, and closed my eyes.

Like flickering snapshots, images of the cemetery in Galveston where Dad was buried flashed through my head. I opened my eyes, and they stopped.

Mom stared at me, her hand on the keys in the ignition. "Are you okay, Lenzi?"

"Yeah, I'm fine, Mom. I just want to get home and shower before Zak takes me out for my birthday."

She started the car. "I'm sorry I have to work tonight, Lenzi. I'll make it up to you next weekend."

"It's fine, Mom. Really." And it was. This was my first birthday without Dad, and hanging out with Zak would make it easier.

I closed my eyes again, and the images flickered. *The gate to the cemetery; the marker on Dad's grave; a tall Celtic cross; a marble angel with a cracked face; a tall, thin guy. The guy was smiling. I liked him. I missed him.* With a gasp, I opened my eyes.

Mom was staring straight ahead, concentrating on the road.

I was losing my mind—no doubt about it. First the voices, and now I was having some kind of hallucinations. My dad had given me a gift this year after all: his schizophrenia.

"Happy birthday, Lenzi," I whispered under my breath.

TWO

At my request, Zak canceled our dinner reservation and picked up sandwiches from my favorite deli. A picnic on my living room floor was the perfect birthday party. Especially with the day I'd had.

"How about a spot under this magnificent oak tree?" he said, gesturing to the support beam across the ceiling. He flipped a blanket in the air, spreading it over the wood floor. "Perfect amount of shade."

I sat cross-legged on the corner of the blanket while he pulled a sandwich out of the bag, unwrapped it, and peeked inside. "Pastrami for me." He pulled another out. "And roast beef for the lady."

I removed my sandwich from the paper wrapper and set it on a napkin. "Thanks for keeping tonight low-key."

"Wanna talk about it?" He popped the top of a Coke and set it next to my knee.

I took a bite and shook my head. He knew I'd been hearing a static buzz for a few days, but the voice thing was different. I wasn't ready to tell him yet.

He shrugged and went to work on his food.

The sandwich wrapper was my favorite texture. Thin and pliable, but stiff enough to hold creases. I closed my eyes and made a fold, then the cross-fold. My fingers slid across the waxy surface as if of their own accord. Folding over, folding under, then a tuck inside a previous pleat. Every piece of paper had its own personality and dictated its shape. This wrapper was a flower. Another petal materialized. I could feel my stress transferring into the hard folds, and I began to relax. The creation of beauty from something formless. I opened my eyes to find Zak smiling. I couldn't help but grin back.

"You do that a lot." He nodded to my hands. "Make stuff out of paper."

I rotated the flower in my hand and folded another petal. "It calms me down. I started doing it when I was twelve, when Dad was hospitalized for the first time."

He popped a couple of chips into his mouth, watching me tuck in the folds of another petal. "So did someone teach you, or did you learn it online or from a book or something?"

I bent the tip of a center petal to curve it. "No. I kind of figured it out on my own, I guess."

"Help me, please," the child's voice cried from right next to me.

I jumped to my feet and backed away, hand over mouth, heart hammering.

Zak was at my side immediately. "What is it, Lenzi?" He placed his hands on my shoulders. "Lenzi?"

"It's, um . . ."

"I need your help."

Not again. I looked in the direction of the voice. "I can't help you."

Zak gave me a little shake. "You okay, babe? Who're you talking to?"

The tears welling in my eyes stung and blurred my vision as the child's sobbing faded to silence.

"Lenzi!" He held my face in his hands. "Lenzi, look at me."

I couldn't bring myself to meet his eyes in case he was giving me the you're-a-crazy-person look, so instead, I wrapped my arms around him and crushed my body to his, feeling safer near his size and warmth.

"It's not just noise in my head anymore," I whispered against his chest. "Now I'm hearing voices. Just like Dad."

I could barely hear him over my sobs. Hearing voices was terrifying, but losing Zak would be worse. He was the only thing anchoring me to reality.

"Shhh," he whispered into my hair. "Hey. 'S gonna be okay. You're not your dad." He rubbed his hands up and down my spine and kissed the top of my head while I caught my breath.

"You're not your dad, Lenzi. You listening? You're not any more like him than I'm like my old man. And I'm not a cokehead, right?"

I nodded, still unable to look him in the eye. I focused on the tingly trail his hands were leaving on my back rather than the churning dread in my chest. Telling him about the voices didn't make me feel better. It just made my worst fear seem more real.

He stopped rubbing my back and leaned down to look at me, smoothing my hair away from my face. "I have a present for you."

We'd agreed he wouldn't get me a present. He was struggling to pay his bills and community college tuition, so we'd decided dinner was enough. But before I could protest, he put his finger to my lips. "Nuh-uh. I didn't pay for anything. I made it myself."

He took my hand and led me to the sofa. "Sit here, and I'll be right back." He flashed a grin, dimples and all, and disappeared through the front door, returning in moments with his guitar case. He snapped it open, pulled out his guitar, and sat on the coffee table in front of me. "Ready?" he asked, tuning it.

I leaned back and took a deep breath. Maybe he was right. Maybe I wasn't like Dad. I nodded and smiled.

I could sort of play the guitar, but Zak was a fantastic musician. He was especially good at Spanish classical, which I couldn't play at all. Dad could a little bit, but not like Zak. I watched in amazement as his fingers flew over the strings, creating a complex, bittersweet tune. Within only a few measures, I found myself breathing in time with the rhythm, heart in sync with the melody line. The song built, and by the end, I was completely engrossed, almost out of breath when the vibrations of the last chord stopped humming through the wood of his guitar.

"Wow," was all I could manage.

Zak smiled and set his guitar in the case. "You like it?"

"Love it. You just made that up?"

He straightened and ran his hands through his thick hair. "Not just now. I've been working on it for a while."

It was the best gift ever—enough to almost make me forget the rotten day I'd had. "That was amazing. Thank you."

"I credit my inspiration." He sat back down on the coffee table. "You do that to me, you know—make me better than I really am." My heart skipped a beat when he knelt in front of me, placing his hands on my thighs. The heat from his palms seeped through my jeans and radiated through my body, making me melt into the sofa cushion. "Glad you liked it." He threaded his fingers through my hair at the back of my neck and pulled me to him. His lips were as warm as his hands. "Happy birthday, babe."

I closed my eyes as he deepened the kiss. Immediately, the images I'd seen in the car ran through my head. They were like vivid memories playing over and over, only other than Dad's tombstone, I didn't recall ever seeing any of these things in real life. When the guy flashed through my brain, there was a strange constriction in my chest, like I'd lost something and I needed to find it. I jerked my eyes open.

Zak stilled and stared at me. "What's wrong?"

"Nothing."

He got up, placed his guitar in the case, and snapped it shut. "Talk to me, Lenzi. We don't keep secrets from each other. What's going on?"

I couldn't answer. It was bad enough I was hearing voices. If I told him I was seeing things, he might tell my mom. Or worse, he might give up on me. I couldn't bear that.

I'd lost all my friends when Dad flipped out, so I didn't really mind it when we had to move to Galveston to be closer to the hospital. We hadn't even finished unpacking when he died. Right after the funeral, Mom and I moved back to Houston. Zak had been through some hard times himself, so he accepted me as I was. I didn't have to pretend or cover up my past. But hallucinations might be a deal breaker.

"I just miss Dad," I said, which was true. "This is my first birthday since he died." I laced my fingers together to keep from fidgeting.

Hands on hips, he studied me. "You sure you're okay? You're acting strange." He sat down next to me and pulled my hands into his lap.

"I'm fine," I said. "I've just been super edgy all day."

He squeezed my fingers. "Did that Xanax you took yesterday make the noises stop?"

I folded my legs under me and shifted to face him. "Yeah."

"Have you tried it on the voices?"

"No."

"Do you have any more?"

I nodded. "There's still more than half a bottle left in my mom's medicine cabinet." Mom had pretty much popped them like candy during Dad's last hospital stay, but she hadn't taken any since the move. He let go of my hands and followed me up the stairs to the bathroom I shared with her. At the back of the medicine cabinet, I found the prescription bottle of Xanax. "Use as directed for anxiety," the label said.

I'd do anything to shut Bogeybaby up. I bit one of the long, white pills on the first score line, stuck my mouth under the sink faucet, and swallowed the quarter of it. Zak took the remainder from me and dropped it into the bottle with the other pills, then handed them to me. "Keep these close, Lenzi, in case it happens again." He brushed my hair behind my shoulder. "Let's hope it doesn't. I'm worried about you." He wrapped me in his arms and stroked my hair.

I was worried too. The images added a whole new layer of crazy. I closed my eyes to see if it would happen again. Right away, the graveyard images began. I needed to go there.

"Zak," I said, "will you help me? There's something I have to do."

THREE

The cemetery was locked up tight with a chain strung through the wrought-iron gate and secured with a rusty padlock. The peeling paint on the sign at the entrance read GATES CLOSE AT DARK. NO TRESPASSING.

After passing me his guitar case through the bars, Zak handed me my dad's and hoisted his leg over the gate. When he dropped next to me, his boots crunched as he hit the gravel. He unscrewed the top on his bottle of Jack Daniels and took a swig while I sent Mom a text message telling her I was out with Zak and would be home late.

The Xanax had made the voice in my head go away, but not the constant noise that sounded like static on an out-of-tune radio. I wondered why the pill had worked on the static yesterday, but not today.

"I'm happy we're here if it makes you feel better," Zak said, taking his guitar from me, "but I can't believe this is how you want to spend your birthday."

I couldn't believe it either, honestly, but something in me *had* to come here.

The cemetery was in a rough part of town, so I'd never been here at night. I didn't know what scared me more—the overall creepiness of the place, the prospect of being busted at any minute by the police for entering the closed cemetery, or the fact that Zak had opened a bottle of Jack Daniels when he crossed the causeway bridge and had been drinking ever since.

We walked down the narrow paved road running through the center of the dilapidated older section of the cemetery and passed a small white and green building, probably a caretaker's shed. I stepped over a low brick retaining wall that defined the newer section where Dad had been buried, and Zak followed.

Even though it was October and the air had begun to cool off from the scorching Texas summer, it was still so humid the air felt liquid. The moon shone bright enough to bathe the cemetery in blue light, causing the monuments to cast long, eerie shadows across the grass.

I inhaled, took in the salty sea breeze, and rubbed my hands over the goose bumps on my arms. I knew the beach was almost a mile away, but it still unnerved me. From the time I was little I'd hated the beach for no apparent reason. Mom called my fear of the beach a childhood phobia, but I didn't seem to be outgrowing it. I zipped up my blue windbreaker and dragged my hair out of my face, determined not to let an irrational fear get the best of me.

Zak reached over and took my hand. "You okay?"

"Yeah, I'm good," I lied. I laced my fingers through his and gave his hand a squeeze. "Thanks for being so cool about bringing me all the way down here to Galveston."

"I just want you to feel better, babe." He set his guitar down and wrapped me in his arms, giving me a slow, tender kiss that made my knees weak. His lips were warm and tasted like whiskey. For a moment, I forgot all about noises, and voices, and hallucinations.

From the corner of my eye, I saw something move in the shadows of the trees lining the perimeter fence. Then there was the distinct pop of a twig snapping. I pulled away from Zak and held my breath, listening and watching the darkness beneath the trees.

Zak stepped into my line of vision. "Something wrong?"

"Shhh. Listen."

"What?"

"Shhh!"

Trembling, I studied the shadows. The sensation of being watched was overwhelming—like insects creeping under my skin. I clutched Zak's large hand and listened, gripping Dad's guitar as tightly as I could.

Nothing.

No movement and no sound other than my frantic heartbeat

and the static in my head. *Fantastic.* Add paranoia to my list of crazies.

I took a deep breath and released his hand. "It was nothing. Just my nerves, I guess."

This was the first time Zak had ever given me the you're-a-crazy-person look—or at least the first time I'd seen it.

Blinking back tears, I picked up my guitar and continued toward the corner where my dad was buried, determined not to look back over my shoulder at the trees.

Dad's headstone was the only one carved from black granite in this section, which made it easy to find. The surface was polished to such a high sheen, you could see your reflection in it. I stopped several yards away and sat on a bench, pulling his guitar case against my chest. My insides churned, and I knew I'd break down if I got too close. Zak plopped down next to me and unscrewed the top of his bottle.

"Want some?" he asked, whiskey sloshing as he pushed it toward me.

"No. Thanks." I bit my lip and fought the urge to ask him to slow down.

"You should tell your mom what's going on," he said, taking another swallow.

"I can't. She might have to lock me up, like she did with my dad—it'd wreck her." I ran my fingers over the guitar case and popped it open, but couldn't bring myself to lift the guitar out.

Zak pulled his out and began tuning. "What're we playing?"

I swept my palm over the surface of Dad's guitar. "'Free Fallin',' " I said. It was Dad's favorite song and the last one we'd played together. This guitar hadn't been touched since. I'd used my own, but hadn't had the guts to even look at his. I lifted the guitar out and laid it in my lap as Zak strummed the first few chords of the song, checking his tuning. Waves of grief swept through me as the crisp smell of mahogany and Dad rose from deep inside the instrument.

"Whoa. Cool guitar," Zak said, shifting on the bench so he was angled toward me.

"Yeah, it's not spruce." It had a natural matte finish and was the color of chocolate. Dad said he bought it because it was the same shade of brown as my eyes. The strings moaned as I ran my hand over them, bumping my fingertips along the frets. It wasn't as out of tune as I'd have expected for having been untouched for nine months. I could almost feel Dad's hand on mine as I adjusted the pegs. The patch of patina where Dad had worn the surface down below the strings was smoother than the rest of the wood, and I ran my palm over it.

"I couldn't help him, Zak."

He stopped strumming, but said nothing. That was one of the things I liked most about Zak: he was a great listener.

I wiped a tear off the top of the guitar with my sleeve. "Mom and I tried everything, but it wasn't enough. Our love wasn't enough to keep him here."

"Oh, babe. I'm so sorry." He tucked my hair behind my ear.

"I couldn't save him." The noise in my head became a little louder, or maybe I just was more aware of it at that moment. "Nobody's going to be able to save me, either."

"I'm here, babe." He laid his hand over mine. "We'll get through this. It'll be different for you. The pills help, right?"

I wanted to believe him. I really did, but something in me knew what was happening was out of my control. Nothing I could do would stop it.

Zak screwed the top off the Jack Daniels. "To your dad," he said, holding the bottle to the moon before taking a gulp. He passed it to me.

"To you, Dad," I whispered to his tombstone before raising the bottle to my lips, shuddering as I swallowed.

I placed the bottle under the bench and strummed the first few chords of "Free Fallin'."

I didn't know how drunk Zak was until we began to play. He knew the song, but his fingering was sloppy and his rhythm was off, which was never the case when he was sober. Eventually, he stopped even trying to play, and I finished the last chorus by myself.

I'd come to the cemetery thinking it would help my restlessness. Singing to Dad hadn't brought the relief I'd expected. In fact, I felt edgier—like I was missing something.

Zak snapped the clasp on his guitar case and scooted closer while I strummed. I didn't struggle when he took the guitar from me because he was pretty messed up, and I didn't want to damage it. After it was safely in the case, I moved to lean against the mausoleum on the other side of Dad's grave.

Zak followed. "I can make you feel better," he whispered in my ear as he put his hands on the pitted marble either side of my head. "Make you forget this."

I looked at the headstones around us. "Zak. Not now," I said, placing my hands on his broad chest.

"C'mon, Lenzi." He ran his hands under my shirt, fingertips grazing my skin.

I grabbed his wrists. "Zak, please. Not at my father's grave."

He froze, then took a couple of steps back and put his hands up in surrender. "You're right, babe. Got carried away. I just wanted to make you feel better." He shoved his hands in his pockets and shrugged. "Sorry."

I exhaled slowly through my nose and relaxed against the mausoleum.

He glanced over his shoulder at Dad's tombstone. "You want some time alone?"

Crossing my arms over my chest, I nodded.

"Whatever you need, babe." He gave me a kiss on the forehead before he shuffled off to a bench in the moon shadow of a vine-covered mausoleum and lay down. Good. In a few hours he'd sober up enough to drive me home.

I stayed leaning against the mausoleum for a few moments, watching Zak's chest rise and fall. I wanted to apologize, but thought better of it.

It worried me when Zak got wasted. His dad died from an overdose when he was a little boy—Zak had been too young to even remember him—and his mom kicked Zak out when he graduated from high school last year. That's probably why we were so good together—he understood loss and loneliness. But I was lucky compared to Zak. At least I'd gotten to know my dad. He never even had that chance.

As his breathing slowed and he drifted into sleep, the shadows of the trees in the moonlight played across his face, accentuating his strong jaw and high cheekbones.

I reached into the compartment under the neck of Dad's guitar and pulled out the lotus flower I'd made from the sandwich wrapper.

I knelt in the grass in front of Dad's tombstone, my reflection in the shiny surface blue and ghostly, and placed my paper flower on his grave. "I'm going nuts, Dad." I ran my fingers over the carved letters of his name. He'd only been forty-five when he parked his car on the train track. And he had started hearing voices when he was in college. It was happening to me much younger. "I don't know what to do. I don't want to end up like you."

I placed my palm flat against the slick blank space where Mom's name would be carved when she died, and the chill of the stone seeped into my hand.

Another face appeared next to mine in the reflective surface of the tombstone. The face of the guy I'd seen in the car when my eyes were closed. Crap. Now I was hallucinating with my eyes open. And even after taking Xanax.

I ran my fingertips over his reflection.

"You've kept me waiting forever, Rose," he said in a smooth, rich voice.

I sat back and stared at the vivid image my mind had conjured in that reflection. He was tall and thin, with longish hair. Well, if I was going to hear bogeymen, I supposed it was better that I could see them too, especially if they looked like this one. But why would I conjure one that called me by my middle name?

I'd had enough weird for one day. It was time to relegate him to my imagination where he belonged.

"Okay, you can just take off now." I waved my hand toward the entrance, shooing him away like a child.

"I can understand if you want me reassigned."

I covered his reflection with my hands. "Back you go. Back to my brain. This isn't really happening."

"Rose, look at me," he said. The grass crunched behind me as if someone were really there.

Oh, God. My hallucinations were taking corporeal form.

I covered my face with my hands and shuddered. No wonder Dad had been terrified. How much of this could I take before I ended up just like him? My heart pounded in my ears.

There was a gentle touch on my shoulder. "Look at me."

I jerked away. "No. This isn't real." I pressed my palms tight to my eyes and took a deep breath. "You're going to go away now," I ordered. Shouldn't a figment of my imagination do what I wanted it to do? "I'm going to open my eyes, and you're going to be gone. Got it? Opening on three. One, two, three."

I opened my eyes and looked straight into the eyes of the guy squatting right next to me.

"Shit!" I jumped up and backed away.

"Rose—"

"Stop calling me that! My name isn't Rose. I told you to go away." I held up my hands to ward him off.

His brow furrowed. "Your name isn't Rose?"

Well, technically it was. Sort of. My mom dreamed she had a daughter named Rose the night before I was born. She thought it was some sort of message, but she and my dad had already agreed on Lenzi, so she stuck it in the middle. But I wasn't telling that to some freaky hallucination. Besides, I'd never told a living soul my middle name. I hated it.

"No. My name isn't Rose."

"How odd . . . It's your seventeenth birthday today, right?"

For a moment, I was startled that he knew stuff about me—but hey, he was just a figment of my imagination, right? He'd know everything I knew. I decided to play along. "Yeah, it's my birthday, why?"

The boy shoved the hair out of his eyes and let out an audible sigh. "What a relief. For a minute, I thought I was too early. I mean, I felt your soul calling, and I came right away. I wasn't really expecting you yet. I'm only seventeen. Usually, I'm at least twenty-one when you show up. I figured I had four more years before you'd emerge. Or maybe even longer. When you denied me, I thought something was wrong." He smiled. "Your sense of humor is seriously lacking, Rose. You've never been very funny."

"Yeah, right. My soul called you." This hallucination might be mildly amusing if this guy would quit calling me Rose.

A troubled look crossed his face. "Of course it did."

Enough is enough. "Look, whoever you are, this—"

"Alden. My name is Alden, Rose. You know that." From the look on his face you'd have thought he was watching a car wreck.

"Okay . . . Alden, this has been a lot of fun and all, but it's time for this little mind trip or whatever it is to end. Time for you to go away."

He shrugged his shoulders. "Maybe you want a different Protector. Say the word, and I can be reassigned. I can certainly understand that, considering how you died."

Well, that scored a perfect ten on the creep-o-meter. "I died?"

"Yes, Rose, yes."

"Very funny. And just how did I die?"

"You drowned, right here on Galveston Island in the Great Storm of 1900. Thousands of people died."

I had no idea I possessed such a vivid imagination. I looked down at Dad's tombstone. Is this what his hallucinations were like?

"I will not end up like that." I pointed at Dad's grave with a trembling finger. "Please, please go away."

"Clearly, you're not ready yet. You know where to find me when you are." He put his warm hands on either side of my neck, and a crazy jolt of current ran through me, causing tingles of electricity to shoot down every nerve in my body. I gasped. He backed up several steps and smiled. "I'm glad you've returned." He then retreated soundlessly into the shadows of the trees.

It took a moment for my pulse to slow enough for me to catch my breath. I placed my hands on either side of my neck where he'd touched me.

I had to get out of this place. Had to get out *now*. It was making things worse.

Zak was sprawled across the bench, bottle of Jack on its side on the ground. He was so wasted, I'd probably have to call my mom. *Please, no,* I groaned inwardly. If I ended up calling her, I'd never hear the end of it. I should have let her teach me to drive last semester when she offered. No. Crazy people shouldn't drive—they end up like Dad.

After pouring out what was left of the whiskey, I nudged Zak on the shoulder. "Zak, wake up. It's time to go." No reaction. "Zak! Come on." I put my hands on his cheeks and shook his head from side to side. He made some snorting sounds, but didn't even open his eyes. Damn.

I pulled out my cell phone to call Mom. Great. No signal. I

knew there was reception near the front gate because I'd texted her there.

Lugging Dad's guitar, I wandered through the older section of the cemetery, making my way to the gate. A strange pang of familiarity flared as I passed a Celtic cross. It was enormous—at least twelve feet tall—looming over the surrounding monuments like a sentinel for the dead. When I reached an angel with a cracked face, it dawned on me why I was having such an intense sense of déjà vu: these were the objects that had flickered through my brain earlier today—these and the guy from my hallucination.

I stopped at the angel. Moss grew from the crack in her white marble face, making her even more tragic in her perpetual state of mourning. I reached up and ran my fingertips over the bristly moss, then crouched down to read the pedestal: ROSE 1831–1875. Underneath, barely legible due to the corrosion of the marble, was carved UNTIL WE MEET AGAIN.

I couldn't help but feel I was supposed to do something. What? Maybe it was part of the craziness. Hell, maybe I was at home asleep and I'd wake up any second, ending this nightmare.

"Looking for someone?" The voice was deep and soft. And *close.*

I shuddered, but didn't scream. When I turned, I found the guy from my imagination a few feet away, leaning casually against a crumbling mausoleum—only now I wasn't so sure he was imaginary. He looked and acted too real. My reaction when he touched me had certainly been no hallucination. The realization that this might not be a dream raged through my body like fire, prickles of fear rolling in waves over my skin. If this was reality, it might be worse than being crazy.

"I knew you'd come, Rose."

I closed my eyes and opened them again, hoping he'd vanish along with my fear.

A troubled look crossed his face. For several moments, he studied me. "You're frightened. This isn't an act. You really don't remember me, do you?"

"No."

"But you knew where to find me."

"No. I just . . ." I looked at the angel, then backed a step away from him.

"Rose, wait." He flipped his hair out of his eyes—a totally futile gesture; the salty, wet wind blew it right back. "I . . . wow. Well, I don't quite know what to do from here. This has never happened to us before. In fact, I've never heard of it happening to anyone before."

I hugged Dad's guitar to my chest. "Yeah, well, lots of things happen to me that don't happen to other people."

"Let me guess." He gave me a half smile. "You think you're crazy. You think you're hearing voices."

I nodded.

He took a step closer. "Well, you're wrong on one of those points." He placed his hand on my shoulder; a warm current flowed from where he touched me and spread through my chest. "You're not crazy. I can prove it if you'll let me."

I took a deep breath as the freaky calm spread through me. "What about the voices?"

"Those are real. That's why I'm here. I can help you."

It was a trick. I jerked my shoulder away and backed up a few steps.

The guy actually believed my voices were real—if he wasn't some figment of my imagination, then he was even nuttier than I was.

I needed to get to the front gate, but part of me wanted to touch him again. To feel that warmth cascade through me. I moved away and pretended to study headstones. My mind kept returning to what he'd said about my death—something about a storm that killed thousands of people. I wandered down the row of graves reading dates on the old, vandalized headstones.

Undaunted, he followed. "Are you looking for something or someone in particular?"

My mind was desperately trying to make sense of this craziness. If I could prove the stuff about the storm wasn't real, maybe I could disprove the other things too. "Well, you mentioned a storm or something. You said that it happened in 1900, right?" I looked over my shoulder to find him following closely, only a foot or so away.

"September 8, 1900," he replied, moving up to walk beside me.

I shifted the guitar to my other hand, putting it between us. "And you said lots of people died."

"Over six thousand on this island alone. You were one of them, Rose."

I pointed to the marble angel. "Is that supposed to be my grave?"

He nodded.

"Why is the date of death 1875 instead of 1900?"

"That was from several cycles ago." He shoved his hands in his pockets and looked at the angel. "Your body was never found after the storm."

I had him now. I stopped and set the guitar down. "Yeah, right. Well, then, if all those other people died too—thousands of them—why aren't there *any* grave markers with that date? I haven't even found one from 1900."

"You won't find many. There were too many bodies to bury. It was a real health hazard," he replied. "Corpses everywhere. Some of them were put on a barge, weighted down, and thrown out in the bay. That didn't work, though, because they washed back up. We ended up burning most of them."

"We?"

"I lived through it. I was here for the aftermath. Fortunately, I don't remember most of what happened right after the storm. I've read about it to fill in the holes. All I really remember is the smell. The horrible smell of death . . . and looking for you, Rose. But that was another lifetime. That's behind me now. And here you are." He touched his fingertips to my cheek, which caused my body to react more than any kiss I'd ever shared with Zak. Gooseflesh broke out on my arms, and my heart thumped so loudly, I could hear it.

"Look, whoever you are—"

"Alden."

"Right. Alden." I picked up the guitar. "My name is *not* Rose. I have no idea who or what you think I am, but clearly you're mistaken. I want you to leave me alone now."

I turned to walk away. He threw himself into my path, arms outstretched. "Wait. How do you plan to get home? Please let me give you a ride. Don't get in a car with that guy tonight," he said.

"You know what? In many ways, you're scarier than he is. I think I'll take my chances. Please leave me alone."

"Help me!" Fear washed through me in a sharp, painful wave. It was the bogeybaby again.

Alden closed his eyes and smiled.

"Did you hear that?" I whispered, setting the guitar down.

He didn't open his eyes. "No, I don't hear hindered spirits. I feel them through you."

"Hindered spirits . . . you mean *ghosts*?"

Still smiling, he opened his eyes and nodded.

"Oh, God. You're saying it's a dead person talking to me? Make it go away." I sidled closer to him, covering my ears with my hands. "Make it leave me alone."

"The intensity of your fear makes it hard to concentrate.

Shhh." He took my hand in his, and I immediately felt better; this time when he touched me, it was like a sedative radiating through my body. Some part of me—the wise part—knew I should jerk my hand back and get away from this boy as fast as possible. The crazy part of me wanted to grab his other hand and never let go.

I flinched when Bogeybaby made another plea for help.

"Rose, all you have to do is tell it to leave you alone. Tell it to go away."

"Go away! Beat it. Get lost!" I commanded the empty air. I held my breath for several moments and waited. "Okay," I said after several more seconds of silence. I slipped my hand from his and slumped down on the bottom step of a mausoleum. "That seems to have worked."

When Alden sat next to me, I scooted to the edge of the concrete step to put some distance between us. What happened when he touched me wasn't normal. Nothing about him was.

"It will only work for a while," he warned. "It will come back until you help it. That's your job."

"My what?"

"Your job." He plucked a long blade of grass growing through a crack in the step. "So, what was it?"

"What was *what*?"

He wrapped the grass around his finger. "The Hindered. The voice you heard. Was it male or female?"

"I don't know. It sounded like a little kid."

"You could resolve a child. What did it want you to do?"

"I have no idea. It just kept asking me for help."

"Call it back. Let's find out what it wants," he suggested.

I jumped up. "What! Are you nuts? Call it back? I want it to go away forever."

Alden chuckled. "What are you afraid of? It can't hurt you while I'm here. Let me show you."

I backed up. "No way. You're crazier than I am—and that says something."

"Come on, Rose. I'll talk you through it. Children are easy."

I grabbed the guitar and headed down the overgrown path that led to the road running through the cemetery. "Zak will be worried. I've gotta get back," I shot over my shoulder.

"Zak's not worried about you at all," Alden called from the step. "He doesn't even know you're gone. Please, don't go back. I can help you."

I slowed my pace. He was right. Zak didn't even know I existed right now. I was hoping he'd sober up, but for all I knew, he'd sleep all night. Ridiculous as it seemed, my chances were probably better with this guy.

"I'll drop it. I won't ask you to call the Hindered. Stay here and talk to me. Don't go back to that guy. He's dangerous."

I stopped. "And you're not?"

"No. And I'm not crazy. Neither are you. Let me prove it. Give me five minutes. Please. Five minutes, and then I'll go away if you still want me to."

FOUR

My options sucked. I didn't feel safe in this part of town alone, so either I returned to Zak, who was completely wasted, or I stayed with Ghost Boy.

How had this happened? I knew one thing for certain: I wouldn't let myself get into a situation like this again. I started walking away from both of them. Once the gate was in sight, I pulled my cell phone out and checked for signal. Yes! It was weak, but at least could I make a call. After a long interrogation, Mom agreed to come get me.

"You have until she gets here to prove you're not crazy," I said as I headed toward the caretaker's shed at the entrance to the cemetery.

"How long will that be?" Alden asked.

"I don't know. Less than an hour, probably." I immediately regretted giving out that much information.

He grinned. "You live in Houston."

"No. Not exactly." How could I have been so freaking stupid?

"My family lives in West University. Maybe we're neighbors?"

"No."

Alden jumped up from his perch on the mausoleum step and followed. "I would have taken you home."

I walked around to the far side of the small stone building. I knew he was right behind me because his boots crunched through the dry grass. "It's kind of far. Mom will love this anyway. She'll have a long time to lecture me on my bad choices."

"Maybe you should listen to her," Alden suggested as he rounded the corner of the shed.

"Maybe you should mind your own business."

"You *are* my business. My job. You are what I do."

I whipped around to face him. "Well, if I'm your job, you're fired. You creep me out."

"That's not my intention." He took several steps back. "This is new to me too. Let me help you, Rose."

"My name is Lenzi. *Lenzi.* Not Rose. Please stop calling me that." It was really irritating.

"I'm sorry. This is the first time you've changed your name. Give me some time to get used to it . . . Lenzi."

I sat down on the sidewalk in front of the caretaker shed. From there I could see Zak if he woke up, plus the entrance gate to the cemetery was close enough that I could get to it if Ghost Boy made a move. But he didn't. He perched on a short, thick grave marker across from me and sat in silence for what felt like forever, closing his eyes occasionally, as if he were listening for something or meditating.

I glanced at my watch. "If you're trying to convince me you're not crazy, you're failing miserably."

"Okay. I'll let the facts prove my sanity. You are a Speaker. I'm your Protector. Every Speaker is paired with a Protector."

"Whatever." I slumped against the shed wall.

"We work for the IC—the Intercessor Council—an entity designed to intercede on behalf of the dead. Your job as a Speaker is to help hindered spirits resolve the problems that are keeping them Earth-bound. Sometimes it's easy. You share your body with them—"

I jumped up. "No way. I don't share my body!"

"Please hear me out. Sometimes the Hindered tell you their problems and then they go on their way. Other times, they aren't simply hindered by something. Sometimes they are impaired. Those souls are called the Malevolent. They try to take your body as their own. If they can force your soul out, they can live again using your body. When you hear about exorcisms and ghosts tearing up houses and paranormal events like that, it's almost always a Malevolent. That's why I'm here. I protect you from the Malevolent when you share your body with another soul. I keep you intact."

He was totally making this stuff up. It was either the most

elaborate come-on ever or he needed serious psychological help. "I share my body with another soul?"

"Yes."

"Look. I'm not sharing my body with anyone." I walked to the entrance gate, pushed Dad's guitar through the bars, and began to scale it. He caught me by the ankle before I reached the top.

"Stop it. Let go of me," I cried.

"Where are you going?" He was gripping my ankle tightly in one hand.

Panic made my voice waver. "To meet my mom. She'll be here soon. Let me go."

"I'll let you go when you come to your senses. A girl like you won't last fifteen minutes outside that gate. Stay with me until your mother arrives."

"Let go. You're scaring me."

"Good," he said. "At least you haven't lost all your common sense." He grabbed me by the waist and easily wrenched me from the iron gate, dropping me roughly to the ground. I didn't get up for fear he'd grab me again.

"Let me tell you something, Rose. This isn't a game I'm playing. It's not me you need to fear. You are in a cemetery in a bad neighborhood in the middle of the night with a guy who's so drunk he passed out, and *I'm* the thing that frightens you? Don't you think I've had ample opportunity to hurt you if that was my plan? I could take you right now, and no one would even hear you scream. If I wanted to hurt you, you'd be hurt."

I remained crouched on the ground by the gate as he stomped several yards down the road that cut through the center of the cemetery. He ran his hands through his hair before sitting on the brick retaining wall that surrounded the southeast section. He was close enough to catch me if I tried to run. He stared straight ahead, avoiding eye contact, which suited me just fine. I pulled Dad's guitar back through the gate and then shifted to a more comfortable position with my legs folded under me.

He was right; I was my own worst enemy. No doubt my mom would tell me all about it the entire way home. *Happy birthday.*

The moon was higher in the sky, providing more light. I couldn't tell what color his eyes were, but Alden had long, light brown, maybe blond hair; it was hard to tell in the moonlight. He had angular features. If it weren't for the fact he was a crazy, creepy ghost boy, I'd have to admit he was totally hot.

"That's better," he said, as if to himself.

"What's better?" I asked.

"You are. You still don't believe me, though, do you?"

"No, I think you're full of crap. And what do you mean, I'm 'better'?"

"I feel your soul responding to your emotions. We're linked. It's how I found you. It's how I protect you."

He could *feel* my emotions? I remained still, trying to get my head around this bizarre scenario. I was less frightened of him now than I was before. I was also pretty convinced that he really believed this whole reincarnated ghost mediator thing.

"I'm sorry, Lenzi," he whispered. "It's frustrating. I know it's hard for you too. I'll try to be more patient. I apologize for losing my cool, but I couldn't risk letting you get hurt."

I moved to the wall across from him, keeping the narrow cemetery road between us, and stared at the broken, vandalized monuments. The windows of the mausoleums were boarded or barred and seemed too low. I noticed the doors were short too. "What's the deal with this place? Is it a graveyard for hobbits or something? The doors are only three feet tall." I plucked a broad-leafed weed from between the bricks.

Alden chuckled. "No. It's because of the storm I told you about."

I turned the leaf over and folded a crease in the center from bottom to tip. "The one where I supposedly died in some past life?"

"Yes." He smiled.

Crazy Ghost Boy. I rolled my eyes. "Were people only a couple of feet tall back then?"

"No. The ground has been raised several feet. The bottom two or three feet of the buildings are underground. The headstones look normal because they were placed on top of the new dirt. The mausoleums were too difficult to raise. Some areas of the island closer to the Gulf are more than fifteen feet higher above sea level than they were in 1900."

Working from the outside in, I folded the leaf into accordion pleats. "Did the storm raise the ground level?"

"No. Men did. After the storm, they built the seawall and raised the level of the island by pumping a slurry of sand and water from the bay and harbor onto the island. They lifted some of the buildings up on screw jacks before they filled underneath. It was amazing."

He didn't seem like a high school boy. "How do you know all of this stuff?"

"I was there," he reminded me as he stood.

I dropped my leaf fan and hopped to my feet. "Oh, no. You stay right where you are."

"I'm not crazy, Rose . . . Lenzi. I can prove it." My heart shifted into overdrive as he moved toward me. "Let me put my soul in your body. It will only take a second. Then you'll believe me." He grasped my hands, and that electrical sensation hummed up my arms and into my chest again. I wanted to lean into him and have that current run all the way through me.

"What the hell do you think you're doing?" Zak yelled from several yards away.

Alden tightened his hold on my hands and only smiled in response.

I jerked my hands away and stepped back from Alden, bumping into Zak, who roughly put his arm around my shoulders, causing me to jump.

"Is this guy giving you trouble, babe?" Zak growled, squeezing me territorially and dropping his guitar case. I could feel his muscles twitching. Zak wasn't totally sober, but he *was* totally pissed. He was going to flatten Alden. A bona fide testosterone fest was not the way I wanted to celebrate my birthday.

"No! No, Zak. Everything's cool. We were just talking. He's, uh . . . an old friend." I was glad my voice didn't squeak.

Alden straightened to his full height. He didn't appear frightened of Zak at all. "Yeah, we've known each other practically forever."

Zak's fingers clenched into a fist on my shoulder.

"It's okay, Zak," I assured him.

"Like hell, it is." Zak took a step toward Alden, who didn't even blink. In fact, he smiled. Zak was no taller than Alden, but he was much larger, industrial strength. I cringed when I pictured the potential outcome if Zak went all tough-guy.

I grabbed the back of his shirt. "No, Zak. Please. It's my birthday." I wrapped my arms around his waist, doing my best to convince him to let it go. "For me?" His muscles relaxed, and I dropped my arms from around him.

Alden held his hand out. "I'm Alden Thomas."

Zak didn't shake his hand, but pulled me to him instead. "I'm Zak Reynolds. Lenzi's boyfriend."

Alden winked at me. "Yeah, I kinda picked up on that."

My phone rang. I wiggled loose from Zak's possessive grip and pulled my cell out of my purse. It was Mom. "Hello?"

Even through the bad connection, my mom's anger came through loud and clear. "I've crossed the causeway and I'm on Broadway. Where in the cemetery are you, Lenzi?"

"I'm at the gate near the corner of Fortieth and Broadway."

My mom disconnected the call. She was in total Momzilla mode. This was going to be bad. I shoved my phone back into my purse.

"She's almost here," I said, walking toward the gate.

"You called your mom to come get you? Why didn't you just wake me up, Lenzi?"

I stopped and turned to face Zak. "I tried."

He strode over and placed his hands on my shoulders. There was none of the electric current I felt when Alden touched me, only weight. "I'm sorry, babe. Really. Just call her back and tell her I'll take you home."

I crossed my arms. "No, Zak. I'm not getting in a car with you. You can ride with Mom and me, or we can follow you to make sure you get home okay."

He looked over his shoulder at Alden, who cocked an eyebrow.

His grip tightened on my shoulders almost to the point of pain. "I'm fine to drive. And I don't need your mom to follow me like I'm some baby who can't find my way home." He pushed me away. "I'm outta here." He staggered to the gate, awkwardly scaled it, and landed with a thud on his feet on the other side, catching the bars for balance. He made it to his car, and after cranking the engine several times before it started, pulled away from the curb.

I rubbed my shoulders where Zak had grabbed me and

watched him round the corner at the end of the block. He'd told me he had a bad temper, but this was the first time I'd really seen it.

"Well. He's quite the catch," Alden said.

I stomped past him and snatched Zak's guitar case handle, jerking it from the pavement where he'd dropped it.

Alden followed me to the gate. "Please let me show you. If you don't believe me after we soul-share, I'll leave you alone forever."

I shoved both guitars through and grabbed the iron bars. "Forget it." I struggled awkwardly over the gate, tearing the seat of my jeans on one of the pointy finials at the top. I shimmied to the ground and watched as Alden scaled the wall as if it were nothing, landing lightly beside me.

Mom's green minivan rounded the corner and came to an abrupt halt in front of us. I could only pick up one guitar at a time because I was covering the hole in my jeans with my free hand. Alden reached in front of me to open the sliding side door of the van and put Zak's guitar in after I'd put Dad's on the seat. Was he snickering? He opened the front passenger door for me, and I flopped into the seat.

Mom leaned over to get a look at him, lowering the window as I slammed the door. "Who are you?"

He leaned in through the window, too close for my comfort. He smelled like mint and the leather coat he was wearing. "I'm Alden Thomas. Lenzi had a problem with Zak, so I stayed with her to make sure she was okay until you arrived. It's a pleasure to meet you." He extended his arm across me while I stifled a groan as my mom shook his hand.

"I'm Julia Anderson, Lenzi's mother." She dropped his hand and immediately lit into me. "Why on earth are you in the cemetery after midnight? Making me drive all the way from Bellaire in the middle of the night! You're lucky it's your birthday, Lenzi. I had half a mind to leave you here!"

Alden rapped his knuckles on the door of the minivan. "Mrs. Anderson, I apologize for interfering, but Lenzi's had a rough night. I doubt she'll do something like this again. Why don't you wait to discuss it until you've both had a good night's sleep and time to reflect?"

Mom and I stared at him openmouthed.

"It was a pleasure to meet you," he continued. "Bellaire. We *are* neighbors. I look forward to seeing you again, Lenzi. Good night." He got into a gray Audi parked farther up the street and drove off.

I crossed my arms defensively across my chest, anticipating the onslaught of mother artillery. None came.

Mom pulled out on the street, looking somewhat dazed. "Alden seems like a very nice boy. The kind of boy I'd like to see you hanging out with."

I almost laughed out loud. If she only knew! A reincarnated, soul-sharing lunatic. Ghost Boy—every mother's dream.

FIVE

I spent the weekend avoiding Mom and doing homework. I'd fallen so far behind in my classes recently, I felt like I'd never get caught up.

I decided to take the Santa Claus approach to Alden's reincarnated ghost mediator story. When I was a little girl, Dad told me that Santa Claus would come as long as I believed he was real. Once I no longer believed, Santa stopped coming. This was how I was going to handle this ghost business. I didn't believe, so they were not real and would stop coming.

The problem was that approach wasn't working. The voices were getting worse, despite my constant mantra that they weren't real. And despite the Xanax too. I couldn't decide which was worse—going crazy or actually hearing ghosts.

My cell rang right as I finished a hideous trig worksheet. A lump formed in my throat as I stared at Zak's name on the screen. I hadn't heard from him in two days.

Zak was the first person I met when I moved back from Galveston three months ago. He was working at a shoe store in the mall and convinced me to buy an outrageous pair of strappy red heels, flirting the whole time. I was immediately attracted to his deep blue eyes and gorgeous smile. I had never worn those shoes, I realized, as his name flickered on the screen.

I decided to not confront him about the cemetery. I couldn't risk losing him too. "Hi, Zak," I answered, tapping my pencil on the table.

There was a long pause, and I thought for a moment he'd hung up. "Hey, babe. I . . . um . . . I'm really sorry about Friday night. I didn't mean for that to happen."

I let out a breath I hadn't realized I'd been holding. "It's okay, Zak."

"Can I make it up to you?"

My fingers touched a piece of paper, and I instinctively began to fold. "Sure."

"How about I take you for seafood in Kemah? You like roller coasters, right?"

I made triangles from the edge moving in, tension ebbing from me into the folds. "Love roller coasters. Sounds fun." I turned the paper over and repeated.

"Awesome. I know you have school tomorrow, so we'll make it an early night. I'll pick you up at six o'clock, okay?"

"Great." I pulled on the edges of the triangles slightly, without looking.

He was quiet for a moment. "You okay? You seem distracted."

I looked down at my hands. My trig worksheet was now a crane. "Yeah, I'm great. I was just finishing some homework." I unraveled the bird and smoothed the worksheet flat. "I'll see you at six."

After changing clothes and strapping on those red heels, I watched for him out the narrow, vertical window next to the front door. Mom was still mad about the cemetery, so to avoid a scene, I didn't tell her good-bye when I took off.

It's a miracle I made it to the car without falling flat on my face. Heels are not my thing, but Zak's grin was worth it. The door to his beat-up Delta 88 heaved a metallic groan as he opened it for me. "Nice shoes!"

"Yeah, this slick salesman at the shoe store convinced me I couldn't live without them."

Zak grinned and wrapped his arms around my waist, pulling me against him. His warmth ran all the way down my body. "What else did he convince you you couldn't live without?"

"Um." I pulled away and slid into the car. "Dinner."

His mood on the surface was light, but he wasn't his usual easygoing self. His smile never reached his eyes. We made small talk on the forty-minute drive to Kemah, covering every subject with the exception of the voices in my head and what had happened at the cemetery.

When we pulled off the highway, the noise in my head became so loud, my eyes watered. I don't know if it was because there wasn't as much road noise or if it was really louder. Individual voices would fade in and out periodically, but I couldn't understand what they were saying.

"You okay, babe?" Zak pulled off into an office parking lot.

The voices continued to crescendo until I clamped my hands over my ears and held my breath to keep from screaming.

"Is it the voices?"

I nodded and uncovered my ears so I could unbuckle and reach my purse on the floor. I was shaking so hard, I couldn't manage the zipper. Zak leaned over, unzipped it, and rooted around until he found the bottle of pills. He handed me a pill and I bit off a quarter and swallowed it dry, dropping the remainder loose in my purse.

"Just relax, okay? Give it time to work," he said.

He rubbed my shoulders while I waited for the pill to take effect, which didn't take very long since I hadn't eaten anything all day. I hated the numbing effect, but it did make the voices return to background static.

"Better?" he said, brushing the hair from my forehead.

I nodded.

He started the car and pulled back out on the road. "You should really tell your mom about this. I'm worried about you."

Just like with the background noises in my head, I pretended not to hear him.

The Kemah Boardwalk was an entertainment complex built on the northwest side of Galveston Bay, far inland from the Gulf, halfway between Houston and Galveston Island. There were clubs, restaurants, and amusement rides.

We sat outside on the second-story deck of a casual seafood restaurant looking over the water. Sailboats, Jet Skis, and wet bikes zipped over the surface of the water below, while seagulls and pigeons bummed food from the restaurant guests. The cool breeze blowing off the water felt good.

Zak usually sat beside me when we ate, but today he sat across from me. The waitress placed our food on the table, and he leaned closer. His eyes were the color of the darkening sky behind him.

"You're still mad at me for what happened in the cemetery, aren't you, Lenzi?"

"I'm not mad." I picked up the ketchup and unscrewed the lid. "I'm disappointed." I tipped the ketchup bottle, wanting to kick myself for how lame that sounded. When nothing came out, I gave the bottle a couple of whacks on the bottom. "I sound like my mom, huh?"

Zak chuckled and took the bottle from me. "I deserve it." He tipped the bottle at a slighter angle and poured a puddle of ketchup next to my fries.

I cut a bite of fish with my fork. "You do stupid things that are totally out of character when you're drinking."

He screwed the top back on and set it down. "Like what?"

"Like trying to make out at my father's grave."

He pushed his fries around. "Yeah, that was pretty stupid."

"It was."

He pointed at me with a shrimp. "But you can't really blame me. Come on, Lenzi. It was your birthday. You were so . . . hot. You *are* so hot. I can't help myself." He dragged his shrimp through my ketchup, winked, and popped it in his mouth.

A blush burned my cheeks. I was probably the color of the ketchup on my plate.

He grinned. "You are especially hot in those shoes." He reached under the table and ran his fingers over my knee, causing tingles to skitter up my leg.

"You're mine," a disembodied male voice said from behind him. I swiveled to the side, pulling out of Zak's reach.

"Why did you pull away?" he asked.

Heart hammering, I rearranged the French fries on my plate and searched for an answer. "Too public" was all I could come up with. I really didn't want Zak to know that even with the Xanax, I was still hearing voices. He might tell Mom. I couldn't bear that.

The voice laughed from behind me, and I flinched.

Zak's brow furrowed. "You okay?"

I reached for my glass to buy more time. "Yeah, I'm just jumpy, that's all."

He held his empty glass up and signaled to the waitress to bring another iced tea. "I need to go to the bathroom." He stood. "You sure you're okay?"

I ran my finger down the condensation on the outside of my glass. "I'm fine. Really."

He leaned over and kissed me. "Okay, then. Be right back." He stopped to look back at me for a minute before disappearing down the patio stairs.

I felt a cold breath on my neck. *"I want you. You will surrender to me,"* the voice hissed. I spun around and found no one.

I didn't know why this voice was so much more terrifying than the others, but I instinctively felt I was in danger. It was hard to breathe, like the air had gotten thicker. The thing's cold respiration continued on my skin, making my flesh crawl. I covered the back of my neck with my hands.

The middle-aged waitress stared at me as she set the tea down on the table and picked up Zak's empty glass. She pulled a straw out of her apron pocket and placed it on the table. "You okay, hon?"

I nodded.

"Well, just let me know if y'all need anything."

As the waitress wandered off to the next table, the thing breathed on the right side of my face. I shuddered, and goose-flesh prickled down my arms.

"Surrender," the voice demanded.

The woman at the table next to me stopped eating and gave me a you-are-totally-nuts look. And she was right. I needed to get another pill down and hide someplace until it took effect.

I sprinted to the bathroom, clutching my purse. Sinking

down to the floor of a stall, I focused on staying in control. My hands shook, making it difficult to unzip the purse. I dug around in the bottom and found the bottle of pills. I fumbled with the childproof cap and instead of just taking a quarter this time, I swallowed a whole pill.

The thing breathed on my neck again. My scream ricocheted off the hard surfaces of the bathroom, amplifying my terror. I jumped to my feet and backed into the corner, wrapping my arms around myself. When I clamped my eyes shut, an image of Alden filled my brain. Alden! In the cemetery, he'd told me to just tell the bogeybaby to go away, and it did. Maybe it would work with this thing too.

My voice sounded like a cartoon character with a speech impediment. Fear personified. "G-g-go away. I w-won't surrender to you. G-go away."

It laughed.

"Now! I mean it."

I stood in the bathroom stall for a long time waiting for the next terrifying assault. The ghost, or whatever it was, seemed to have taken off. Maybe it was gone, or maybe the Xanax had taken effect and I'd stopped hallucinating. Either way, I washed my face at the sink, praying the voice wouldn't return.

I took a deep breath as I made it up the stairs to the restaurant deck, but before I could round the corner to the patio, something scratched my back and cold air blasted my neck. It stung like the scratch had broken the skin. I clapped a hand to my spine under my windbreaker. Blood. Terrified, I stared at my crimson fingers.

"Surrender to me."

"Never!" I yelled.

The thing's laughter rang over the pounding pulse in my ears. I realized in horror that I hadn't told my mom good-bye. I was going to die, and I hadn't even said good-bye. . . . Just like Dad.

"I will have you. You are mine. Surrender."

"You'll never have me! I'll never surrender!"

A sharp pain shot up my abdomen. I watched as drops of blood seeped through my shirt. *Run!* I yanked off the high-heeled shoes. I could hear it laughing as I bounded down the patio stairs two at a time into the parking lot. *Run!* I had to get away. Another slash across my stomach.

"Never!" I screamed as I ran between the cars toward the Ferris wheel. A horrible ripping sensation filled my body—like Velcro ripping out my insides. Alden was right. These weren't just voices. Somehow this voice was making me bleed. It had entered my body. And now I was housing its soul.

SIX

I collapsed next to a pickup truck in the parking lot and curled in a ball on the pavement.

Get out! the voice in my head shouted.

I remembered Alden telling me that a Malevolent would take my body to use as its own if it could force me out. "No," I gasped, barely able to speak because of the burning pain filling me from head to toe. I focused on staying conscious and in control. It felt like the thing was trying to make me move against my will.

I could see the steps to the restaurant where I had been attacked. People were laughing on the patio, unaware that things like this lived among them. Or lived inside me, as it were. What would it do if I let go and allowed it to take over? Would it kill someone? Would it live as me?

Now that I wasn't struggling to stay on my feet, I felt stronger. Maybe knowing the stakes allowed me to control it.

"What do you want?" I asked it.

You.

Gee, I'd have never guessed that one. "Why?"

To kill my cheating wife.

Was I supposed to try to talk him out of it? Alden had mentioned resolving issues for these dead guys. "I'm not going to help you with that."

You don't need to. Get out.

A painful tugging sensation began at my extremities, like I was being pulled on from the inside. He was trying to force me out. I tried to scream, but nothing came out, at least nothing I could hear over the carnival music and the rattling and roars of the roller-coaster cars as they plummeted, packed with screaming passengers.

The orange glow of the setting sun reflected off the sparkles in the concrete and shiny car surfaces. It would be so easy to let go and allow him to take over. *No.* I had to hang on.

"Rose?" Alden's voice sounded close. Maybe a row over. "I feel you; don't give up. I'm here."

"Alden." My lips moved, but no sound came out.

He rounded the corner of the aisle of cars, running toward me like a beautiful avenging angel.

"Rose, I'm here. Hold on."

I made a groaning sound. It wasn't my voice. It was deeper.

"She's gone," it said through my mouth as my body sat up against my will.

Alden took me by the shoulders, but I didn't feel his touch. "Rose! Are you ready for me to come in?"

"She's gone!" the foreign voice screamed from my body.

"Rose!" He shook me. "Rose. Let me in!"

I sucked in a deep breath and concentrated on regaining control of my body. "Alden." The voice was weak, but mine. The thing seemed to be getting weaker.

He took my face in his hands. "Rose. Now?" I had no idea what he was asking me. Everything was garbled and fuzzy. "I'm sorry." His voice broke. "I should have told you the protocol. You have to say yes. I need permission to enter the vessel. Consent. You have to be ready to end negotiations with the Malevolent."

Negotiations? I closed my eyes. It was taking too much effort to keep them open.

"Don't you dare give up on me!" he shouted. "Rose . . . Lenzi! Now? Say yes, dammit!"

He'd used my real name. My voice was soft, frail. "Yes."

I felt like a punching bag turned inside out. I'd no idea what Alden was doing, but the thing in my body screamed like it was being hurt.

After a ripping sensation, the screaming and jostling stopped, and I opened my eyes. The translucent form of a middle-aged man stood over me, his face contorted with hate. I watched with morbid amazement as he was swallowed up in a cloud of blackness, all the time cursing me. Impenetrable, opaque, final blackness.

It was over. I was safe.

I sat up and leaned on the door of the pickup. Alden was sitting on the concrete next to me. Another wave of pain shot through me, then Alden took a deep breath.

"Are you okay?" he asked as he stood and brushed the gravel off of the back of his jeans.

"Yeah, I think so. Is it gone?"

"You bet. So gone. As gone as they get."

I began to cry. "I tried. I really tried, Alden. I didn't know what to do. He just kept telling me to get out." I wanted him to comfort me. I needed him to put his arms around me and hold me. Instead, he pulled out his car keys.

"You did your best. That's all you can do. Move on. You'll get the next one." He held his hand out to help me up. I stood without it.

"I don't want a next one. One is enough." My body ached like I was covered in bruises.

He sighed. "Let's go. You need to go home and clean up."

I straightened my skirt. "I need to go back to Zak. Thanks anyway."

"You need to let me help you. You can't do this alone, and your boyfriend won't be able to help." Alden reached for me, but dropped his hand when I took a step away. "Your soul feels wrong. And you look terrible."

The extra Xanax must have been too much. I squinted to pull him back into focus. "Thanks, you really know how to compliment a girl." I wobbled slightly as I spun around to return to the restaurant. Zak had probably freaked out when he found me gone.

Alden fell into step beside me. "We need to stay together. Something's not right."

I swayed as exhaustion trickled through my limbs. "Ow." I stopped to knock off a tiny pebble that had stuck to the ball of my bare foot. A wave of nausea rolled through me when I saw the raw bottoms of my feet.

"Do you want me to carry you?" Alden offered.

"No. She doesn't." Zak's low voice rumbled. I took a deep breath and straightened. Zak was right in front of me, holding my red shoes. He looped his finger through the heel straps and held them out to me. "Kinda like Cinderella, but different, huh, Lenzi?"

I took the shoes and looked from one guy to the other. The air almost crackled with testosterone.

"You're the guy from the cemetery," Zak said, fists clenched.

Alden moved closer to me and smiled. "Yes, I am. Very good, Zak."

Everything seemed fuzzy. So tired. "Zak. He was helping me."

Zak took another step closer, shaking with rage. "I bet he was."

The dizziness made it hard to stand. "I had a bad episode

with the voices. I freaked out and ran down here. He found me and helped me."

"That's quite a coincidence, isn't it, lenzi?" Zak said.

I swayed a little bit. Alden put his hands on my waist and leaned me against a truck. I held on to the edge of the truck bed for balance.

"Get your hands off of her," Zak growled. "I'll take it from here."

This was a disaster. Panic squeezed my chest, and I gulped for air. I had to do something before they started fighting.

Alden placed his hand over mine on the truck bed and a soothing calm radiated up my arm. The panic ebbed away, and I could breathe. Alden gave my hand a squeeze. "Now, listen to me, Zak. I'm taking Lenzi home, and you're going to just walk away. You can't help her, but I can."

"Walk away, huh?" Zak squared off like he was going to throw a punch. "She's coming with me."

The soothing energy flowing up my arm increased as Alden spoke. "I've known her a long time and understand what's happening. You can't help her."

Zak took a stride closer. "I said get your hands off of her."

"Why don't we let Lenzi decide?" Alden's stance was casual, but his voice had a hard edge.

"There is no decision," Zak said. "She's here with me."

I pulled my hand away from Alden. "Shut up! Both of you!" To my amazement, they did. My vision blurred. I squinted to focus on Zak's face. He wanted to help me, but the Xanax wasn't working on the voices anymore. Alden knew something about all of this. He made the thing leave my body. I needed answers so I didn't end up like Dad. "I'm sorry, Zak. This isn't about being my boyfriend. This is about stopping the voices. Alden can help me with that."

As Zak's face faded in and out of focus, I realized I'd probably just lost not only my boyfriend, but the only real friend I had left.

Even holding on to the truck, I couldn't remain upright. Before I crumpled, Alden scooped me up in his arms. I wanted to protest, but couldn't remember why. I tried to speak, but found myself unable to do anything except lay my head against Alden's shoulder and close my eyes.

SEVEN

The familiar lullaby of my ticking clock made it hard to open my eyes as the sweet smell of Mom's lilac shampoo drifted into my room. Time for school. I raised my arms over my head until the sharp pain on my belly cut my stretch short.

"Good morning." Alden's voice was barely above a whisper.

I froze, heart racing, then rolled over. He was sitting in the corner at my desk, barely visible in the dim light. I shot a look at my open door. Mom would freak if she knew a guy was in my bedroom.

"It's all right. She's in the shower."

I pulled the covers up to my chin. "What are you doing here?" I whispered.

"My job." He picked up an origami frog I'd made from a report card and held it in his palm. "Don't worry. Everything's okay."

The shower knob squeaked as Mom turned it off. My belly stung when I sat up. "You've gotta get out of here. Mom'll kill me if she finds you. I'm not allowed to have boys in my room."

"I like that policy." He grinned and gently placed the frog back on my desk next to the menagerie of other origami figures.

Mom's dresser drawer creaked open, then slammed shut. "Lenzi! Time to get up and get dressed for school," she called from her bedroom.

"Not today," Alden whispered, backing into the shadows in the corner of my room.

"What am I supposed to do?" I whispered as the latch on my closet clicked. Oh, great. I had a guy hiding in my closet. Perfect.

The light flipped on with a snap. "Lenzi. Time for school."

I squinted and shaded my eyes from what seemed like a billion watts of light to find Mom in my doorway with her hand on the switch. "Are you okay? You look pale." I fought the urge to check to see if the closet door was closed when she placed her palm on my forehead. "You're all clammy."

"Yeah, I don't feel so good." It wasn't a lie.

"Maybe you'll feel better after a shower. Come on." She pulled the covers off. "Oh, Lenzi." Her brow furrowed. "You were asleep when I got home. If I'd known you were still in your clothes, I'd have woken you up to change."

I slid to the edge of the bed. I had to get her out of the room before she figured out Alden was hiding out in my closet. "Yeah, I was really tired when I got in last night." I followed Mom's troubled look down to my rumpled clothes. There was a bloodstain on the blouse. "And I spilled ketchup on myself."

She took a step closer. "It doesn't look like ketchup."

It didn't. The blood had dried a dark maroon—almost brown. I couldn't let her know I'd been hurt or she'd never leave. "It was shrimp sauce. Worcestershire in it, or something."

I grabbed my bathrobe and pushed by her. I didn't realize how weak I was until I lost my balance in the hallway. Bracing myself against the wall, I waited for the floor to stay in one place. The faint click of my closet latch drove my heart into hyper-drive.

Mom brushed my hair out of my face. "Lenzi, honey, you're sick. Do you want me to take you to the doctor?"

"No!" It came out much louder than I'd intended. "No. Thanks. I just need a shower and some sleep."

She took my face in her palms and looked in my eyes—searching for something like she did with Dad. My heart knotted in my chest. She knew.

Her eyes brimmed with tears. "You can always talk to me. You know that, right?"

I nodded, afraid to say anything.

"I can't be late to the office today. I'll call the school on my way to work and tell them you're sick. Call me if you need anything."

She held me for a long time. Her lilac scent and familiar arms made me feel like I did when I was little. Before Dad got so sick. Before the voices. When I was safe.

I showered as quickly as I could, considering, and once I was sure Mom had left for work, I padded down the hallway to my room.

The sun streaming through my open blinds lit the gold highlights in Alden's hair. This was the first time I'd seen him in the light. His eyes were pale gray, almost silver. Beautiful and unearthly. He was the most attractive boy I'd ever met, and he looked way too comfortable lying on my bed.

My heart did a flip-flop and I pulled my bathrobe tighter when he looked me up and down with those crazy silver eyes. I winced when the robe brushed the stitches. It had been a shock during my shower to discover five dark blue tidy knots on my upper abdomen just under my rib cage. I didn't remember going to the hospital. I didn't remember anything after I'd collapsed. I'd clearly overdone the Xanax.

"How do you feel?" he asked, propping up on an elbow.

I shifted my weight from foot to foot, feeling vulnerable in my robe. "I'm okay."

He sat up. "You don't feel okay. You feel conflicted."

Conflicted summed it up pretty well. Being attacked by whatever that thing was in Kemah last night convinced me I wasn't imagining things, and this boy on my bed had some answers. I took several steps into the room.

"How do you know how I feel?"

He lay back down and put his hands behind his head. "I told you in the cemetery that our souls are linked. I feel your emotions." He rolled onto his side. "It's how I found you last night. You were in danger. Your soul called."

I tightened my robe belt. "I thought you were just stalking me."

He smiled. "That too."

"How did you get in here?"

He reached in his pocket, pulled out my house key, and set it on my nightstand. Obviously, he'd taken it from my purse when I was unconscious. Clever Ghost Boy. "I tucked you in before your mother came home and hung around to be sure you were okay."

I looked around and groaned. He'd been in my pigsty of a room all night.

The noises in my head bounced to the foreground. I pressed my palms to my temples. "Stop. Stop it," I whispered. The voices dimmed at once.

Alden and I stared at each other in silence for a tense moment before he closed his eyes as if listening to something. My soul?

I pulled the collar of the bathrobe closer. "It's real, right? What's happening to me—it's not in my head. Dead people are really talking to me."

He moved to the edge of the bed. "Yes."

A lifetime of this would be intolerable. There had to be a way out. I crossed my arms. "I can't do it. You need to make it stop."

"I can't." His voice was soft. Almost apologetic.

Tears stung my eyes. "Why?"

He stood, and for a moment I thought he was going to take me in his arms, but he put his hands in his pockets. "Lenzi, we're just people. We're different from most people, admittedly, but we don't hold the cards. You can't change what you are any more than any other creature on this planet."

It took everything in me not to cry. "I don't want to do it. I'm scared."

He shuffled foot to foot as if he were uncomfortable. "I know. Knowledge alleviates fear. Maybe if you ask me questions, I can help you understand. What do you want to know?"

I sat on the edge of the bed. "How do I make them go away?"

He sat next to me. Close, but not touching. "You ask them to clarify their needs and then you help them find resolution. They aren't trying to frighten you. They just want your attention."

"That thing last night wanted more than my attention."

"Yeah, that was unfortunate. And totally my fault. I shouldn't have left you unprepared." He ran his hands through his hair. "I'm sorry about that."

I swiveled to face him. "Okay, why does the temperature go nutty sometimes, like an arctic blast?"

He smiled. "They have all kinds of gimmicks to catch your

attention. That's one of their favorites. Some of them can even give off smells. They can manipulate the physical environment, like knock things off shelves and lock doors and stuff like that."

I fiddled with the end of my robe belt. "Oh. So I'm not really in danger."

Alden paused for a moment before answering. "No. You really *are* in danger. Not from the run-of-the-mill Hindered, but from the Malevolent like last night. There aren't many of them, but they'd love to have your body. They'd kick you out if they could."

I shuddered, recalling last night's attack. "So that's why I need you."

He stared into my eyes and paused before answering. "Yes."

"And we've been together for generations."

"Yes."

That, more than the thing about ghosts, made me uneasy. What was he to me in past lives? What did he know about me?

He stood and stretched. "How about some breakfast? You could use some fuel after last night."

As if on cue, my stomach rumbled. "We have some Pop-Tarts."

He gave me a thumbs-up. "Perfect! The breakfast of champions. Get dressed, and I'll meet you downstairs."

I sat on my bed for a moment after he left, trying to grasp my new reality. Being nuts was easier.

EIGHT

I felt better after some milk and a strawberry Pop-Tart. Better, but still uneasy. I could tell Alden was waiting for me to lead the conversation, but I had so many questions, I didn't know where to start.

I slid off my bar stool and unwrapped two more Pop-Tarts. "So, I guess you took me to the hospital while I was unconscious."

Alden held his finger up while he finished chewing and swallowed. "No. I sewed the stitches."

I slid my hand under my shirt and ran my fingers over the stitches. "You did it?"

He turned on his stool to face me. "It's hard to explain that kind of injury to doctors. The wounds you have right now are pretty innocuous, but sometimes they're not. Sometimes the

Malevolent carve words into your skin. I'm trained to handle most of the types of injuries you'll receive. Sutures are my least favorite. Fortunately, you only needed a few at the top of one of the scratches."

"Sometimes they carve words in my skin?" I crumpled the foil pastry wrapper in my fist. "Carve words? And you're trained to handle that? Trained by whom?" I dropped the balled-up wrapper on the counter.

"Calm down. When you have the full picture, it won't be as scary." He moved next to me and pulled the Pop-Tarts out of the toaster.

I carried my plate to the island and slid onto my stool. "Okay. Enlighten me, then, because it's pretty freaking scary."

He sat next to me and took a bite of his pastry. "We need to start at the beginning."

"And where is that?"

"Soul-sharing. It's the foundation of the system." He took a few more bites and a gulp of milk.

No longer hungry, I placed my plate on the counter next to the sink. Embracing any part of this as a possibility was a terrible idea. I needed to get out of this, not find out how it worked.

Alden joined me and set his plate in the sink. "Your job is to serve as a conduit for Hindered resolutions. We have to soul-share in order for you to do that. Two souls in one body."

"Whose body?"

He grabbed the Pop-Tart off my plate and took a big bite. "Yours."

"No way." I wadded up my napkin and threw it in the trash can. "Forget it."

"Wait," Alden said, crossing the kitchen in huge strides. "Please wait." He touched my elbow and that funky soothing thing started.

I yanked my arm away. "Stop it. Whatever that is . . . stop it."

He held his hands up and backed away. "It's okay. I'm trying to help you, Lenzi. There's a lot at stake here. A lot more than you being afraid of voices or getting some cuts from a Malevolent." He ran his hands through his hair. "I understand your frustration. Your past-life amnesia makes this complicated for both of us. But we can get through this if you'll just let me help you. Please."

I leaned against the door frame. He was so sincere. There was something about him—something different from anyone I'd ever met. As much as I hated to admit it, Ghost Boy fascinated me.

"Okay," I said. "Get on with it, but I want you to know, I don't like this."

He followed me into the living room and began strolling around checking out photos and memorabilia. His uninvited scrutiny made me feel naked. I never felt this self-conscious with Zak.

He picked up my framed third-grade class photo from the

bookcase and smiled. *Ugh.* Why did he have to pick that one? That was the year I decided to give myself a haircut before picture day. My bangs stuck up like a science fair exhibit on the effect of static electricity.

"So cute," he said.

I rolled my eyes.

He took a deep breath through his nose. "The house smells like you."

I put my hands on my hips. "What does *that* mean?"

"You have a distinctive smell. I've known you so long, I'd recognize it anywhere."

That was one step too far over the perv line. "Okay, I've heard enough."

"No, calm down. It's a compliment. You smell good. I'm not being weird. It's part of the Protector-Speaker thing. Sorry." He plopped down on the sofa. "Please sit down," he said, patting the cushion next to him.

I strode to a chair on the opposite side of the coffee table and sat.

"No. It will be hard for us to do it in that chair. The sofa will work much better."

I stood. "That's it. We're done."

"Whoa. Okay. You stay over there, and I'll stay here. I'm not talking about sex. I'm talking about keeping you alive." He leaned forward, voice quiet and calm. "I want you to share your body with my soul, nothing else." Those strange eyes of his were mesmerizing. "Please. Let me show you, then all of this will make sense." He stood and held his hand out to me. "If you touch me, it will be easier. It's . . . uncomfortable without contact."

I put my hand in his. "Let's get this over with, Ghost Boy."

"Okay, I'll consider that consent." He took a deep breath and closed his eyes. I studied him as his brow furrowed in concentration. His hair was blond, but his long eyelashes were almost black. Why was it that guys always got the Maybelline lashes? He opened his eyes and focused on my face.

"Out," he whispered.

I watched his eyes glaze over, and my stomach churned. Almost immediately, it felt like my insides were being ripped apart. I screamed. The fear was as bad as the pain, and the pain was intense. It felt like hot water pouring into my body, beginning with my chest and radiating all the way out into my toes and fingertips. I kept screaming, but I couldn't hear it.

Stop it, Lenzi! Relax. The hard part is over, he assured me. *Listen to me. I'm in. It will stop hurting now. Stop!*

It sounded like he was talking from inside my head, which was impossible, of course, because he was standing right in front of me. I stared at him. He was right: the pain was gone.

See? It's okay now. I'm in, and you're fine. You'll get used to it.

His mouth hadn't moved. The voice really was inside my head. My panic rose again. Shoving his shoulder caused no reaction. He looked like a standing corpse.

I'm not there, Lenzi. That's just an empty shell. I'm in your body.

It felt claustrophobic, like I was too full and there wasn't enough room for me.

You're okay. Relax and just get used to it.

I stood panting in the middle of the room. "I'm freaking out, Alden. I don't like this."

It gets easier. You're not in danger.

It wasn't like he was just a little voice in my head—he was a complete presence throughout my being. It felt like I was being consumed. "Alden, I can't take it anymore. Please. You've got to get out."

Okay. I'll leave your body now. It will be easier if you touch me.

I put my hands on his shoulders.

Out, I heard him command his soul.

There was a distinct ripping sensation throughout my entire body. I dug my fingers into his shoulder and hung on.

His glazed gray eyes came to life as he drew a deep breath and smiled.

I released my death grip on his shoulder and backed away. I hadn't expected it to be so intense—in fact, I hadn't truly believed it was possible at all. I slumped onto the sofa and stared at him. He stood still as if he were afraid to move for fear I'd bolt.

His voice was soft and gentle. "Are you okay? I didn't mean to frighten you."

I took a deep shaky breath and nodded. "I'm fine."

He sat down right where he was in the middle of the floor,

and we stared at each other for what felt like forever. "Do you have any questions for me?"

I laughed. Totally lost it and flew into a giggling fit. I'm not sure why that question set me off. Perhaps it was because he was so sincere. It could have been a post-trauma adrenaline rush. Or maybe it was because my reality was crazier than any nuthouse diagnosis. Crazier than Dad.

After a moment, he smiled and then laughed too.

I patted the sofa cushion next to me and repeated his words. "It will be hard for us to do it in that chair. The sofa will work much better."

He joined me on the sofa, and we laughed until my sides hurt.

"Do I have any questions?" I said, wiping a tear away. "About a billion."

He leaned back with his hands behind his head and closed his eyes. "Shoot."

"Is this what my dad had? Did he hear ghosts too?"

"No. Your dad was not a Speaker. He was really sick." He opened his eyes and looked into mine. "It's totally unrelated. You are not like your dad. You're supposed to hear voices. It's your job."

"It's a weird job."

"It's a wonderful job," he said, closing his eyes again.

As turned off as I was by the prospect of talking to ghosts, I still found myself drawn to Alden more than anyone I'd ever met. A strange pang of familiarity shot through me as I scanned his long body. It was like my memories of him were right at the tip of my brain, just out of reach. I bit my lip. "Um . . . in our past lives . . . were we . . . What was our relationship?"

He sat up and stared directly into my eyes. "Our relationship varies. It's dictated by your mood."

My mood? "Have we ever been . . . ?" I looked down at my hands, which were folded in my lap. I could feel his eyes on me.

"The relationship is defined by the Speaker. The Protector has no say in it." He got up and walked to the bookcase, keeping his back to me. "Sometimes we're just business partners. A couple of times we got married. Occasionally, you were romantically involved with someone else." His grip tightened on the bookshelf. ". . . Like you are in this cycle."

His answer took me by surprise. "Did you ever get involved with someone else?"

He kept his back to me. "No."

I couldn't believe he wouldn't date. "No?"

He turned and met my eyes directly. "I'm your Protector. Once you emerge, I'm here solely for you. I can't let myself be distracted. If I don't focus, you'll be killed. My purpose is to protect the vessel. That's the only reason I exist."

His sudden intensity made my heart hammer in my ears. "That sucks."

"Not at all." He sat next to me on the sofa and smiled.

I returned his smile and leaned a little closer. "What do we do now?"

His gaze fell to my lips then returned to my eyes. He reached over, and for a moment, I thought he was going to pull me to him. Instead, he brushed my hair behind my shoulder. "I'll teach you how to help the Hindered."

"I don't want to do that. It's disturbing."

"It's not disturbing. It's natural."

"Natural?" I got up and began pacing. "What do you mean it's natural? You're like this minion who follows me around so that ghosts can't shove my soul out of my body. You have no free will. You have to subject yourself to my *mood*? That's what you said, isn't it? That's not natural."

He looked so comfortable and confident, arms draped across the back of the sofa. "I have an inordinate amount of free will. I *choose* to be your Protector. I choose to let you lead. I choose to let you decide how to handle each particular lifetime."

I stared at him openmouthed from across the coffee table. "How can a guy who can kick a bogeyman's butt be such a wimp?"

"I'm anything but a wimp." He leaned forward. "Let me show you. Let me in again, so that you can understand me better."

"It hurts."

He got up and crossed to me, taking my hands. "Lots of things hurt. You get used to the pain of accommodating another soul. Sometimes pain is good. It lets you know you're alive. And the cool part? I can show you my memories."

Maybe seeing his memories would trigger mine. "Why don't I remember, Alden?"

He dropped my hands and shoved them in his pockets. "I

don't know." He stared at the floor. "It's probably related to your absence. Maybe being gone longer affects memory." He met my gaze. "Please, Lenzi. Let me in again."

I gnawed on my bottom lip, considering. "Can you show me things from past lives? Can you show me . . . *me*?"

"Absolutely."

NINE

I couldn't believe I'd actually agreed to let Alden put his soul in my body again, but I was too curious to pass up the chance to see myself in another life. I sat on the sofa and nervously gestured him over.

He lowered himself next to me, close but not touching. "If you just relax and trust me, it won't hurt too much."

"I bet you say that to all the girls," I joked in a feeble attempt to mask my fear. He blushed and looked away.

"Oh, my gosh, Alden. Did I embarrass you?" His blush darkened, and I laughed. "I did! I embarrassed you!"

He glanced at me, then stared at the arm of the sofa. "I'm just surprised, that's all. I don't expect you to find double entendres in everything. You're funny. It's new."

New? It was hard to accept the fact that he had known me in other lifetimes.

"What? Was I some boring loser or something?"

"No. Oh, no. Never boring, just intense. You took your job very seriously. You took the rules seriously. You were the best Speaker on the planet. No one could beat your record. Very few Malevolent made it through you unresolved."

"What does that mean?"

"Heaven and Hell really exist, Lenzi. As long as the soul is Earth-bound, it isn't too late for redemption. There's hope until the last second."

My insides churned like they were being dissolved and sucked down a drain. "Don't tell me I was in charge of saving souls. That's *way* out of my league."

Alden took my hand, and the calming thing began immediately. "No, no. You were the best at pointing souls in the right direction, that's all. You were amazing."

I pulled my hand away. Amazing. I had been amazing. And now I was just . . . funny.

"Show me. Show me what I was like."

He stood and faced me. "I obey my master Speaker, to whom I am subordinate, because I have no will of my own under the natural law of subjugation and oppression." He bowed low, chuckling.

"Okay. I'm the one who's supposed to be funny. Cut that out. What do we do to accomplish this with as little pain as possible? Laughter is good. Pain isn't."

"Both are good," he said. "You should stand up and put your arms around me."

"You're only making that up."

He smiled. "Sort of. Contact really does help. Here, just take my hands."

Maybe it wouldn't be as bad this time because I knew what to expect. I placed my trembling hands in his. He squeezed my fingers, transmitting warmth through the contact.

"It'll be okay. You get used to it."

I closed my eyes. "Let's get this over with."

He enveloped both of my hands in his and pressed them to his chest. I could feel his heart beating. *Come on. Do it before I chicken out.*

"Out," he whispered.

I didn't open my eyes; I was too frightened. But this time I didn't scream as his soul poured into my body like scalding water. I controlled myself to the point that I only squeaked.

In a matter of seconds, the pain stopped. His heart still beat under my palms. *What happened? Why didn't it work?* I opened my lids and stared up at his empty, hollow, silver-gray eyes.

"Alden?"

Right here.

I flinched. The voice was in my head.

Are you okay?

"Um. Yeah. It's weird. It's like I'm thinking in *your* voice." My hands remained over his heart, the rhythm of life still beating in his chest. I dropped my hands, backed up several steps, and pointed at his body. "Alden, if you're not there, are you dead?"

No. The autonomic nervous system still operates. Everything is intact. Only part of the soul is missing.

"Part of the soul?"

Yeah, I split my soul. A tendril remains behind to keep my body closed. Protectors are closed vessels and can't be possessed by another spirit as long as part of the soul remains. Unlike Speakers, Protectors' bodies can only accommodate one soul at a time.

It still freaked me out when he talked or communicated or whatever it would be called in this situation. "That makes no sense whatsoever."

It will.

"So, will you just stand there forever like that?"

I can only do this where my body is safe. If I know I'm going to be gone for a while, I'm particularly careful. I usually leave my body sitting or lying down so that it doesn't get knocked over or damaged. We'll be here next to it the whole time, so it's okay.

I sat down and stared at his empty body. Even lifeless, he was hot.

Thank you.

"Oh, great. You can hear what I'm thinking."

No, I can only feel your soul respond to your emotions.

"Watch it, minion, or you'll be banished from my kingdom."

Yes, master.

I laughed. "Okay. What's it like? Are we really sharing my body?"

I can't feel anything at all in a tactile sense. No physical sensation whatsoever after the pain of entering. Because my soul isn't complete, I don't have enough power to control your body, but I can get some of your emotions, and I hear exactly what you hear. I also see through your eyes. I can't access any of your memories, but I can give you mine. Are you ready?

"Are you in a hurry?"

Well, sort of. I don't like leaving my body soulless for long. There's a risk of discovery. It would be awkward if your mom came home or something. A Protector is not allowed to let his soulless body be discovered. It's one of the rules.

There seemed to be a lot of rules, but that one made sense. "Okay, go for it."

The transfer of memories was like a high-def slide show in my brain. I could hear and feel Alden's memories as if they were my own, but I was limited to the memories he showed me. I could repeat and slow them down myself. It was like the images had been downloaded onto my hard drive and I was manipulating the data. I was flooded with images of me or, rather, Rose and Alden. When the rain started, I slowed everything down. Alden hadn't lied. These were memories from the Great Storm of 1900.

"Hurry, Rose, we need to get out before the structure fails," the Alden from the past shouted. He was perched in a dormer window, extending his free hand to her. "Rose, please." He was just as beautiful in the memory as the lifeless Alden standing in front of me, and he looked pretty much the same except for the shorter hair and long sideburns. He was also older in the memory.

Rose yanked off her petticoat and waded through the ankle-deep water to grasp Alden's hand. It was like watching myself in an elaborate play. Her face looked just like mine, and she appeared to be about my age—younger than the Alden in the memory. Her hair was the same dark brown and her eyes were almost black, like mine. The similarity between us was striking, but she seemed different somehow. Dignified or something.

She crawled onto the writing desk under the window and then onto the ledge.

"Stay here. I'll find a secure place," he shouted in her ear. With both hands, Rose clung to the window frame as Alden climbed out onto the roof.

Alden's voice pierced through the howls of the storm. "Here, Rose! Now!"

She clambered up the slate shingles as he pulled her to where he was balanced on the apex of the window dormer. A churning brew of brown water swirled around the house at the roofline. Wooden debris, mixed with the bodies of animals and humans, passed by as all around them people clung to parts of houses and buildings floating in the water. Their faces were twisted in agony as the storm swallowed their screams.

"We must get to the other side," Alden yelled. He wrapped an arm around Rose's waist and pulled her with him over the top of their two-story home to the gentler slope at the back of the house. Wedging himself into the valley of the roof where the porch met the bedroom, Alden tucked Rose in against him, protecting her from the debris hurtling through the air.

That was definitely Alden, but Rose was not me. We looked alike, but she seemed so foreign—the grace in her movements, her voice.

Rose asked Alden to find her in the future if something happened. Then they kissed. Really kissed. It was a passionate, desperate embrace like I'd only seen in movies.

It was odd watching their intimate moment. Awkward and wrong. Like I shouldn't be seeing it. But I wanted to. I wanted to put myself in her place.

I realized, as I watched them, that my heart was pounding in my chest.

The memories stopped as if someone had pulled the power plug from the projector.

"What happened?" I whispered. "Why did you stop?"

Touch the body, please. It's time to go back.

"I want to see more."

Not now. Please let me out. Touch the body, or my exit will be unnecessarily painful.

I stood up and put my hands on his chest. This time I did scream. I'd forgotten to brace myself. Alden's chest heaved under my palms.

Avoiding eye contact, he picked up my phone from the coffee table and punched buttons. "I need to get home. Here's my number if you have any questions. I'll feel the pull of your soul if you need protection."

I couldn't believe it. One minute he was playful and funny,

the next he was all business. I was embarrassed and angry. I wasn't quite sure why, but I felt used. How could he kiss me like that and just blow me off?

. . . But he hadn't really kissed me. That was just a memory from a long time ago. He had kissed someone else. He had kissed Rose.

I opened the door for him without speaking, afraid of saying something stupid.

I was jealous. The problem was that the other woman was *me*.

He paused in the doorway and handed me my phone.

I shoved it into my back pocket. "I'm not cut out for this, Alden."

He stared into my eyes for an uncomfortably long time. "The Intercessor Council won't take no for an answer. Stop fighting who you are, Rose."

TEN

The minute Alden left, the Hindered began calling out to me. I almost ran after him to beg him to stay, but then took a breath. I was fine before he came along. I'd be fine again. I would ignore the voices and act like nothing weird was happening. At least now I knew I didn't have Dad's schizophrenia.

"Help me," a voice cried over the others. It was the child again.

"Get lost, ghoul!" I shoved the coffee table with my foot before bounding up the stairs two at a time. "All of you can leave. I'm not going to play with you, so go haunt somebody else. I'm sick of this. Go away! I'm not Rose. You've got the wrong girl."

Slamming the door of my room felt good—so good, I did it again. "Get out of my life!"

The ghost thing was terrifying. So was Alden. He made me feel out of control and inadequate. After seeing Rose, I knew there was no way I could ever compete with her.

I slipped into my desk chair and picked up the origami frog Alden had held. His scent still lingered in my room—peppermint and leather—causing my pulse to quicken. The whole reincarnation thing was over the top, but it explained why I was so drawn to him. Still, I had a bad case of information overload. I'd gone from crazy girl to the ghost hunter in a flash.

I set the frog down.

Alden couldn't possibly expect me just to jump right into something this bizarre. I opened my top desk drawer and pulled out a square of the special paper Mom had bought online. This sheet was jet-black, which suited.

I folded the paper into sixteen even squares. Deliberate and exact, like I wished my life could be. Folding the corners on the diagonal, I closed my eyes and let the shape guide me, pinching the center crease and pleating out to the edges.

I hadn't spoken with Zak since leaving with Alden from Kemah last night. I knew he was short tempered, but I didn't peg him for the jealous type. No doubt he was furious with me. I turned the paper over and made valley folds from the corners to the center. Tension seeped from my fingers into the paper.

Just as my heart rate slowed and my breathing returned to normal, my cell rang. Alden's name popped up on the screen, causing my heart to hammer again. He must have called or texted his phone from mine to get my number. My fingertips passed over the paper. I creased it several more times, creating a mountain fold while the phone rang. I wasn't up to talking to him, so I let it roll over to voice mail. The screen on the phone went dark and I took a deep, cleansing breath, letting my fingers skim the paper.

I needed to get my mind off Ghost Boy and the bogeyman business. I had only one constant in my life, and I might have ruined it last night. For the sake of my sanity, I hoped not. I put down the origami and picked up my phone.

Dialing Zak was almost as scary as soul-sharing and potentially as painful. I thought for a moment he wasn't going to answer, but he picked up just as I was about to hang up. He didn't say anything, but I could hear music in the background.

I had no clue how to begin. "Hi, Zak."

"Hey." It sounded like he was at a club or something, but it was too early for clubs to open.

I balanced the phone on my shoulder and picked up the paper, tucking the corners under toward the center. "I'm really sorry about last night, Zak. I should have explained things better."

"What's to explain? It's pretty obvious what's going on." The thrumming of a bass guitar vibrated through my ear.

"It's not what you think, Zak."

He didn't answer.

"Alden's just an old friend who knows about Dad and the voices."

Still, nothing but the bass chords.

"Can we meet up and talk about it?"

"I can't. I'm practicing for a gig tonight at Last Concert Café."

"How about afterward?"

Someone in the background yelled his name. "Sorry, Lenzi, I've gotta go. Bye." The line went dead—and so did my heart.

When I looked down at the paper, it was a pinwheel. I'd never made this shape before. Most people had to practice origami, but it came naturally to me, like my hands just knew what to do.

I tugged on the folds, forming wedges. I needed to talk to Zak in person. This could be cleared up if he'd just hear me out.

My phone chirped, letting me know I had a voice mail. I dialed it up, expecting it to be an apology from Alden. Instead, it was a bossy message from him telling me not to reveal anything regarding Speakers, Protectors, or the Intercessor Council to Zak or anyone else. Like I'd do that. It was nuttier than schizophrenia.

I decided to go to the Last Concert Café. I needed normal. I needed Zak.

Turning the paper over, I curled the edges and tucked the corners in. Like my mood, the harsh paper softened.

I closed my eyes and pulled down the edges of the folds. Images flickered. The memory of the storm Alden had given me replayed. When it reached the kiss, I jerked my eyes open and stared down at the black paper rose resting in my palm.

ELEVEN

I stood on the sidewalk for a long time after the cab drove away. The Last Concert Café had been built in the late forties, and the modern glass and chrome city of Houston had popped up around it, leaving it as an untouched time capsule right at the base of the interstate off-ramp. There wasn't a sign out front, and you had to knock twice on the red arched door to be let in.

I brushed my fingertips over the hedge in the planter between the two doors, waiting for the lump in my throat to shrink down.

Local musicians were booked on weeknights, and Zak played here sometimes to earn extra money. Music did for Zak what folding paper did for me. If I were going to get through to Zak, this was probably the right place and time.

Taking a deep breath, I knocked twice and waited until a guy opened the door. In decent weather, bands would play on the patio, which is where I found Zak. He was riffing away on his bright red electric guitar while a bassist and drummer played along. He didn't notice as I took a seat at a wooden picnic table near the stage.

Eyes closed, he hammered out a song from the seventies, drawing out chords and creating his own syncopation. Dad would have loved hearing Zak play—more than that, he would have loved playing with Zak.

A waitress dressed in a bright Mexican smock and skirt brought a basket of tortilla chips and some salsa. My stomach was in knots, and there was no way I could eat, so instead of my usual chicken enchiladas, I ordered some crab-stuffed jalapeños—Zak's favorite.

Zak noticed me when he looked up at the end of the song. His face was unreadable. I clasped my hands together under the table and held my breath, waiting for his reaction. My heart did a flip-flop when he nodded to me.

He leaned into the microphone. "We're gonna take a short break." The guys onstage with Zak didn't look happy, but after he chatted with them a moment, they left the stage and headed into the restaurant.

"Hey, babe." The way he said it didn't sound like an endearment. He sat facing out next to me on the bench and leaned back against the table.

I traced the wood grain with my finger. "You sound great up there."

His smile was more of a smirk. "New group. I figured it was time to try new things. Kinda like you."

"Zak, I—"

The waitress plunked down a glass of water, a huge plate of stuffed jalapeños, and a bowl of *queso*.

Once she was out of earshot, I continued. "I'm really sorry about Kemah."

He stared straight into my eyes. I'd never noticed his blue eyes were peppered with gold flecks. "So am I, Lenzi."

"It's not what you think."

He shifted and straddled the bench so he faced me. "And what do I think?"

I thought he'd blow up, but instead he was creepy calm. I unrolled the silverware and pressed the napkin flat. "Alden's an old friend, that's all. Nothing more."

He simply stared at me, waiting, drumming his fingers on his thighs. He leaned forward so his face was inches from mine. "Is that so?"

"Yes."

He glanced at the plate in front of me. "I thought you didn't like jalapeños."

I slid the plate closer to him. "I ordered them for you."

He lifted an eyebrow and leaned in even closer so that our faces touched. "Really?" He brushed his lips against mine as he spoke. "Because I thought they were for the guy at the table behind you."

I jerked away and twisted on the bench to find Alden watching us from a table in the back corner. *Fantastic.* This was the last thing I needed right now.

Alden didn't react to my glare.

"Does he like jalapeños too, Lenzi?" Zak asked as he dragged one through the *queso.*

"I have no idea, but he's about to wear some." Getting out of the picnic table wasn't graceful, and I'm sure steam was coming out of my ears as I walked over to Alden. "What are you doing here?"

He didn't move a muscle. "My job."

I pointed to the exit and whispered, "Do it somewhere else."

He looked past me to Zak and then back at me. "I'll leave if that's what you really want, but that's a bad decision."

I put my hands on my hips. "That's what I want."

He stood and grabbed his jacket from the bench. "I'm not allowed to interfere with the outside relationships of my Speaker, but I want you to know that this guy's not right. Be careful, Lenzi." After shrugging into his jacket, he gave Zak a nod and strode through the exit.

Zak was biting into another jalapeño when I stepped over the bench and sat next to him. "He won't bother us again," I said, raking my hair back with my fingers.

He chuckled. "Wanna bet? That guy's totally into you."

My face flushed hot. "No, he's not. He's just an old friend."

"From Galveston?"

I'd hoped Zak wouldn't ask a bunch of questions. I was a pathetic liar. I pulled a hair band off my wrist and wrapped it around my hair several twists. "Yeah."

"I need you to be honest with me, Lenzi. How *well* do you know him?" He took a drink from my water glass.

I felt trapped. I'd chosen Alden over Zak yesterday, so I had to say we had some kind of real friendship, but not that kind. "It's not like that, Zak. He's just a friend. He knows all about Dad."

"Have you kissed him?"

Alden and Rose kissing on the roof flashed through my mind. I shifted on the bench. "No. Zak, let it go. He's gone. I'm here to be with you."

"You weren't with me last night. You chose him." His voice was strained, and the veins in his neck were visible.

"Zak." I ran my hand through his thick hair. "Tonight, I chose you."

He closed his eyes, hands balled into fists. "I won't share you, Lenzi. Get rid of him. I don't do jealous well. When you left with him last night, I wanted to . . ." He took a deep breath and let it out.

I placed my hands over his fists. "I'm sorry." His hands relaxed, and I threaded my fingers through his. "The voices were really bad. Alden knew what to do to help me. That's all."

His brow furrowed as he studied my face. "Let *me* help you, Lenzi. Tell me what you need."

What I need. I needed normal.

"Please let last night go. You're the only sane thing in my life. The only really good thing." I squeezed his hands. "I get why you're mad, but nothing happened, and he won't be an issue again."

"Okay." He ran his fingers down my neck and over my shoulder, sending chills up my spine. "Okay, I'll drop it." He placed his warm lips to my neck, and my heart rate doubled.

The drummer and bassist climbed up on the stage and one of them whistled to Zak. He gave them a thumbs-up and swung his leg over the bench so his back was against the table again. He wrapped his arms around my waist just under my cut and slid me next to him. The bass tuning thrummed in my head as Zak's kiss coursed through my body. He tasted delicious and spicy; I started to laugh.

He pulled away and smiled. "What?"

"I just might learn to appreciate jalapeños after all."

The sun had set before the end of his last song, and the strands of decorative lights draped around the patio made the place seem magical. The patio was almost full now of people dropping in for some music, margaritas, and dinner before the commute home to the suburbs.

Zak's voice sounded even deeper in the microphone. "This is for someone very special to me. This is for my girlfriend, Lenzi."

I must have turned a million shades of red when he pointed at me and people clapped. He picked up his acoustic guitar from the rack behind him and played the classical piece he had written for my birthday.

I became completely lost in the song. Closing my eyes, I ran my fingers over my napkin. For the first time in a long time, there was no shape inside trying to get out. No folds. No pleats. It was just a paper napkin, and I was just a girl with a cool boyfriend. This is what I wanted.

Zak stood during the applause and pulled another guitar from the rack. "I owe that girlfriend of mine something."

I gripped the edge of the bench, aware that everyone was looking at me.

"I owe her another song. But it will only work if she plays with me." He grinned. "Come on, Lenzi."

The people on the patio applauded, and Zak pulled another stool next to his. "Come on, babe. 'Free Fallin'' again, but this time I promise to do it right." He was tuning the second guitar when I climbed the steps, heart hammering. I'd never played in public before.

I slid onto the stool, and Zak handed me the guitar. Unlike Dad's, this guitar was shiny and slick. I ran my hand over the polished surface and focused on Zak. The minute he began to play, the audience seemed to melt away. I joined in when he began to sing.

This was the first time I'd felt happy—really happy—since

Dad died. The music was a release, and Zak's gorgeous grin was a gift.

Zak had asked me what I needed. *This* was what I needed. Something Alden and the Intercessor Council and all the bogeymen on the planet couldn't provide.

TWELVE

The evening was perfect until we rounded the corner onto my street.

Zak was laughing and telling me about a drummer friend getting so high he fell asleep onstage while I tried to act interested so he wouldn't notice Alden's car parked at the far end of my street.

If he could really feel my emotions, Alden knew I was pissed at him. If he blew my best date ever, I'd make him a *real* ghost boy.

Zak pulled into my driveway. I needed Zak to leave before Alden popped out of the bushes or did something stupid to set him off.

"Thanks for an amazing time," I said, fighting the urge to

look at Alden's car or check to see where he was lurking. I grabbed my purse from the floorboard. "It was a lot of fun."

"Hey." He leaned across the console and crooked his finger. "It's not over yet."

A good-bye kiss and he'd be gone before anything bad happened. I leaned in and met him over the parking brake, cup holder between us. The whole situation was awkward. I tried to act like I was into Zak's kiss while really I was terrified that Alden might appear and make Zak go crazy.

The hard plastic of the console bit into my thigh and hip when Zak shifted and pulled me closer. "Let's go inside." His voice was husky. "Your mom is never home this early."

That was even worse! "No." I couldn't let him know I was panicked. "She said she'd be home early tonight," I lied.

He ran his finger from my chin down my throat to the bottom of the low-cut V-neck of my shirt. "Let's stay right here, then."

I took his hands in mine. "Really, Zak. I have a ton of homework."

He sighed. "Okay. Wanna hang out tomorrow, then?"

"Yeah. I'd love that." I gave him a quick kiss. "Thanks for an awesome night." I twisted my purse strap around my palm and pushed the car door open. Where was Alden? I zipped my eyes to the right, but didn't see him outside anywhere.

My skin prickled with dread as Zak got out of his car and

walked me to the door. I just knew that any minute Alden would pop out from wherever he was hiding. I barely felt it when Zak kissed me good night one last time.

There was no click when I turned my key in the knob. Mom must have forgotten to lock up.

Once inside, I leaned back against the front door and waited for the rumble of Zak's car to fade away down the street before I allowed myself to relax a little.

"Coast clear?" Alden's voice came from the kitchen.

That explained why the front door was unlocked. How did he get inside? I had the urge to growl like an animal, but I answered as sweetly as I could. "No. *You're* here."

He entered the family room and sat on the edge of the sofa. "I have to be here. It's my job."

"Yeah, I know." I pitched my purse onto the coffee table on my way to the kitchen. "I told you I'm not interested."

As I pulled on the fridge handle, he pushed it shut. "Let's make a deal."

I tried to be nonchalant, leaning against the counter. Even as mad as I was, the nearness of him affected me. I wanted to lean into him. Have him touch me. "What kind of deal?"

"I'm going to tell you more about your job. I believe you'll change your mind once you understand the importance of what you do."

He stepped back when I tugged the refrigerator door open. "And what if I don't change my mind?"

"You're the Speaker. You control the relationship. If you want to ignore your job and hang out playing guitar with your boyfriend, I have to defer to you, but you need to know the consequences of that." He crossed his arms over his chest.

I glanced at the clock on the microwave. Mom wouldn't be home for at least an hour. I shrugged and pulled two Cokes out of the fridge and tossed him one. "Deal. Enlighten me."

His smile was beautiful. My stomach made an excited churn like I was on a roller-coaster climb before a huge fall.

I popped the top on my Coke. *Zak has a gorgeous smile too,* I reminded myself.

Alden moved close to me—close enough for me to feel the body heat rolling off him. "Being a Speaker is an amazing calling. You make the world better—safer."

I perched on a bar stool at the island counter. "Why me? How did this happen?"

"Speakers are born. It's a gift." He pulled a stool from the far end of the island and placed it close to mine, facing me.

"It doesn't feel like one," I grumbled.

He sat on the stool, knees outside of mine, but not touching. "A great gift. The Intercessor Council recruits them from the general population. Speakers in their first cycle are usually discovered among the ranks of fortune-tellers and mediums, most of whom are total scam artists, but some are legitimate. Protectors can identify the genuine Speakers."

"How?"

He popped the top of his soda. "You know how you can hear the Hindered? Well, Protectors hear Speakers. It's not really hearing. I've told you that I feel your soul. I can do it with other people too if they have a sensitivity to the Hindered. Most potential Speakers are drawn to the paranormal in one way or another. Some start up or join ghost-hunting agencies, some join the clergy, some find a way to cope with the voices, and some go insane. In fact, some of our best Speakers have come from asylums. When you hear about people who say they are reincarnated, they are probably Speakers or Protectors who haven't been called into duty yet."

"Couldn't they be retired Speakers or Protectors? Maybe they got sick of doing it."

He put the can down on the counter. "They wouldn't have come back if they had retired. Their souls wouldn't have recycled."

I stiffened. "Don't tell me they kill someone if they don't want to do it."

"Absolutely not. They just live out a normal lifetime like everyone else. They don't recycle in the next generation—at least that's what I've read. I've never heard of it really happening. The only time the IC terminates a life before the end of a natural cycle is if one of the primary rules is broken."

"And those are?"

He sat up straight and looked up at the ceiling like a kid reciting a memorized passage of text. "A Protector can be removed from the cycle for intentionally not informing, protecting, and serving the Speaker, entering the body of the Speaker without permission, or entering the body of any living human outside of an exorcism."

I stared at him in silence for a moment. "What about the 'letting the Speaker lead' thing?"

He smiled. "A breach there won't get someone executed, just reprimanded."

"All of those rules apply to the Protector," I said. "What about the Speaker?"

"The primary thing that could get you removed from the cycle is intentionally allowing your body to be used by the Hindered or Malevolent for purposes other than resolution." He shifted his gaze away from my eyes. "Speakers can also be discontinued for lack of productivity."

I tore a piece of paper from the notepad next to the telephone. "What does that mean?"

"Speakers must intercede on behalf of the Hindered and average a certain number of resolutions in order to recycle in the next lifetime. I've never heard of a Speaker being discontinued for a breach of this rule. It's very rare."

I folded the paper into squares. "What about the Protectors? Is it rare for them to break the rules?"

"It isn't common, but it happens."

I stood up. "What happens? I mean, if people blow it, what really happens?"

"There's a hearing, and if the transgression is serious enough, they are discontinued on the spot."

I put the kitchen island defensively between us. "That's a nice way of saying they're murdered."

"No, Lenzi. They aren't murdered. Justice is carried out."

"I don't want to do this, Alden. I don't want to be part of a system like this."

He picked up my discarded piece of paper and handed it to me. "You used to love the system. In fact, you sat on the Rule Development Panel in the mid-1800s. The rules have been established over centuries. This is the way it has to be."

"I'm not Rose," I said, reorienting the piece of paper in my hand.

His eyes followed my fingers as I tucked a flap under a corner crease. "I know that."

"Whatever happened to democracy and equality?"

He leaned across the counter. "It's not about holding hands, feeling good, and singing 'Kumbaya.' It's about staying alive!"

I climbed back on the stool and covered my face. "I don't think I'm up to this."

He placed his hands on my shoulders. "Lenzi. You are more than up to this. The Hindered need you. The Intercessor Council needs you. Imagine what would happen if there weren't Speakers. Unaided, all the Hindered would become Malevolent and they'd quickly outnumber living humans. It would cause an apocalypse."

Well, that certainly put a new spin on the weirdness. I lowered my hands from my face and took a deep breath.

"Please, Lenzi. I'm not asking you to commit. Just give it a trial run." I swiveled on the stool to face him. He leaned close and placed his hands lightly on my knees. "Do one resolution and see how it goes." It felt like an electric charge shooting up my thighs to my belly as he rubbed his thumbs in circles on the inside of my knees. Desire swirled through me to the point I couldn't sit still, and when I shifted on my stool, he froze. He shook his head once and backed away a couple of steps. "Sorry," he whispered.

We stared at each other for a moment, then he half smiled and picked up the folded paper. "This goes like this, I think," he said, making a reverse fold to form the frog's back leg.

I took it from his hand, pulse still hammering in my ears. "You make origami too?"

He shook his head. "No. But I've watched you do it for lifetimes."

Rose. I placed the frog on the counter.

He squatted in front of my stool. "Lenzi. Please give soul sharing a try. Just once and I think you'll understand. You can make a difference—a life and death, Heaven and Hell kind of difference. It's an opportunity very few are privileged to have. One resolution—an easy one—and you'll see what I mean."

I glanced at the clock on the microwave. "Mom's going to be home soon."

“Tomorrow, then.” He stood up. “How about I pick you up after school?”

Staring into his pale eyes, I realized I might just be making the dumbest decision ever, but clearly there was something to this Speaker business—something bigger than me. I had to give it a try.

“Okay. It’s a deal.”

THIRTEEN

Rain trailed in narrow rivulets down the classroom window. As always, Ms. Mueller, my history teacher, yabbered from her podium. Her voice droned on and on like a hive of bees. *Bzzz.*

All I could think about was last night, which made school seem insignificant. My time with Zak at the Last Concert Café had been incredible. My heart raced every time I thought about playing together onstage and how easy it was to be with him—how normal he made me feel.

And then there was Alden, who made me feel anything but normal. He fascinated me. The Speaker thing, though, gave me the creeps. "It's a gift," Alden had said. I shifted in my hard plastic chair, trying to find a more comfortable position. The cuts on my belly hurt again, and the stitches pulled when I moved.

Bzzz. Bzzz. Bzzzzzz.

There were only fifteen minutes left, but the closer it got to when I'd see Alden, the slower the clock seemed to move. I doodled on the cover of my binder and killed time until the bell finally rang.

The social scene at the bank of lockers didn't slow me down at all. I was the new girl and didn't fit in—and the episode in the bathroom hadn't helped. The other students talked about me, but not to me, which was probably my fault. I'd made no attempt to even be friendly. My mom had enrolled me in this snooty private school because my grades had dropped before we moved and she thought a lower student/teacher ratio would help.

My problems had nothing to do with student/teacher ratios.

Ignoring other students' curious stares, I left everything in my locker, including my backpack. I wasn't going to do homework anyway, so why bother? I slipped my jacket on over my purse so it would stay dry and headed to the front doors of the school. Before I made it outside, Zak texted telling me he'd had a great time last night. I replied that I'd had a blast and couldn't wait to see him again. Grinning, I slipped my phone back under my jacket into my purse before braving the carpool line.

Rainy days were the worst. The line was always long, and it took more time for people to load into cars. The rain hammered on the corrugated aluminum overhang, drowning out everyone's voices as they waited to dash to the cars pulling into the drive.

"Help me." It didn't drown out Bogeybaby, though.

Alden's gray Audi pulled up in front of the covered area. "No. Go away!" I shouted at the ghost, shoving my way through the students to get to the front of the group. Alden got out and walked around the front of his car through the downpour to open my door. I sprinted through the cold, stinging rain and ducked into the car.

Drenched, Alden slipped into the driver's seat and stared at my face for what seemed like an eternity.

"You feel troubled. You okay?" he asked.

Nodding was the only safe response. Why, I wondered, did being around Alden turn me into a member of the Moron Club? I slid my shoes off and pushed my feet closer to the warm air coming out of the vent at the base of the dash.

It was an awkward silence as he pulled onto the freeway. I would have made small talk, but there was nothing we could talk about that was small.

I couldn't help but sneak glances at him. He was beautiful. His hair was soaked and stuck to his neck and cheek.

Turning off the freeway, we entered West University. The streets were lined with ancient oak trees whose branches met in the middle of the street, forming a living tunnel.

We parked in front of a large house that looked like it would be more at home in New England than Texas. It was gorgeous, with large, dark green shutters framing banks of French windows. I slipped back into my cold, soggy shoes.

Water seeped through the neck of the jacket as I dashed after Alden to the front porch. I tugged the collar up, and cold raindrops slithered down my back between my shoulder blades. The small overhang forced me to stand so close that I could feel his warmth as he unlocked the door. I resisted the urge to lean into him.

We stepped inside, and I followed Alden to the kitchen, where he took my coat and hung it on a hook by the back door. We were both dripping on the hardwood floor.

"We're a mess," he remarked as he pitched me a kitchen towel. I rubbed it around with my foot to sop up the water that had dripped off of my jacket. A small dog with a long face and wiry hair trotted in and barked happily at him. "Hey, Spook!" He reached down and scratched her behind the ear. "Let's get out of these wet clothes. I'm sure I've got something that'll fit you, Lenzi."

I felt too awkward to say anything, so I nodded. Full Moron Club membership with benefits. I followed him up the stairs to the first room on the right.

"Welcome to your minion's domain," Alden said, opening the top drawer of a tall dresser.

I peeked in from the doorway. The furniture was dark and formal. Not the room of a typical seventeen-year-old boy.

"Not my taste, necessarily," he said as he threw some clothes on the bed. "Mom used it as a guest room while I was away at school. This is my first year back."

I wandered over to his desk. This was more like it. Untidy stacks of papers were piled up on the edges. In the center of the desk was a stack of black files. The top one had a seal with the letters *IC* in gold. The bookshelves above the desk were stuffed with classical literature and books about paranormal phenomena. I picked up a small, ragged teddy bear from the bottom shelf.

"Ah, that's Joe Bear," Alden said. "We were inseparable through second grade. He likes milk and animal cookies."

I smiled and put the bear back.

He passed me some dry clothes. Warm-up pants and a T-shirt. "There's a bathroom right across the hallway. Make yourself at home."

The little dog, Spook, growled at a door at the end of the hallway that had a bright pink letter *E* painted on it, then followed me into a pink and purple bathroom with princess accents. I squatted down and rubbed the dog's neck. I'd always wanted a dog, but Mom said that it would be too much trouble. Spook tilted her head and leaned into my scratching. "Hey, there, sweetie."

She lay down on a purple rug with pink hearts around the edge, put her head between her paws, and watched me slip into Alden's warm, soft clothes. The warm-ups had a drawstring, so they stayed up even though they were way too long. The thick, oversized shirt smelled like Alden and was so loose that it didn't rub against my cut. I couldn't help but smile as I pulled the collar up to my nose and inhaled. *Mmm.* I closed my eyes and remembered the way he had kissed Rose—the passion I'd seen on that roof while hell raged around them.

I dropped my wet things in the sink and found a brush in the top drawer. After towel drying my hair, I stepped into the hallway barefooted.

"Alden?"

"Down here. I'm in the kitchen."

Spook gave the door at the end of the hall a parting growl before bouncing down the stairs ahead of me. Alden was stirring something in a pot on the stove.

"Hot chocolate," he announced. "The real kind. The powdered stuff is disgusting."

His hair was still wet, and he was in a black long-sleeved T-shirt and tattered blue jeans. His feet were bare. Casual. Comfortable. Gorgeous.

I hadn't felt this calm in ages. My body almost hummed with peace.

"You're better," he said as he handed me a cup of chocolate.

I took the cup and wrapped my fingers around it, knocking off the last bit of chill. "Yeah, I feel a lot better. Bogeybaby was hassling me when you pulled up."

He smiled and put the pot in the sink. "Ah, that explains it. I thought maybe you were having boyfriend troubles."

"No, we're fine. Fantastic, in fact."

His smile faded. "Glad to hear it."

I took a sip of chocolate. It was rich and delicious. He was right—compared to this, the powdered stuff Mom and I made at home was disgusting. "Is that your Cinderella hairbrush in the bathroom?"

Alden laughed. "No. That belongs to my sister, Elizabeth. She's four." He walked into the next room and plopped down on a sofa.

I followed him and sat in an overstuffed chair. "Where's she?"

He set his cup down on the coffee table. "Early learning center."

I looked around the large family room. It could have been the cover shot for an interior design magazine. The back of the room was a wall of French doors accented with floral drapes that puddled into folds of fabric on the floor. No doubt his parents were loaded. "This is a great house. What do your parents do?" I asked.

"Doctors. Mom's an oncologist, and Dad's a general surgeon." He put his feet up on the coffee table. "I won the parent lottery this time." Spook jumped in his lap. "I hope it's okay I brought you here instead of your house. When this storm stops, I'll take you home."

"No. This is fine."

Alden scratched the dog behind the ear, and she made an *oof oof* sound.

"Spook is a funny name," I said.

"Yeah. She senses Hindered. Spooks drive her nuts. I got her when I was away at school."

I put my feet on the coffee table too. I figured since he was doing it, it was okay. "Where did you go to school?"

"Wilkingham Military Academy. It's actually just a cover for a Protector training facility that's run by the Intercessor Council." Spook climbed off his lap and padded in circles on the sofa cushion next to him and settled down with her head on his thigh. "When I was fourteen years old, I got a letter telling me I'd earned a scholarship, and my parents let me go. The brochure was slick, and they bought into it completely. I knew exactly what it was, of course. I'd already begun having memories of my past lives."

I finished off my chocolate and set the cup on the coffee table. "So if I were normal . . . or rather appropriately abnormal, I would have started having past life memories when I was younger?"

He nodded.

"I wish I could remember. This is driving me crazy."

"You and me both." Spook grumbled when Alden stood and picked up our cups.

I followed him into the kitchen. "Do Speakers go to school?"

"No. Speakers go through an apprenticeship their first few cycles under an experienced mentor. From then on, their job pretty much stays the same generation after generation. It's not affected by technology like my job is." He set the cups in the sink and ran water into them.

I leaned on the granite counter next to him. "What kind of technology?"

"Medicine is totally different each cycle. Things were pretty rough before antibiotics and sterilization. My past life memories don't help me with that. School gets me up to speed with the era's advances. Laws change too. I can't just run around with a sword strapped to my hip anymore, much as I'd like to." He winked and pulled out a sponge from under the sink.

"So, are you going back there?"

He squirted soap on the sponge and scrubbed the cups and pan. "No. I've been released for duty. Now my parents think I'm so brilliant, the school has allowed me to do a correspondence course by computer." He rinsed the dishes and set them in a drain rack next to the sink.

"So, the academy is where you learned to be Ghost Boy."

He smiled. "Yes, Ghost Boy and Doctor Boy. Let me see your stitches."

I put my hands over my abdomen. "Why?"

He groaned. "Come on, Lenzi. . . . I put them there. Get over it. I need to be sure there isn't an infection starting up. It's just your stomach. It's not like I haven't seen it before."

That last little bit irked me. How much of my— No. How much of *Rose's* body had he seen, and in what context?

He groaned again.

"Fine." If he wanted to play doctor, I could go with that. I had to lift my shirt almost to my bra to expose the scratches because they extended so high on my abdomen.

He leaned closer, running his fingers along either side of the sutures. His gentle touch caused my heart to race and the cut to ache. I winced. He pulled my shirt down and straightened up. "It's a little red. You need some antibiotics, and I need to treat it. I'll be right back, okay?"

"Okay." I gripped the edge of the counter. Treat it how? I'd always been terrified of all things medical and this home-doctoring routine was no exception. His emotion-feeling stuff must have kicked in because he stopped at the base of the stairs.

"Lenzi, it'll be fine. I know what I'm doing. You need to trust me."

I nodded.

He returned from upstairs with a cardboard pack of giant pills and a small vial of clear liquid. After punching the first two capsules through the foil on the bottom of the pack, he placed them in my hand. "Here, take both of these antibiotics now and follow the schedule on the inside for the rest." He pulled a bottle of water out of the fridge and led me to the sofa in the family room.

I took a swig from my water bottle and swallowed the pills. He shifted the sofa cushions and had me lie down. When he sat next to me and began to pull up the bottom of my shirt, I inhaled sharply, one step short of a gasp.

"Trust me," he said, opening the top of the vial full of clear liquid. "That thing was demonic."

I nodded. He sprinkled the liquid from the vial over the wound. A small area bubbled like it was hydrogen peroxide, but it had no odor. He pulled my shirt back down and moved away.

"What was that stuff?"

"It was holy water. The antibiotics will fight infections with earthly causes. The holy water will kill off infections caused by evil. The Malevolent you dealt with was evil. Its wound can infect not just your body, but your soul."

I bit my lower lip. "Am I going to get sick?"

"Not a chance."

I stood. "Alden, I'm really not cut out for this kind of thing. I'm not made for bogeymen and stitches and evil spirits and—"

He placed his hands on my shoulders. "Stop! We had a deal. You said you'd give it a try. Just once, remember?"

Tears filled my eyes, and I trembled. Alden pulled me into his arms and held me against his chest. "Just once, Lenzi. You can do this."

He smelled delicious, like rain and chocolate, and his embrace was so right. I wrapped my arms around him and closed my eyes. I wasn't addicted to Xanax, but I could certainly become addicted to Alden.

Still clinging to him, I drew a ragged breath. "I'd better let Mom know where I am, though. She'll freak if I'm not home when she calls to check on me."

He opened his arms, and reluctantly, I stepped out of his warmth. I went to the kitchen, pulled my cell phone out of my purse, and texted Mom. A message from Zak came through as I was putting my phone away. He wanted me to come see him play again tonight. I could still feel the warmth of Alden's embrace as I texted Zak that I couldn't make it. I took a deep breath and turned my phone off. Alden was right. I'd made a deal to give being a Speaker a shot, and I needed to carry through with it.

When I returned to the family room, I found Alden just outside the open French door. The rain had stopped, and he was standing with his back to me, looking out over a small, landscaped yard—well, more of a courtyard, really, with a tiny sparkling pool and ornate fountain. He had his hands on his hips, and Spook was sitting at his bare feet.

"Alden," I said softly. "You'll have to cut me some slack. I'm really new at this."

He remained facing away. "It's hard to play follow-the-leader when the leader doesn't know where she's going. I'm spoiled. It's usually so easy to predict your needs and follow you. I'm not being very helpful. I apologize."

"Teach me how to deal with the bogeymen. I don't want to be attacked by a Malevolent again."

He studied my face. All business. The calm tutor.

"That's a good start," he said. "Keep telling me what you need. That's the essence of this relationship. I'm here to help you. You are the real power. Only you can hear the Hindered.

Only you can help them. Let's start there, okay? Are they talking to you now?" He shoved his hands in his jean pockets.

I sat on the concrete surround of the fountain. "No."

"Let them."

"How?"

He sat next to me. "Listen. They're always there, waiting for you to listen. Really powerful ones will break through regardless. If the timing is bad, just tell them to go away. They're persistent, but usually they'll obey you. The one in Kemah was rare and unfortunate. It was my fault, really. I should never have left you alone untrained."

I shifted to face him. "Alden. That's ridiculous. I told you to go away and leave me alone. How could that possibly be your fault?"

"Rules. There are rules. Clear, concise, concrete rules. It is my duty to inform, protect, and serve the Speaker. I facilitate your success. That's why I exist. If you don't get tough soon, the Intercessor Council is going to wonder what's wrong."

He stood and paced along the edge of the pool. "No offense, but your little hundred-year vacation caused some trouble. We did our best to cover the region, but with you gone, we got pretty backed up around here."

"Do all people who die become Hindered?"

"No. Only those with unresolved issues. Most souls just move on."

"Issues like my dad had?"

He stopped pacing, but said nothing. He just stared at me with those clear gray eyes.

"What if Dad is out there somewhere? I could talk to him. Tell him good-bye. Ask him why—"

Alden put his hands on my shoulders. "He's gone, Lenzi."

My chest ached. "But he killed himself. Obviously he had issues."

He shook his head. "Perhaps they weren't issues that kept him Earth-bound. Maybe they were internal within himself or maybe his death solved his problems. Not all suicide victims become Hindered."

The thought of being with Dad again, even as a ghost, made my heart speed up. "What if he was, though? Couldn't he still be out there somewhere?"

"Very few spirits linger, Lenzi. He would have contacted you by now if he were still here. Family bonds have a strong pull." I could tell it was hard for Alden to discuss this with me. He spoke slowly and carefully. "He died several months ago. You hadn't emerged as a Speaker yet. If he had been Earth-bound, he would have approached the nearest Speaker, and there isn't a record of that. I checked. Chances are, he just moved on without needing help." He released my shoulders and flipped the hair out of his eyes. "I'm sorry, Lenzi."

I sat on the edge of the fountain and ran my fingertips in the cool water. Knowing Dad was at peace made me feel a little better.

He stopped within a few feet of me and met my eyes directly. "You okay?"

I nodded.

"If you're up to it, we really need to get to work now."

"Okay," I said, willing my heart rate to slow. The way he looked at me made me uncomfortable—as if he could see inside me. "You want me to call out a Hindered?"

"That would be a good start, if you feel up to it. But it's not really about what *I* want, is it?"

I rolled my eyes. I hated the hierarchy involved with this. I wanted a friend, not a subordinate. "Alden, stop with the minion crap. Can't you just be my friend?"

"I'll be whatever you want me to be. Define my role and begin doing your job."

"I want you to be my friend, Alden. I need a friend."

His expression didn't change. "A friend it is. Let's do this first resolution in the living room."

"Great." At least he wasn't just going to act like he should be my servant anymore.

Alden made Spook stay outside so she wouldn't bark and growl at the Hindered the whole time.

We sat on the sofa.

"Okay, Lenzi, you should focus on one voice at a time. Pick the one that's most persistent because it will calm the others down to get rid of the troublemaker. As long as you're resolving problems for them, the Hindered should remain peaceful. Call me if you need me because I can't hear what's going on in your body. I can feel the fear, but I'm not allowed to enter the vessel unless invited. Remember to ask me in when it's time for the extra soul to leave. My entrance alone will dislodge them. The vessel can't accommodate three souls for long. The weakest one is forced out. Malevolent are an entirely different situation, but don't worry about that right now.

"Make it easy this first time," he advised. "Pick one that can clearly define its needs."

I tucked up into a ball and hugged my knees. I was terrified, but didn't want Alden to know. I wanted him to think that I was brave and tough. I wanted to impress him—like Rose did.

FOURTEEN

I closed my eyes and concentrated on singling out a Hindered. It was easy, really. The bogeybaby, who told me her name was Suzanne, started whining at me right away.

"Okay, I've got one," I said, stifling a nervous giggle.

Alden grinned. "What's funny?"

"I sound like I'm trying to land a fish!"

"Well, reel it in, Captain Ahab!"

"I don't know how," I mumbled.

"Invite it in. It'll give you a clear picture of what it wants. Let me know if it gives you any trouble, and I'll help you."

A jolt of panic shot through me.

"It's okay, Lenzi. I'm right here. Go ahead. You'll know what to do."

I felt like a little kid about to jump off of the diving board for the first time. I reached over and took Alden's hand. I needed his magic calm-down thing. Instead, his touch delivered a type of electric shock that caused my entire body to tingle and buzz with energy. *What the heck?* I looked over at him. "What's going on?"

"I . . . um . . . It's complicated. Give me a moment." He closed his eyes and took a deep breath. The current running up my arm dimmed and mellowed into that peaceful hum I'd experienced when he touched me before. I knew for sure now that he was doing it on purpose.

"What is that, Alden? Are you doing that intentionally?"

"Yes and no." He took a deep breath. "Yes, I am doing that intentionally, but I'm having trouble controlling it. I'm pretty young this cycle, and it's harder to keep it together. You're feeling what I want you to feel. You're also sometimes feeling what I'm experiencing myself. As I get older, I'll be able to mask my own emotions completely and gift you with what you need. As I said, you came four years earlier than usual, and you took my hand before I was ready."

I stared at him for a moment, baffled. "So what exactly was that?"

"It was . . . well, it was what I was feeling at the time."

"Which is what?" When it appeared he wasn't going to answer, I pushed harder. "You told me your job was to inform the Speaker. Well, I'm the Speaker, so inform."

He fidgeted and then ran his hands through his hair. "Okay. Your fear is a turn-on. Protectors are stimulated when their Speakers are afraid. It's what makes it possible to put you in harm's way. Otherwise, our instinct to protect would trump everything and we'd never allow you to do your job, which is to put yourself in danger in order to resolve the issues that keep the Hindered Earth-bound."

Well, that certainly wasn't what I expected. "Get out! You're turned on by fear?"

"And pain to some extent." He winked and pulled his hand away.

I turned on the sofa to face him. "That's totally sick. Whose pain?"

"It's irrelevant." He made a shooing motion with his hand.

I gave him my best imitation of Mom's glare. "Whose pain, Alden?"

He leaned back and put his arms across the back of the sofa. "Isn't there a Hindered waiting for you, Captain Ahab?"

"Help me, please! You have to help me." Bogeybaby sounded frantic.

"Fine. Ghost time, but we're not finished with this discussion." I turned my head to where the voice was. "Okay, Suzanne. I'll help you now."

"Tell her she can enter the vessel," Alden prompted.

"You can enter and tell me what you need me to do, Suzanne," I said as I took Alden's hand again. This time his touch was reassuring.

I cried out as the Hindered entered my body. I hadn't thought about the pain involved, or I'd have braced myself for it. Fortunately, it only lasted a second. A jolt from Alden jumped up my arm. Well, that answered my question—*my* pain. Fantastic.

"The worst part is over, Lenzi. You did great. Is she talking to you?"

I nodded as the little girl went on and on in a loud shrill voice about her sister and a cat and a Christmas tree and shots and needles and dying. I could barely understand her. "She wants to tell her sister something." I kept my eyes on Alden. "She wants to give her something. Oh, no, Alden. She's talking too fast!"

"She's just a person without a body, Lenzi. Tell her to slow it down. You're in control. Tell her what to do."

It was too much. Suzanne was getting louder and talking faster. I stood up and put my hands on either side of my head. "I can't do it, Alden. I need her to get out."

He stood and pulled my hands away from my ears, holding me by my shoulders. "No. Lenzi. Listen to me. Are you listening? Tune her out and focus on *my* voice only." I nodded and he continued. "You are in control of this situation. The Hindered need you. You must take charge. Be strong. Do you hear me?"

I nodded.

"Tell her to slow down and do what you say."

"Suzanne, I want you to slow down and tell me the story from the beginning. Wait until I tell you to start." To my amazement, she shut up.

He tightened his grip on my shoulders. "Good, Lenzi. Yes, that's right."

I made a halfhearted attempt to smile. He let go of my shoulders and sat back down. I sat next to him and curled my legs under me. It was a bizarre sensation to house another person's soul in my body. Almost overwhelming. *Be strong like Rose,* I told myself.

"It's all right, Lenzi. Go ahead. I'm right here." He patted my leg.

"Okay, Suzanne, tell me slowly," I whispered. I closed my eyes and listened as the child spoke to me about her death and what she needed from me.

"Stop for a minute, Suzanne. I'll let you continue in a sec, okay?" I got on my knees facing Alden. "It's a kid—a little girl—she wants to draw something for her mom. What do I do?"

"You let her have your body. Let her draw or whatever she wants. I'll get some of Elizabeth's crayons. Hold on." He leapt up and strode to the kitchen, returning with a pad of paper and a handful of crayons.

I took the supplies with trembling hands. "How do I give her my body?"

"Invite her to use your hands to draw. She'll know how to do it. Just stay close to the surface so you can hear me. Don't retreat in too far." He stroked my face with his fingertips. "You're doing great, Lenzi. I'm proud of you."

A tear rolled down my cheek. Alden wiped it away with his thumb and gave me a reassuring smile.

"Okay, Suzanne. You can use my body to color a picture if you want to."

Oh, yay! Thank you, thank you, thank you!

"You're welcome."

"I'm right here," Alden said.

My body began to move as if on its own. I knew it was Suzanne controlling the motion, but it was still weird to the point of being scary. Not of my own accord, I nibbled my lip and my shoulders slumped. Clutching the art supplies, I slid off the sofa onto the floor. Alden moved to the edge of the sofa watching with interest. Suzanne grabbed the blue crayon in my fist and began making dramatic strokes across the paper.

"That's the sky!" Suzanne announced proudly from my mouth in a child's voice.

"Very nice, Suzanne," Alden said.

Next came jagged vertical green strokes at the bottom of the page.

"Grass?" Alden prompted.

"Mmm-hmm. Watch this!" Using my hand, she picked up the black crayon and whacked the tip on the paper, making spots in the grass. "Ants!"

Alden chuckled. "You okay in there, Lenzi?"

"Yes," my own voice answered. Cool. I could control which one of us was in charge of my body.

"Nuh-uh. Go 'way! It's my turn," the child's voice retorted from my mouth. Well, I could sort of control it, anyway.

"Play nice, Suzanne," Alden warned, "or I'll have to make

you leave. You can't play with Lenzi unless you're willing to share. Okay?"

"Okay, I'll share," she grumbled. "I need an orange crayon. I don't have one."

Alden shrugged. "I'm sorry, Suzanne, but there isn't an orange crayon."

"B-b-but I need one for Mr. Sun. I g-g-g-gotta have orange," the tiny voice wailed.

"I'll have to remember to get a new box of crayons before we take on a child again, Lenzi. The old charcoal and slate days were easier," he said.

The child was nearly hysterical. I had to do something so she'd finish her picture and get out. Through thought, I told her how to mix colors. Eventually, the wailing stopped and she picked up the yellow crayon and drew "Mr. Sun." Then she got the red and lightly shaded over him.

"Wow, Suzanne. That was a good idea," Alden remarked.

She made my body grin. "Yeah, Lenzi told me how. I like Lenzi."

"I do too," Alden said.

"Now for Mr. Jinx," Suzanne's voice called from my body. She had me on all fours, rocking back and forth, looking at her drawing.

"I've always loved resolutions with children. They make you do such random things," Alden remarked.

"Not helpful, Alden," I said, trying unsuccessfully to stop the rocking.

I gave up fighting her, hoping it would end sooner. She sniffled and wiped my nose with the back of my hand. *Gross.* At least she hadn't picked my nose or anything.

Alden was grinning when she rolled me over on my back and held the picture up so that he could see.

"I like your picture, Suzanne. Who's Mr. Jinx?"

"My best friend. I told my little sister, Becky, she could have him when I died." She rolled back over and picked up the purple crayon. She began drawing vigorously, chewing on my lip the entire time. I hoped she wouldn't gnaw my lip hard enough to draw blood.

"You still okay, Lenzi?" Alden called.

"Yes."

"Done!" the voice of Suzanne proclaimed proudly. She held the picture up for Alden to see. Mr. Jinx appeared to be a stuffed purple cat. He had a huge grin and was sitting on the ant-filled grass. "I love Mommy" was scribbled across the sky.

"It's beautiful, Suzanne. We'll deliver it to your mommy. Let Lenzi come up to play now, okay?"

"NO!"

Alden stood up. "Lenzi?"

"I'm here. It's okay. Give me a second," my own voice answered as I sat on the sofa holding the drawing. I closed my eyes and regained control of my body, relegating Suzanne back to a voice in my head. Alden was right; I could do this.

I remained still for a few moments and through thought convinced Suzanne to cooperate.

"Okay," I said. "She's going to be a good girl, Alden, because she's very sweet. Aren't you, Suzanne?"

Yep.

"Tell me where you were when you died."

Mommy and Daddy called it MD Anderson Hospital.

"Where did you live?"

In a brown house with a red door.

Great. That really narrowed it down. "What street did you live on?"

I don't know.

Fantastic. There were over four million people in Houston. "When did you die?"

I don't know.

"What school did you go to?"

Wildcat Way.

"Is there anything else?"

Give Mr. Jinx to my sister.

That was it, I marveled. That's all that was keeping her here. She needed to give her mommy a picture and a stuffed cat to her little sister. I wondered if resolutions were all this simple. After some more questions, I had all the information she was going to give me about where Mr. Jinx was and how we could find her sister. She sounded weak and tired. By this time, her voice was barely a whisper. I assured her we'd take care of what she asked. Then I couldn't hear her at all, but I could feel her presence in my body.

"Now, Suzanne, it's time for you to go, okay?" There was no response, but I knew it was time. "It's my friend Alden's turn, so you need to go. Are you ready? Okay, Alden, let's do it."

Alden released his soul from his body and slid into mine. Across the room, a tiny girl in a ruffled dress waved. Her body seemed to glow blue from the inside, making her appear translucent. She blew a kiss to me and skipped into a shaft of brilliant white light.

That's what it's all about. Well done, Alden said.

"Thanks, now get out. I'm feeling claustrophobic. One soul in here is enough."

As you wish, my master, he joked. *You'd better go touch me, though, unless you're starting to like pain.*

I huddled on the sofa next to his lifeless body and wrapped my arms around him. "Get out, my oppressed minion. . . . Be gentle."

He exited with little pain.

"Hello, friend," he said.

"Hey." My head was against his chest. I didn't look up or move other than to tremble all over. I clung to him as I rode a wave of emotion. Suzanne's resolution was the scariest, most incredible experience of my life. The intense pull I felt toward Alden was overwhelming.

"Hey, it's over now. Relax. You did great. Perfect. Textbook perfect," he said.

I loosened my grip and shifted so that I faced him. I'd never felt this charged and confident. The resolution was a huge rush, and my strange, unearthly attraction to him was more than I could resist. I entwined my fingers in Alden's thick, silky hair, and before I thought through what I was doing, I kissed him on his gorgeous mouth. Not a gentle kiss, either.

To my astonishment, he laughed. I pulled back, mortified.

"Well, you wanted to be friends," he said, eyes twinkling. "That was friendly, I suppose."

FIFTEEN

Stupid, I thought as Alden laughed. I couldn't believe I had so little self-control. I'd been "friendly," all right.

"I'm so sorry, Alden. I don't know why I did that," I whispered. An image of Zak flashed through my head, and I cringed even more.

"It's fine, Lenzi. I guess that's what friends do."

I couldn't tell whether he was kidding or not. I seriously wanted to crawl under the sofa. Instead, I walked over to the back door and let in Spook, who trotted over, jumped on Alden's lap, and licked his face.

"See, Lenzi? Spook and I are just friends, and she kisses me too."

If he was trying to make me feel better, it wasn't working.

Spook barked and wagged her nubby tail—a tail so minimal she had to wag her whole back half to get the point across. The cute boy/cute dog combination was too much to resist. I smiled in spite of my misery.

Alden patted Spook and put her down on the floor, then stood up and stretched. "You did a great job, Lenzi. How do you feel?"

Other than mortified over acting totally out of character and pouncing on him? "Good. It wasn't as awful as I thought it would be."

"Do you need to go home, or can I take you to dinner?"

He still wanted to take me out to dinner after that? "Um, dinner would be great. I'm starving."

"Fantastic." He scanned me from head to toe. "Oh, wait, change of plans. Why don't I call for Chinese takeout instead?"

I glanced down at his baggy T-shirt and too-long warm-up pants. "What? Are you telling me my wet school uniform or my chic cross-gender athletic garb isn't the height of fashion?" I strutted across the floor like a runway model and almost tripped on the warm-ups on my turn.

Alden applauded. "I'll buy the entire collection. I don't see how you could look better, honestly, but I think it is a little too sophisticated for the restaurants around here. How about moo goo gai pan and an order of fried rice?"

"Great."

"Egg roll?"

"Sure."

"Any special requests?"

I sat back down. "No. Anything you want is fine." He stared at me awhile. "What?" I asked.

"Nothing. You're just really easy to get along with."

"Why? Because I'm not a picky eater?"

"No. You're just . . . different."

Rose again. "I'm sorry."

"Why are you sorry, Lenzi?" he asked, sitting down next to me.

I didn't really have an answer that wouldn't make me sound stupid. He looked at me until I could feel the blood heating up my face. He shook his head and dialed the Chinese restaurant. I was glad he'd dropped the subject. It would have been pretty hard to explain that I was jealous of myself.

Alden was a master with chopsticks. I finally gave up and used a fork. Between the two of us, we finished everything, including four fortune cookies.

"What do we do with Suzanne's drawing?" I asked.

He picked up the fortune cookie wrappers and pitched them into an empty takeout container I was holding. "We deliver it to her mother and tell her little sister where the purple thing is."

"Mr. Jinx. How do we find the mother?" I dropped the containers into the kitchen trash can.

"We have the name of the hospital and her school. Did she tell you her last name?"

I sat down next to him on the sofa. "Yes. It's Lawrence. Suzanne Lawrence. She died of cancer. The sister is three. Suzanne was almost five. Mom goes by Susie. Probably Suzanne also. She has a dog named Fluffy. The toy is named after some cat that died when she was a baby."

"Wow. Good job. Where's Mr. Jinx?"

"In a shoe box behind the fake Christmas tree in the attic. She hid him so that he didn't have to go back." Hard as I tried, I couldn't hold back tears. "Mr. Jinx was scared of needles."

"Hey," he whispered as he put his arm around me. "Hey. You saw her. She's fine. She's released. You helped her."

I nodded and wiped my eyes. "Sorry. I'm just a wimp, I guess. It kind of got to me."

The front door opened. Alden smiled. "Mom must be home. Good, she'll get to meet you."

Oh, no! I looked awful. Blotchy from blubbering, and wearing Alden's clothes. I wiped my eyes on my sleeve, straightened my shirt, and finger combed my hair.

I was probably blushing purple by the time his mom walked in wearing a long, white lab coat with CAROLYN THOMAS, MD embroidered in navy blue on the pocket. I tried to wiggle out from under Alden's arm, but he held me tighter.

"Hey, Alden. Is this Lenzi?" his mother asked with a smile.

"In the flesh," he said cheerfully. "Lenzi, this is my mom, Carolyn."

Even without the lab coat, Dr. Thomas would have been intimidating. She was tall, blond, and gorgeous. Shoulder-length hair framed a high-cheek-boned face.

"Hi," I said.

"It's nice to meet you at last, Lenzi. You're all he's talked about for the past week."

I smiled. Dr. Thomas smiled back and strolled into the kitchen.

I glanced at my watch. Time had passed faster than I realized. Mom would be home by now. I pointed at my wrist and whispered, "I need to go."

"Alden, don't you have a report due tomorrow?" his mother called from the kitchen.

He rolled his eyes and grinned at me. "Yes, Mom, I do. I'll get right on it. I'm taking Lenzi home first."

"Be sure you get back soon enough to finish that report before the sun comes up. If they're going to let you earn a degree by correspondence, you need to stay on top of it."

Alden walked to the kitchen and kissed his mother on the cheek. "Don't you have a cauldron to stir or a broomstick to ride around on or something?"

She laughed and ruffled his hair.

I felt silly returning home barefooted, wearing a raincoat over Alden's clothes, and carrying a plastic bag containing my soggy uniform. It reminded me of the time I'd wet my pants in preschool.

Alden walked me to the door and we stood outside uncomfortably—like it was the end of a first date. Was letting a ghost share your body and then chowing down on Chinese takeout a date? He was waiting for me to say good-bye, looking as nervous as I felt. Should I shake his hand or kiss him good night on the cheek? Maybe I should act like Spook and just lick his face.

I didn't know what to do. I had a boyfriend. A great boyfriend, but something in me needed Alden.

"What is this we're doing?" I asked, shifting my weight foot to foot.

"I don't know," he said. "You tell me."

My mom opened the door and saved the day. Whew. A graceful exit.

"Oh, Alden," Mom gushed. "Please come in."

Forget the graceful exit.

"Thanks, Ms. Anderson, but I have to get home. I have a report due tomorrow. Good night, Lenzi. It was . . . fun."

"Yeah. Thanks for dinner."

Alden smiled and shoved his hands into his pockets. "You're welcome. It was my pleasure."

Mom put her arm around me as we watched Alden drive off. "I'm glad you are finally making friends," she said.

A *friend.* Is that really what Alden was?

Zak's set at the Last Concert Café wouldn't be over until eleven. He was probably disappointed I didn't come watch him play, and he'd go ballistic if he found out where I'd been, so I left my phone off to avoid having to lie . . . again. Guilt pinched the pit of my stomach.

After changing and brushing my teeth, I lay in bed waiting for my post-resolution jitters to settle. I'd finally done something that mattered—something significant. Alden was right. It made sense now. I *had* to be a Speaker. It was the first time in my life I'd felt completely right. I hadn't been able to help my dad, but I could help the Hindered make things right so they could be at peace. And hanging out with Alden was a definite job perk. If only he would see *me* instead of Rose every time he looked at me.

Just as I closed my eyes, a sound came from my window, like when the June bugs knock against it in the summer months. *Tap. Tap-tap. Tap.*

Were the Hindered drawn to light like bugs? "Go away. Ghost Busters Inc. is closed for the night!"

Tap. Tap.

Dang. I was never going to get any rest. I got out of bed and shuffled to the window.

Tap tappity tap.

It wasn't bugs or Hindered. It looked like . . . pebbles? I opened the window and stared down at Alden, who shot me a heart-melting grin.

"Took you long enough. I was about to start serenading if you didn't notice me."

I stared down at him, mystified.

"Please, Lenzi. Let me in before the neighbors call the cops."

I wished I'd grabbed a bathrobe or something when the cool air gusted in the front door. The shorts and cami were fine as long as I was under my down comforter. Alden walked by me into the entry hall.

"Where's your mom?" he whispered.

I pointed over my shoulder to the stairs. "Asleep in her room."

"Perfect." He brushed by me and started climbing to the second floor.

Oh, no! Not my room again! It was a disaster. In addition to the bathroom, there were three rooms upstairs: mine, at the top of the stairs, Mom's bedroom at the far end, and a tiny bedroom where Mom stored her old client files and tax returns. Maybe I could steer him in there. "Alden, don't—" Too late. He was in my room before I could finish my sentence.

"Don't what?" he asked, sitting on the bed.

"You dare to enter the inner sanctum of the Speaker?" I joked, looking around.

"The oppressed subordinate is feeling brave." He chuckled and patted the spot next to him. "If you'd leave your phone on, this would be much easier."

And much less embarrassing, I thought as I shoved a pair of underwear under the bed with my foot. "Is something wrong?"

He stared at me with his odd, gray eyes. "No. Well, yes, actually. I need you to leave your phone on all the time. Since we're in the twenty-first century, we should take advantage of the technology."

"Okay, I'll leave it on." I stood awkwardly near the doorway. I never felt this way with Zak. My attraction to Alden was unnatural. So intense it was painful. *Pain lets you know you're alive,* Alden had said when we soul-shared. I'd been walking around numb for the last three months, and for the first time since Dad's death, I felt truly alive. "Is that all?"

"No. I didn't really get to say good-bye to you properly when I dropped you off," he said, scanning me from head to toe.

Was he finally starting to accept me as Lenzi? I didn't respond for fear my heart would be successful in its attempt to escape from the confines of my rib cage. I knew what *I'd* consider a proper good-bye. I took a step closer, hoping he had the same thing in mind.

"Well, we didn't have closure to the resolution, and we didn't make plans for the next one. I'm not supposed to leave business unfinished like that," he explained. A peculiar look crossed his face. "Are you okay?"

Business. It had nothing to do with me. It was business. "I'm great. Finish it. Let's have closure."

He stood up. "What's wrong? You feel off."

Well, that was a good way of wording it. "I'm fine, Alden. Just get on with it. I'm tired."

"I'm sorry. We can do the interview for the resolution report later, but we have to come up with a strategy to fulfill the promise tonight."

"Report? I thought it was a school report."

"No. I don't go to school, Lenzi. I've graduated. IC training ends when the Speaker emerges."

I leaned against the closed door. "But you told me you were taking a correspondence course."

"No, I told you my parents *thought* I was taking a correspondence course. I'm doing the paperwork for us. It's part of my job. The IC keeps track of resolutions. You know, trends in Hindered requests and duration of negotiations—stuff like that."

I gasped. "You've gotta be kidding me. They keep bogeyman statistics?"

He sat back down on the edge of my bed. "Mm-hm. There's an entire department at the IC devoted to it."

"Why on earth would someone keep up with something like that?"

"As the population increases, so do the death rates, and logically, so do the Hindered. The Intercessor Council ensures that the Speaker-Hindered ratio is balanced. There are a lot more of us now than there were the last time you did this."

Always Rose. "I haven't done this before," I whispered. Ratios. Reports. What in the world had I gotten myself into?

"There are more of us than ever before."

"I can just imagine the recruiting poster. 'Ghost whisperers wanted: no experience necessary. Death wish and masochistic tendencies a must.'"

He smiled. "Yeah, something like that."

"So, what else did you need to do to wrap up our little business transaction?" I asked, fidgeting with the bottom of my shirt.

He checked me out again before he answered. "We have to keep our promise to Suzanne. I'll go to the hospital while you're at school tomorrow and see if I can get an address on her. I doubt it, though. Hospitals are pretty tight with information like that. Sometimes I can chat people up and get them to tell me stuff."

I raised an eyebrow. "I bet you can."

He stood and strode the door. "Please leave your phone on. I'll pick you up after school so we can close the file."

"Is that an order?"

"No. It's a request—an invitation. Lenzi, will you please allow me to pick you up after school so that we can close Suzannc's file?" He gifted me with a gorgeous smile.

"I'd love that."

I sat on my bed long after he left, staring at Dad's guitar in the corner. Thc melody Zak wrote for me ran through my mind. When I closed my eyes, I could see Zak sitting on the coffee table with his guitar, giving me his heart in a song.

"What am I doing, Dad?" I asked. I held my breath, waiting for a reply that didn't come. Deep down, I knew the answer.

SIXTEEN

The clock in my American history classroom moved in slow motion. I fidgeted, willing time to speed up so I could see Alden again. I'd hardly slept last night.

Maybe Alden was right. Maybe being a Speaker was a gift.

"Help me," a woman's voice whispered in my ear.

A gift with drawbacks.

"She stole it," the disembodied voice continued.

"Not now. Go away," I whispered.

"You must help me retrieve it."

"Go haunt someone else. I said, not now!"

"Miss Anderson?" The entire class was looking at me. "Is there a problem?" Ms. Mueller asked.

"Um, no, ma'am." I'd always done my best to be invisible and not draw attention to myself. I shifted in my chair as all eyes in the room appraised me.

"Who were you talking to, Miss Anderson?" Ms. Mueller waddled close enough for me to see the coffee stains on her lavender polka-dotted blouse. She appeared to enjoy my discomfort. "I thought for a minute you might be talking to a ghost or something."

Titters and giggles erupted.

Apparently satisfied, Ms. Mueller resumed her mind-numbingly boring lecture about the Battle of Gettysburg, and one by one, my classmates stopped gawking. I relaxed and let my mind wander back to Alden. My snobby classmates might have lots of things I didn't have, but they didn't have anything like *him*—a hot, mysterious ghost boy. My feelings for Alden were intense and dangerous, just like the life he was encouraging me to embrace. So different from Zak, who represented everything I thought I wanted in a boyfriend—until now.

At last the bell rang.

It took no time at all to force my way to my locker, stuff my backpack, and fly out the front door. Alden wasn't in the line yet, which gave me time to return Zak's text. He'd sent me a message during trig asking me to hang out this afternoon.

I can't, I wrote. **I'm going to study with a friend. I'll call you when I get home.**

I couldn't keep lying like this. Maybe Alden was right: it was easier not to be with anyone if you were in the ghost-hunting business—well, except for maybe another ghost hunter.

I pushed Send right as Alden pulled up. I took a deep breath, shoved aside my guilt over lying to Zak again, and dropped my phone into my purse. Alden grinned at me through the windshield, causing my heart to lurch.

"Sorry I'm late. The medical center traffic was a nightmare," he said, opening the passenger door for me.

"She stole it. You must help me," the female voice demanded as I buckled my seat belt.

"Leave me alone! I told you to go away and leave me alone!" I shouted.

Alden closed his door. "Wow. I thought we were making some progress. I sure hope there's someone else in the car with us and that ugliness wasn't directed at me."

I was certain Alden was the only person in the world who would wish a voice with no body was in the car with him. "Of course it's not directed at you. This bogeywoman's driving me nuts. I got busted in class because of her."

He brushed my hair behind my shoulder. "Hi. It's nice to see you too, Lenzi. I'm fine, thanks for asking."

I laughed. "Sorry. Hi. She *is* driving me crazy, though."

He started the car. "What does she want?"

"She says that someone stole something from her."

"Cool! I love it when they've been wronged. The resolution can be exciting. It's worth a lot of points. Not as many as a Malevolent, but not as dangerous, either."

"Points?"

"There has to be some kind of grading scale, doesn't there?

If not, every Speaker-Protector pair would pick the easy ones to pump up their statistics." He turned onto the freeway service road. "You and I had the highest score three cycles running."

"I've never done this before, Alden."

He grinned. "Yes, you have—you just don't remember." He pulled into a coffee shop parking lot around the corner from the school. "I want you to meet some friends of mine, and yours too, sort of."

I pulled the handle on my door as Alden walked around the front of the car. "I can open my own door, Alden," I said as he held the door open for me.

"Of course you can. Would you like to open mine for me, instead?"

I squinted as I stepped out into the sunshine. "No. It's just old-fashioned, that's all."

"*I'm* old-fashioned, Lenzi." He laughed, pulling a computer case out of the backseat. "I'm old. *Really* old. Humor me, okay?" He gestured for me to lead to the door of the small, trendy coffee shop.

"Wait, Alden. I really don't want to meet your friends dressed like this."

"They're your friends too. And you look fantastic. I love the school uniform. You have great legs."

"Shut up!" I gasped. "I thought you were an old man!"

"Old soul. Young man. Big difference. It's okay, though; we're just friends, remember?"

Man, did I ever.

The coffee shop smelled delicious. Coffee, chocolate, and cinnamon. A couple at a small table began waving the minute we walked in the door. Both of them looked like weight lifters. Neither was tall, but both were muscled. The boy stood. Alden gestured for me to lead. The girl in the pair ran up and hugged me with gusto.

"Rose! You look great! I'm so glad you're back. Come on and join us." The girl bounded back to her companion. "She looks great. Doesn't she, Race?"

The short, redheaded boy stepped out from behind the table and kissed my cheek. "She has always looked great. It's good to see you, Rose."

Alden pulled out my chair. "She goes by Lenzi now."

"Why?" the boy, Race, asked.

Alden leaned forward. "For the same reason you two go by Race and Maddi. She doesn't like her real name."

"Yeah, but Rose is a timeless name. Our names are dated," the girl said.

"What are your real names?" I asked.

Both of them stared at me in astonishment.

Alden put his arm around me. "Okay, guys. I told you on the phone that I needed to tell you something. This is it. She has no memory of her past lives at all. None."

Race and Maddi were studying me with a combination of pity and amazement. I felt like I was a science experiment gone wrong.

Alden stood. "Lenzi, I apologize for not introducing you properly. This is Maude Wilson and Horace McLain. Maude and Horace prefer to go by Maddi and Race. Both of them are Protectors, like me. Maddi and Race, this is Lenzi Anderson."

Race stood. "I'm pleased to meet you, Lenzi."

Maddi remained seated, studying me.

"Wow," Race said. "This is weird. I've never heard of this happening before. Is it in the rule book, Alden?"

"No. I can't find another case of past-life amnesia in any of the IC documents I've read. I don't think the IC knows about it yet. And I hope if we become productive, they won't care." Alden slumped back into his chair.

"What do you mean, 'become productive'? Can't she intercede?" Race asked, not taking his eyes off me as he sat back down.

Alden took my hand. "She's fine. She battled a Malevolent and resolved a juvenile Hindered."

"A Malevolent," Race repeated. "Was it—"

"No," Alden cut him off. "It wasn't. Not yet, anyway. Subject closed."

"Got it." Race gave Alden a conspiratorial wink.

To me, the only thing weirder than having past lives I didn't remember was meeting people who knew things about me from those lives. I was intrigued and repelled at the same time.

Maddi and Race seemed nice enough, and though they seemed familiar to me somehow, I'd no definite recollection of ever meeting them before. In contrast to her muscular build and spiky short haircut, Maddi had a sweet, feminine face. She wore a floral western shirt with pearlized snaps down the front. Race had freckles that were set off perfectly by his thick red hair. Eyelashes in matching red framed his blue eyes. He had on a Rolling Stones T-shirt.

"How long ago did she emerge?" Maddi asked.

Alden squeezed my hand. "This is day five."

Maddi and Race gave each other a sideways glance.

"Have you closed the cases yet?" Maddi asked Alden.

Alden shook his head.

"Nothing in five days? I'm surprised the IC hasn't called a session. You'd better do something quick, Alden. It would be a shame to lose her."

I shifted in my chair. "Do what quick? Lose who? Me?"

"*Inform,* Alden. Inform, protect, and serve," Race scolded. "You're in pretty deep if they call a session. You'd better get your act together and tell her what's going on before it's too late."

Alden gripped the edge of the tiny round table. "When was the last time you trained a Speaker from scratch, Race? How about you, Maddi? I'm doing the best I can. Both of you are much younger than your Speakers. Generations younger. They trained *you* . . . just like Rose trained me. I have no idea what I'm doing here. I need your help, not your condemnation." He buried his face in his hands.

I shifted my gaze from Race to Maddi to Alden in astonishment. Why hadn't he told me there was some time limit? What in the world was a session?

"Alden, tell me what to do." I ran my fingers through his hair. "Tell me how to help you."

Race let out a whoop. "You're right, Alden! She doesn't remember a thing. The Rose I know would never ask you to tell her what to do!"

Maddi laughed. "Yeah, she was too busy telling *you* what to do!"

Both of them giggled and gave each other a high five.

Race reached across and patted his shoulder. "Why haven't you finished the paperwork?"

"The first Hindered resolution only happened last night, and she was so upset by the Malevolent before that, I didn't want to interview her yet. We're going to close the first resolution file after I pick up my little sister, and then we'll take on a Hindered that's been hassling her today about retrieving some kind of stolen item."

Maddi clapped her hands. "Ooooh. Restitution. Those are my favorites. Worth a lot of points. You'll love it, Lenzi. It's really exciting. Nothing better than a justifiably angry Hindered. Has it been haunting the perpetrator? Those are the best ones."

"I have no idea." I couldn't believe anyone could be stoked about something so creepy.

Race jumped up. "I've got it! You work on the first resolution file, Alden, and I'll interview Rose . . . Lenzi about the Malevolent. You're up to it, aren't you, Lenzi?"

Race's enthusiasm was contagious. I nodded.

"Ha! See?" Race pulled out Maddi's chair. "Maddi, darling, will you go get something wonderful for Lenzi so that we can fill her full of sugar and caffeine to get her ready for her busy schedule? We're gonna make a significant dent in the Hindered population around here!"

Before long, I was at a separate table with Race, sipping on a mocha latte, answering questions about my encounter with the Malevolent in Kemah. Race entered my answers on his laptop into a document that looked like a standard form for a normal business, except it had strange questions. At the top of the form, I noticed a grading scale.

Exorcism with resolution, no loss of life	100 points
Exorcism with resolution, death of possessed	80 points
Exorcism, no resolution, no loss of life	70 points
Exorcism, no resolution, death of possessed	60 points
Malevolent, positive outcome	50 points
Malevolent, negative outcome	30 points
Hindered seeking restitution	25 points
Hindered seeking resolution	10–15 points

Alden and Maddi were at a table across from us. She was reading out information from a paper file while he entered the data on his own laptop. Occasionally, Alden would look over at me, causing my heart to beat a little faster.

"Done," Race proclaimed right as Alden's phone rang.

Alden's face clouded as he inspected the caller ID screen. He turned the phone toward Race, Maddi, and me. "ICDC" appeared on the screen.

"Oh, no! We weren't fast enough!" Maddi gasped.

"Wait!" Race said. He pushed Send on the form he had just completed, and his computer made a whooshing sound. "Okay. Go ahead."

Alden gave me a significant look and answered the phone. "This is Protector 438."

Maddi squeezed her eyes shut, and Race took my hand.

Alden stared straight ahead while he spoke. "Yes, sir, I understand. . . . No, everything is fine; I'm simply behind in my paperwork. . . . Yes, sir, I am at fault. . . . No, sir, I believe she is not at zero. I have just submitted a Malevolent with Negative Outcome Form. I'm holding a Standard Hindered Form. . . . Yes, sir. Completely my error. . . . Yes, I anticipate resolution of a Hindered seeking restitution before midnight— Tomorrow?" He shot me a frightened look. "Yes, sir. We would be available to meet with a representative tomorrow. . . . Noon in Galveston at the Seawall historical marker. Yes, sir, we'll be there." Alden ended the call and continued staring straight ahead.

"Is it a formal session?" Maddi asked, breaking the tense silence. "Will it be a hearing?"

Alden glanced over at me and then at Maddi. "No. They just want to talk to us."

"That can't be a good thing," Race said.

"Frankly, I'm surprised it took them this long." Alden began packing up his laptop.

"What is ICDC?" I asked Race.

"Intercessor Council Disciplinary Committee."

The name alone was scary. I put on my best game face in an attempt to appear unconcerned in front of Maddi and Race. But fear surged through me like ungrounded current. Maddi and Race stopped what they were doing and stared at me. Alden closed his eyes.

"Intense, isn't it?" Alden remarked.

"Wow. How often does she do that?" Race asked.

"All the time." Alden's eyes were still closed.

Maddi laughed and punched him on the shoulder. "No wonder you haven't finished your paperwork."

"How often do I do *what*?" I asked.

The three Protectors laughed. Alden zipped up his computer bag and glanced at his watch. "We've got to go. Thanks for helping us out. I'll call you tomorrow after the meeting. They probably just want to see her and make sure she's intact. It takes a formal session to sentence a Speaker to be discontinued."

"Or a Protector, for that matter," Race added. "Keep it together, Alden. Inform, protect, serve, no matter how much fear she throws at you."

After hugs and handshakes, Maddi and Race got in a blue

Dodge Ram pickup truck, leaving me alone with Alden, who was politely holding my car door open.

"You should have told me we were in trouble, Alden."

After he pulled out onto the service road, he glanced over at me. "You weren't ready. If I had told you about the ICDC, you would have taken off. I'm not one hundred percent sure you're on board even now."

"Well, I am on board, Alden. And if we're going to be a team, you can't keep secrets from me."

"Deal," he said as he pulled into a day-care facility. Not the average day care—a huge, elegant exclusive one. He parked under the covered pick-up area. Immediately, a woman escorted a little girl with bouncing blond curls out to the car. Alden got out and walked around the front of the car to meet them. The little girl ran into his arms as he opened the door. He picked her up and twirled her around before setting her in the booster seat in the back of his car.

Alden spoke with the woman briefly before turning his attention to the little girl, who was grinning hugely at me.

"Izzy, this is Lenzi. Lenzi, this is my little sister, Elizabeth."

Alden got in the driver's seat and waited patiently for Elizabeth to buckle her seat belt. "Do you want help, Izzy?"

"No! Charlotte says I'm a big girl and I don't need boys to do stuff for me."

Alden rolled his eyes. "Charlotte says a lot of things. Miss Mason told me that you're upsetting the other kids by talking about Charlotte too much. You need to tone it down, Izzy."

"Miss Mason is just jealous 'cause she doesn't have a friend like Charlotte."

Alden sighed. "Buckle up so we can go."

"Who is Charlotte?" I asked.

"My bestest friend in the whoooole world," Elizabeth volunteered from the backseat while she wrestled with the seat belt.

Alden reached back and helped her buckle up. "Charlotte is Izzy's imaginary friend."

"She's not 'maginary. She's real!"

Alden winked at me and started the car. "Izzy, you're going to play with Miss Aurora until Dad gets home, okay?"

"I want to play with Lenzi!" she said, grinning.

"Yeah, well, so do I, so you can play with her tomorrow. Where's Boo Bear?"

She dug through her backpack and produced a tattered pink bear. "Here!"

"Good afternoon, Boo Bear. How was your day?" Alden asked, glancing briefly in his rearview mirror.

"He doesn't want to talk to you, Alden. He wants to talk to Lenzi."

"Hello, Boo. Where did you get your name?" I asked.

"He got it from Alden," Izzy said, kissing the pink bear's nose. "Alden says Boo Bear can scare the ghosts away."

I smiled. "Maybe you'll let me borrow him sometime. Boo's talent could come in handy."

I watched Alden while Izzy chattered from the backseat. He

had his arm on the console between us. In my mind, I took his hand in mine. Before my imagination could explore a wider range of possibilities, Alden pulled into the driveway of his house. He escorted Izzy to the door and turned her over to a pleasant-looking woman in her mid-fifties with graying black hair pulled back into a bun. She waved at me from the doorway.

"Where to now?" I asked when we were back on the road.

He smiled. "I hate to ask you to cheat on your boyfriend, Zak, but I believe you have a date with a purple cat named Jinx."

SEVENTEEN

Alden pulled into a preschool with a sweeping circular drive and aqua columns decorated with zoo animals on either side of the front door.

My phone chirped to let me know I'd received a new text as he parked the car.

He unbuckled. "Let's go find out where Mr. Jinx is." As Alden walked around to open my door, I read Zak's message asking if he could pick me up from where I was studying. A chill ran through me at the prospect of Zak discovering I was with Alden. I really couldn't keep this up much longer. Being with Zak was not going to work. He'd never accept or understand this ghost-hunting gig.

I'll call you when I'm free, I texted. **We need to talk.**

Alden, still holding my door open, cleared his throat. "Let's get to work now.

"Just like the hospital, the school will have privacy rules," Alden whispered as we entered the office. The receptionist was nowhere to be seen. As Alden unfolded Suzanne's picture, a heavyset woman bustled in from an office nearby.

She immediately teared up when she saw the drawing. "Suzanne was a favorite of everyone here. Mr. Jinx was a fixture of the school," she said.

But even after Alden turned on all his considerable charm, she said she couldn't give out any information regarding students or their addresses. Luck was on our side, though, because the school nurse passed through as we were being given this disappointing news. She was wearing blue hospital scrubs with rainbows all over them. She paused when she noticed the drawing on the receptionist's desk.

"That's Mr. Jinx," she said with a wistful smile. "She drew him all the time."

"Yeah, I promised Suzanne Lawrence I'd give this drawing to her mother," Alden explained, giving the nurse his most charming smile.

"I could mail it for you," she suggested.

"It was very important to Suzanne we deliver it in person. I promised her we would. I also told her I'd pet Fluffy for her and tell Becky where Mr. Jinx is. She hid him so that he wouldn't have to go to the hospital with her the last time. Mr. Jinx was scared of needles."

"We're not allowed to give out addresses," she said, glancing at the receptionist. "Why don't you give me your number, and I'll contact the family for you? Come into my office, and I'll take your information."

We followed the nurse into her office. She pulled a file out of a gray metal cabinet and placed it on her desk, open to the first page. She pulled out a pad and got a pencil. "What is your phone number?" she asked loud enough for the receptionist in the next room to hear as she wrote down the address from the file. Alden matched her volume as he recited his phone number while she finished copying the address and handed it to him.

He put his hand on hers. "Thank you," he whispered.

We walked out of the office and, once outside the doors, practically ran to the car. Making it through the parking lot without touching Alden was a true test of willpower. It seemed like I was becoming more and more aware of him. There really was a link between us that was beyond normal—a link from centuries of knowing each other.

"I can't believe we got it!" I said as we closed the car doors. I read the address scribbled on the piece of paper. "I know right where this is. It's behind the neighborhood pool around the corner where I used to take swimming lessons when I was little. Turn right out of the parking lot."

The house looked just like Suzanne had described it—one-story brown brick with black shutters and a bright red door.

"You should do this alone," Alden said, parking at the curb.

"Mothers of dead children respond better to women. She'd probably close the door in my face."

"Come with me. Please, Alden. I'm scared."

"No, you're not." He passed me the drawing.

The soul-feeling thing was a pain. "Okay. I'm nervous. Please come with me. I need you there with me."

He shot me a skeptical look. "You are not experiencing a trace of fear or nervousness. All I feel from you is excitement. Go take care of this. You can do it."

Something in me needed to be with him. "Please, Alden. Share this experience with me."

He sighed and opened the door. "I've never been able to say no to you."

Suzanne's mother was far more receptive than I'd expected. I told her that we'd met Suzanne in the hospital while we were there visiting a friend. Before fifteen minutes were up, we'd fulfilled both of our promises to Suzanne. Becky was on the floor playing with Mr. Jinx when we left.

Back at the car, I was elated. This was what I was put on earth to do—help souls find closure. Happiness buzzed through my body.

Alden put his head back against the headrest and closed his eyes without pulling out his key.

I snapped my seat belt. "Is something wrong?"

"Shhh. No. Give me a minute."

Something was definitely wrong. "Was it something I said or did?"

After some deep breaths, he opened his eyes and pulled out his key. "No, Lenzi. You were wonderful. Magnificent. Congratulations on your very first closure."

"Why were you acting weird just now?"

"I've never felt you like this. Closure in the past resulted in happiness that bordered on gloating—the thrill of success. This was different. You were transmitting joy."

"That's a good thing, right?"

A big grin crossed his face. "Even better than the fear." He started the car. "Are you hungry?"

"Starving. Do you like French food? There's a bistro around the corner."

The restaurant had rustic French decor complete with a fireplace, which suited me just fine because I was still in my short uniform skirt and the October wind was chilly. The high from helping Suzanne hadn't worn off yet, and I chatted nonstop through dinner while Alden's eyes kept straying to my legs, which I intentionally kept visible. I'd decided to see if I could make him see me in the same light as Rose. Maybe I wasn't the smart, tough, kick-ass woman Rose was, but I was here now. Although my knowledge of men was minimal, from Alden's behavior I guessed that I was on the right track.

I took a bite of quiche and made a series of pleats in my napkin. "Tell me about Rose, Alden."

He lifted an eyebrow. "What do you want to know?"

"Tell me about when you were married to her." I put my feet up on the empty chair next to him and turned the napkin ninety degrees and repeated the pleats.

He glanced at my legs, then at his bowl of soup. "What do you want to know about it?"

"What was it like?" I folded a corner of the napkin in on the diagonal.

His reticence surprised me. For a minute, I thought he wasn't going to answer. "The job was much easier when you . . . she and I lived under the same roof."

I rotated the napkin and folded another corner over. "Did you get married because you loved each other?"

My phone chirped in my purse, and Alden looked directly into my eyes. "Rose married me because it was convenient. Will you excuse me for a moment?" He seemed agitated as he strode to the bathroom. Maybe I'd struck a raw nerve. Convenience seemed like a lame reason to marry someone. He wasn't telling me the whole story.

Zak's message was hostile. He accused me of, well, doing exactly what I was doing: hanging out with Alden and lying to him about it. I didn't respond other than to turn the volume off on my phone.

Alden sat back down, let out a deep breath, and took a sip of his coffee. "Lenzi, thank you for stopping the pills."

How did he know? Was it the linked-soul thing? "Um, Alden, did you feel high when I was?"

Taking my hands in his, he smiled. "No. Your soul just

seemed out of focus. Not right. It's like hearing my favorite song played by a marginal cover band. I like the song. I just prefer the real thing." He squeezed my hands and leaned closer. "I'm glad you are giving being a Speaker a chance. I'm proud of you."

Our faces were only inches apart across the small table. I was sure he was going to kiss me. Instead, he sighed, released my hands, and leaned back in his chair.

"Okay, where do you want to take on that Hindered who was complaining about the stolen property?"

Back to business. I flattened the napkin on the table and smoothed out the pleats. "I don't care. Where do you want to do it?"

"My little sister will drive us crazy at my house. Will your mom leave us alone at yours?"

"Mom has some deadline at her office and won't be home until after ten o'clock. She said if I'm not home when she gets there, she'll ground me, so we're better off there."

He stood and slipped into his coat. "Perfect. That gives us plenty of time."

EIGHTEEN

I made Alden stay downstairs by telling him I needed to change clothes, but I really wanted to straighten my room before he came up. I slipped on some jeans and a tight, red cashmere sweater I thought he'd like before scrambling around shoving things under the bed and into drawers. His room looked like an antique showroom, and mine resembled a Dumpster. Rose was probably perfect and tidy.

"Do you need help?" he called up the stairs. "It's taking you a long time to change clothes. It's not a prom, you know—it's a resolution."

"Come on up," I said as I stuffed a pile of clean clothes in my closet.

He sat on my bed. "Ready?"

"Yeah. Let's get this resolution over with." I sat next to him. "Why is this one worth more points?"

"Because restitution is usually more complicated. Call the Hindered. We have to close this one before the meeting tomorrow—which reminds me, we have to be in Galveston by noon. What will it take to get your mother to call you in sick?"

My mom had already made an excuse for me this week. "It would take my death."

"We're trying to avoid that." He pulled out his wallet and removed a slip of paper. "How about a doctor's note?" He scribbled on it with a pen from my desk. "I'll pick you up at ten o'clock. Bring a change of clothes if you don't want to wear the uniform." He placed the note in my hand. It was an appointment slip to a doctor I'd never heard of.

"It's an IC front," he explained. "They actually have someone who poses as a front desk receptionist at a doctor's office to cover in situations where Speakers and Protectors have to miss work or school."

"So, this is a super-secret society, this ghost-busting business?"

He slipped his wallet back into his jeans. "As much as possible. If it got out as general knowledge, it might cause panic because ghosts tend to freak people out. We share our existence with people on a need-to-know basis. Like, there may come a time when your mom or your boyfriend needs to know, but the fewer, the better."

"Yeah, I can understand that." I stuffed the note in my pocket, wondering what Zak's reaction would be if I told him I could talk to bogeymen. "Zak's not my boyfriend anymore, Alden."

His strange silver eyes met mine, and I felt as if frozen in place. "Your soul is troubled by that."

"I haven't really talked to him about it yet."

"Well, that would certainly trouble a soul." He shrugged and a hint of a smile touched his lips. "Call the Hindered, Lenzi."

I wasn't as nervous as I'd been with Suzanne, but I was anxious to get the ghost stuff over with so we could be alone. I gave Alden a big smile and then cupped my hands around my mouth. "Here, Hindered, Hindered, Hindered. Come out, come out, wherever you are!" I called.

I was immediately flooded with voices calling for help from all around me. They were everywhere, and the voices were so loud it hurt my ears. I staggered backward off the bed and slid to the floor.

Alden laughed. "I bet that got their attention. You won't do that again, huh?"

"What do I do now?"

"You'll have to seek out the one you want, specifically." He sat on the floor next to me. "It's okay. I should've warned you." He took my hand and started the soothing thing. "Go ahead. Call it."

"They're so loud, I can't even hear myself think." I got on my knees and sat back on my heels, still clutching his hand. "Okay, ghouls, everyone quiet down. I want to talk to the woman who hassled me in history class and got me busted. She wanted me to help her with something someone stole. Everyone else, scram to some other happy haunting ground!"

"She stole my mother's necklace!" The voice was behind Alden's shoulder.

"Who stole your mother's necklace?" I asked.

"My sister."

"Her sister jacked her mother's necklace," I explained to Alden.

"Why is that significant enough to keep her Earth-bound?" he prompted.

"What's the big deal about that? Why is that keeping you here?"

The voice came from behind me, which made me flinch. I'd never get used to this. *"I promised my mother on her deathbed that I would keep it in the family. It had been passed down for three generations. My sister is childless. I have a daughter. My mother left it to me in her will, but Karen stole it from her house the day of the funeral. She has it. I've seen it."*

I squeezed Alden's hand. "Did you catch that?"

"No. I only hear them when my soul is in your body. What did she say?"

"Her sister stole it. I'll fill you in on motive later."

"Don't go to any trouble on my account," Alden said, chuckling. "Is she haunting the sister?"

"She can't hear you, either, can she?"

"No. You are the Speaker."

"Being the middleman sucks." I looked at the spot behind me where the Hindered had last spoken. "Are you haunting your sister?"

From the other side of the room, a pile of papers from my desk flew in all directions. *"Yes!"* the voice howled.

I stood up. "Cut that out! My room is messy enough. If you want me to help you, stay in one place and don't mess with my stuff."

"You tell her!" Alden said with a smirk as he lay back on the floor with his hands behind his head like he was watching a movie rather than a ghost mediation.

"It's a good thing she can't hear you."

"It's a good thing *you* can. Where does the sister live, what does the necklace look like, and where is the rightful owner?"

I faced the desk. "Okay. Where does your sister—"

Alden tugged on the leg of my jeans. "Lenzi. Let her in. Save yourself time and irritation. She'll give you all that and more if you let her in. I'll get the information too. I can talk to her while she's sharing your body. We both can."

I lowered myself onto the floor next to him. "I was really hoping to do it without the soul-sharing thing. Do I have to?"

"Yep. Sorry." He propped up on his elbow. "We have less than three hours. An interview could take all night. We need these points before the meeting tomorrow. Please, Lenzi. I'd do it for you if I could." He reached over and touched my hand.

That was incentive enough. "Okay, come on in. Tell it to me quick; we've got a deadline."

I wasn't sure whether the entrance of a soul was becoming less painful or if I was just getting used to it. Before long, the Hindered named Georgia had filled me in on the details of the theft of the family necklace and its whereabouts in her sister's house. I listened as Alden quizzed her, which was weird, because it was my body Georgia was using to draw a map and write addresses.

"Are you okay in there, Lenzi?" Alden would ask occasionally.

Once Georgia had spilled the whole story about her sister, Karen Black, I gave the okay for Alden to help her soul out. I expected to see Georgia when she exited, like I'd seen the Malevolent and Suzanne, but there was no trace of her.

"Where's Georgia, Alden?"

You only see them if they are moving on. She's probably hanging around to see her promise fulfilled.

"Oh." That made sense, I supposed.

You asked about our marriage. Want to see a memory?

Unexpected lotto win. "Yes!"

A vision of the two of them, Rose and Alden, standing at a church altar getting married, flashed through my head. Rose was in a white dress with gauzy sleeves. The front of the dress bloused loosely. Her waist was so tiny, it was obvious she was wearing a corset. Her hair was piled on the top of her head under a multitiered veil. Alden had short hair and sideburns.

He was wearing a black suit, a white, stiff-collared shirt, and a white funny-looking tie. He reminded me of Mr. Darcy from *Pride and Prejudice*. There were only a few people in attendance. I recognized Maddi and Race, but the other guests were unfamiliar. Rose was beautiful. Jealousy surged through me.

Wait, there's more, Alden said as the image fast-forwarded to the point after they walked out of the church. Rose looked up at Alden. "Remember, we are only doing this for the sake of convenience. You are a marvelous Protector. If this will make it more convenient for you, then it is the right thing to do. Don't get any ideas, Alden. This is a marriage in name only. Anything else would make you less effective. We will never be more than business partners in this lifetime or any other. Are we clear?"

"As crystal," Alden said as he touched his lips to hers in a light, platonic kiss.

I was furious with Rose. The frigid witch.

Seen enough, Lenzi? Does that answer your question?

"Yes." I reached over and touched his body on the shoulder. "I'm ready."

I was so shaken by Rose's words, the sensation of his soul's exit didn't even faze me.

Alden's eyes burned to life and he gasped a breath of air. He smiled. "It gets easier, doesn't it?"

I was determined not to cry. "Yes." I stood up. "Alden, I—"

He put his finger to my lips. "Shhh. If this is about the memory you saw, don't. Don't react to it yet. An emotional response would be wrong. Think about it first. Rose was right: anything more would have made me less effective. More importantly, it would have made *her* less effective. I promised to follow her dictate. Your dictate." He traced my lips with his finger. "There's a lot at stake here, Lenzi. I think you'll see her side if you just think about it."

"Why did you show me that right now?" I asked.

"Because you were coming on to me earlier. Because you're . . . making me crazy."

"What's wrong with that?"

He took my face in his hands. "I have lifetimes of memories you don't have. I know more about you than you know about yourself. I have an unfair advantage, so I'm trying to level the playing field—the field you used to control. The rules state that I must follow the Speaker. You must lead. I want you to know where you're going, Lenzi. That's why I showed it to you."

He hugged me to him. I wrapped my arms around his waist, glad to finally be in his embrace, whatever the conditions.

Alden glanced at his watch. "We've got to get moving. We need to break into this house as soon as possible."

"Break in?"

"Whatever it takes." He grabbed the map and addresses and shoved them into his pocket. "Don't worry, Lenzi. This first trip is just to check the place out. You'll stay in the car with my body while I go in alone."

"You're going in without your body?" I stopped short at the

top of the stairs. He climbed back up and pulled me down by the hand.

"Yes, Lenzi. She'll never know I'm there. I'll be like a Hindered . . . only not dead. Gawk later. Let's go. Call Georgia. We'll need her for this one."

I stared at Alden's body in complete disbelief. Part of his soul was out there somewhere, breaking into a house to steal a stolen necklace. The whole thing was crazy. He had exited about fifteen minutes ago, leaving his body seat-belted in the passenger seat. He'd given me instructions to drive straight to his house if something happened and to use his phone to call the IC to report a problem for Speaker 102 and Protector 438.

The street was a cul-de-sac. Karen Black's home was four houses from the cross-street. Alden had parked on the opposite side of the street several houses away, leaving the car windows cracked open about an inch. I blamed the cool night air for my trembling hands. Rifling through the glove box, I searched for something to fold, but the Audi owner's manual was the only paper in his car. I clamped my hands between my knees. What was taking him so long?

Alden's body came to life with a gasp at his soul's return. "I got the alarm code and the location of the necklace." He appeared proud of himself, keyed up. "Plus, we lucked out. She's leaving in half an hour for the store, in case we have to steal it."

"What are you talking about?" I asked. "Where's the necklace?"

"It's in a drawer that has a false bottom."

"Why didn't you get it?"

Alden furrowed his brow. "It's hard to pick stuff up when you don't have hands, Lenzi."

Moron Club president for life. "Oh, duh."

"Yeah, duh." He ruffled my hair. "Before we break in for real, let's see if she'll hand it over willingly."

I liked this better when I thought that Ghost Alden would handle the hard stuff. "I guess so. Do you think she'll give it to us?"

He shrugged. "It depends on how sick she is of being haunted by Georgia."

What if the woman had a gun or something? I grabbed his hand, and he shot some calming current my way. My fears dissolved when the tiny elderly lady opened the door. She was wearing a pink and yellow floral print housecoat with her hair in a style that looked like it took a lot of hair spray to maintain. She squinted at us from behind her oversized gold-rimmed glasses.

Alden smiled politely. "Miss Karen Black?"

"What do you want?" she grumbled.

"Georgia sent us."

She slammed the door in our faces. Alden scowled and knocked on the door. "Please, Miss Black. We just want to talk to you. Georgia will go away if you give the necklace back."

“I don’t know anyone named Georgia,” her wavering voice called out.

“Yes, you do. We know the entire story. Give the necklace to your niece, and this will all be over.”

“Never!” she shouted from the other side of the door. “Never. It should have been mine. I’m the oldest. I’m going to be buried in it. It’s mine.”

Alden groaned. “Come on, Miss Black. Georgia made a promise to your dying mother. She can’t move on until she fulfills that promise. That’s why she’s haunting you. She’ll go away if you do the right thing.”

“Get off my property, or I’ll call the police.”

“Obstinate old bag,” he muttered as we walked back down the sidewalk. A neighbor to the east of Miss Black’s house peered out her front window at us. Alden opened the driver’s side door before he walked around the front of the car and slid in the passenger side. I stood in the middle of the street, looking at him through the open door.

“Drive us to my house, Lenzi.”

“I don’t have a license.”

“I don’t care.”

Other than driver’s ed, I’d never even been behind the wheel of a car. “I don’t really know how to drive very well.”

He laughed. “That’s a problem, because you’re going to be driving yourself back here.”

“Where are you going to be?”

"In your body. We're leaving my body at my house. We need to do this together in case we get caught. Two souls are better than one." He put on the passenger-side seat belt.

Get caught? Oh, great. I leaned over to get a better look at him. I really didn't want to drive his snazzy car and smack it into something. "Why don't we just do it from here?"

He heaved a theatrical sigh. "Because someone might find my soulless body, resulting in my discontinuance by the IC. The objective is to stay *alive*."

"If the objective is to stay alive, then you don't want me to drive."

Alden shifted in his seat to face me. "Lenzi, listen to me. We have less than two hours before your mother gets back and less than fourteen hours before we meet with the ICDC representative. We need this resolution. Not obtaining it will be far more deadly for both of us than a car wreck. Besides, the car is insured," he added with a smile.

I studied him for a moment, letting his words sink in. "Will they kill us if we don't succeed tonight?"

"Our situation is unprecedented. I have no idea what they'll do. You emerged five days ago. An experienced Speaker, which is what you're supposed to be, should average twenty points a day. Fifteen is low-range acceptable. Tomorrow will be day six. You should have at least ninety points by noon tomorrow. We only have forty points right now. This one is worth twenty-five. We'll still be under the average, but I think that will be enough to satisfy them. We need this, Lenzi."

I slid into the driver's seat, shaking. "Why can't you just drive using my body?"

"Because part of my soul remains in my body when we soul-share. Only a complete soul—a dead person—can control another body."

"And why do I have to drive now instead of just driving us back here?"

"It's a practice run. I thought it would make you more comfortable. And if you suck as bad as you say you do, I can take over and we'll call a cab for the return trip. I'd rather not do that because it's just one more witness."

As much as I hated it, that made sense. I held my breath and turned the key in the ignition. At least the Audi was an automatic.

After averaging around twenty miles an hour, I finally pulled into Alden's driveway, managing not to take out the mailbox in the process. Go, me.

"Maybe we'd be faster walking next time," Alden kidded as he got out and opened my door. "Mom's at a conference, and Dad's working the ER shift tonight, so Aurora is home with Izzy, who should be asleep if we're lucky."

"Aurora is the woman you left her with earlier."

"Our housekeeper. She spends the night when my parents are out of town or on call. She won't give us any trouble."

I followed him into the entry hall. "Wait here," he whispered.

I could hear his warm, rich voice as he spoke with Aurora from somewhere in the back of the house. He apologized for coming home late and told her that he would see her in the morning. Then he grabbed my hand and ran up the stairs, dragging me behind him. After he closed and locked his door, he grinned at me and took off his shoes. "Exciting, isn't it?" He slid under the covers of his bed.

It certainly could be. "Uh, yeah," I murmured. "Exciting." What in the world was he up to?

He held out his arms. "Come here, Lenzi."

Now, this looked promising. "What do you want, Alden?"

"What I want and what I'm going to do are two different things. I need to transfer my soul to your body. Take my hands so it won't hurt as much."

When I grabbed his hands, a jolt of energy surged from him through me—not the calming kind of energy. He was feeling the same way I was. Warning or no warning, I leaned down to kiss him. Before my lips touched his, his soul entered my body.

Stop, Lenzi. I told you to think first.

"Ow! That hurt . . . and I *did* think."

Obviously not. What you were about to do was impulsive and emotional. We don't have time for that right now. Miss Black will be leaving in less than five minutes. Climb out the window. There's a trellis that's easy to climb. I do it all the time.

I slid the window open and peered out. I crawled onto the sill and poked around with my foot to explore the vine-covered wall for the trellis he had mentioned. After some fumbling, I managed to climb down the side of the house without hurting myself. The dense vine left my hands sticky. I wiped them on my pants.

Alden gave me driving pointers the whole way to Georgia's sister's house, which was beyond irritating. Driving was traumatic enough as it was. His backseat driving from inside my head made it a nightmare.

"Now what?" I snapped as I turned the car off.

We're going to break in.

"Fantastic. My mom will be so proud."

Let's hope Georgia's right about the spare key under the back doormat.

I crept around to the back of the house and lifted the mat, knocking over a ceramic bowl full of water that had GOOD KITTY painted on it. I pulled out the key. "Now what?"

Unlock the door. When we're in, I'll give you the alarm code.

I entered the code he gave me on the keypad inside the door. All the lights were out, but from the faint light coming in through the windows from the streetlights, I could tell the house had been ransacked. Paper was everywhere, and the smaller pieces of furniture were overturned. "What happened in here?" I whispered.

Georgia, most likely. She's here somewhere. If you call her, she'll come.

"No, thanks. One disembodied voice is enough right now. Where's the necklace?"

In her bedroom. Third drawer down in the tall dresser by the window. It has a false bottom. The necklace is underneath.

The hardwood floor groaned under my tennis shoes as I tiptoed down the narrow hallway toward Miss Black's room at the back of the house. The silence was painful. The only other noise was the rhythmic ticking of a clock somewhere in the house. I found myself creeping along in rhythm.

Tick-tock, creak. Tick-tock, creak.

The phone rang, causing me to jump and nearly wet my pants. I flattened against the wall and held my breath until it finally stopped ringing. My skin was prickly all over, like bugs were crawling under the surface. I closed my eyes and tried to calm down enough to get a full breath. I wasn't sure whether Alden could feel my panic while we were soul-sharing. But if he could and my fear really turned him on, he must have been having a great time.

Once my legs weren't Jell-O, I continued down the hallway to Miss Black's bedroom.

I wrinkled my nose when I entered. The small, cramped space smelled like mothballs, hair spray, and Chanel No. 5.

I crept to the tall dresser and gave the third drawer a pull. It was stuck. Why couldn't something be easy just once? After a couple of sharp tugs, I cracked it open just enough to slip my arm inside. I shoved the folded clothes aside and found a lift hole in the center of the bottom. I pulled it up and felt around with my trembling fingers. Stupid drawer. I would have been out already if it had opened all the way. Ah, cold metal.

"I've got it!" It was an opal pendant on a heavy gold chain. Hard to believe one little thing could be the cause of so much trouble. I needed to pocket it and get out before the old woman got back. I shoved the drawer closed and folded the chain in my hand.

"Yes! That's it. It belongs to my daughter." Georgia's voice from behind my shoulder freaked me out so much I almost dropped the necklace. It took a moment for me to stop shaking enough to cram the necklace in my pocket. Now, I just needed to get out and drive to Alden's house without totaling his car. Piece of cake.

I reset the alarm. Almost out.

As my fingers wrapped around the door handle, blue and red lights pulsed and flashed through the windows at the front of the house.

Cops! "Oh, no, Alden . . ."

Don't panic, Lenzi. Call out for Georgia, I need to talk to her.

I couldn't control my trembling. This was bad. As bad as it got. My mom was going to ground me for all eternity.

Lenzi. Concentrate. We need Georgia.

I called her, and through me, Alden explained the game plan. She was supposed to scare Ms. Black before she ever got out of her car—like, really freak her out. That was fine with me if it worked, but who knew if it would?

Say as little as possible to the police, do you understand? Don't answer a single question; don't even give them your name. I'll prompt you from in here. Try not to act schizophrenic because I'm in here. This is why we did it this way. If I had come in my own body, they would have separated us. This way, we stay together.

"I'm scared, Alden."

I know. I'm sorry. It'll be okay. Walk out the back door and down the driveway. Move slowly and keep your hands visible. Do everything they tell you to do, but don't answer any questions.

I took a deep breath, stepped out onto the driveway, and without incident found myself, along with Alden's soul, sitting in the back of a police cruiser, trying not to break down, hoping to heaven that Mom didn't find out I'd been arrested for burglary.

NINETEEN

Handcuffs are the most uncomfortable contraptions ever. I'd been in the back of the police cruiser for what felt like a lifetime. Through the window, I watched Miss Black's neighbor talking to the police officers. The woman gestured wildly as she spoke, causing the belt on her lime-green bathrobe to come untied repeatedly. She would jerk it back in place and go right back to talking and flapping her arms like a giant, green flightless bird. She was the woman I'd seen peering out the window at us earlier. Probably the one who'd called the cops.

It appeared the police were waiting for Miss Black. This was going to be bad. Alden had nearly given the old woman a coronary when he hassled her through the door. She would love to see us locked up.

"My mom's going to kill me," I moaned for the millionth time.

She'll never know it happened. If we're lucky, my plan will work. If not, the IC will have it cleared up in no time.

"Are they going to lock me up?"

No. This kind of thing happens all the time to Speakers. The IC has a great relationship with the police. We've helped them solve several high-profile murder cases in this city over the past two years. So, even if we get taken to the station, nothing will happen to you.

"Wait a minute. You said the whole Speaker-Protector thing was a secret."

I said it was need-to-know. We have a symbiotic relationship with upper-level law enforcement, sort of like a paranormal secret service. Most cops don't have a clue. We'll call the IC if we get taken in, and they'll know who to talk to and will clear it up. Please trust me. I won't let anything bad happen to you.

"Too late. You did, Alden! I'm sitting here in handcuffs like a criminal. You let something bad happen to me!"

Lenzi, calm down, or they'll think you have a mental illness. From their perspective, you're sitting here alone, remember? Get control of yourself.

"That's easy for you to say. You're not the one going to jail."

You're not going to jail, either.

Miss Black pulled up in front of the house in her old-model Cadillac. The two police officers abandoned bird lady and strolled toward her car. Before they got to the curb, though, the old woman, who was still behind the wheel, began waving her arms over her head as if fending off a swarm of wasps. The lights inside the car flickered as the windows rolled up and down.

Atta girl, Georgia! Alden cheered from inside my head. Maybe the plan would work.

Her car rocked back and forth as if being pushed by an invisible force. Miss Black covered her ears and screamed while the radio cranked an elevator version of an Elton John tune at full volume.

It was a full-on multisensory bogeyman boogie, courtesy of Georgia, who didn't hold anything back, including flashing headlights and a blasting horn. If I hadn't been just one policeman's phone call away from the longest grounding in history, it might have been funny.

The cops stopped a few feet away from the car, unsure of what to do.

As quickly as it started, the craziness came to a halt. Miss Black sat panting behind the wheel for a few moments until one of the police officers ran around to open her door and help her out. I couldn't hear what they were saying, but she pointed at me repeatedly.

After a few tense minutes, in which I was positive my heart would stop beating, Miss Black signed a paper on a clipboard the officer handed her. He then gave her an envelope and walked over to lean against a tree while he finished filling out the piece of paper. The other cop opened the back door of the police cruiser.

"Well, young lady, it appears this was all a mistake. You should have told us you were Miss Black's niece and that the necklace was yours. I guess that makes sense, considering you knew the alarm code and everything. Why didn't you tell us?"

"I was scared," I answered honestly.

"Well, you are free to go. Please turn your back to me so that I can remove the handcuffs." The officer unlocked the metal cuffs from my wrists. He handed me Alden's car key and my cell phone, but not the necklace they'd taken at the same time when I was arrested.

Ask him where the necklace is, Lenzi. We need to get it back, Alden prompted.

"Um, sir? Where is my necklace now?"

The officer put the cuffs in a holster on his belt. "We just released it to your aunt."

Oh, no! This is bad.

"Hush! I know it's bad!"

The officer studied me. "I beg your pardon?"

I made a show of rubbing my wrists where they'd been cuffed. "Oh, um. I was talking about my wrists. I said, 'They hurt bad,' that's all."

"Sorry about that," the officer said, turning my wrists over to examine them. "They look okay to me. You're free to join your aunt now. Stay out of trouble, okay?"

"That's my goal."

"Oh, and be sure your aunt gets that car checked out.

Looks like it has an electrical short or something. Probably not safe."

"I sure will. Thanks." I stepped onto the lawn and watched with relief as the two police officers got in their car and drove away.

I can't believe it worked! Alden said.

The neighbor in the green robe crossed into the yard and spoke with Miss Black conspiratorially behind her hand. Miss Black shook her head and struck out in my direction, leaving the gossipy neighbor behind.

"Now I just need to get that necklace back in the right hands so Georgia will move on," I muttered, hoping Miss Black was calmer than she looked.

"Out! I want her out of my life and gone. I don't care what it takes," Miss Black said.

"She has it. She has the necklace. You must get it. You must give it to my daughter, Cindy. Then I can rest. It belongs to Cindy!" Georgia nagged.

"Oh, shut up!" I shouted.

Miss Black's jaw dropped in surprise.

Oh, great. Now I'd done it. "I was talking to the ghost, not you." I shifted my weight from foot to foot. "Sorry. Georgia's being a pain. Miss Black, I'm really sorry about all of this. I'm not here to judge what happened years ago—I just want to help Georgia make good on her promise. I want her to move on. I know that you do too."

"Darn right I do. I've had enough. Where is she?" Miss Black asked. "I want to talk to her."

"Georgia! Where are you?" I called.

"Here," Georgia responded from behind her sister's shoulder.

Miss Black looked around nervously. "Is she here? Where is she?"

"She's right behind you," I said.

Miss Black jumped and looked behind her. She shook her finger as she spoke. "I want to talk to you, Georgia. You and I need to settle this."

She can't hear her, Lenzi. Either you need to interpret or let Georgia talk through you. I can clear out, so that Georgia can come in.

"Oh, no you don't, Alden. You stay right where you are. I don't want you to be floating around out there where I can't see you. It's bad enough when dead people do it." I tapped Miss Black's shoulder. "Miss Black. She can't hear you. I'll have to speak for you."

The tiny old woman wrinkled her face. "Well, you tell her that I'm going to give this necklace to her daughter, not because of what she's done to my house or my car, but because it's what Mama wanted. If Georgia had asked me properly, instead of being so pushy, I'd have given it to her when she was alive."

"Georgia, Karen says she's going to deliver the necklace to your daughter in keeping with your mother's wishes."

"You tell Karen that she's a hard-hearted old bat and she's lucky I didn't tump that car over on her thieving hide."

It was a good thing that Alden was soul-sharing with me right now so that I didn't have to allow Georgia to speak through me and screw everything up. If I'd gone through all of this for nothing, I'd be royally pissed. "Georgia says she appreciates it, Karen."

"I said no such thing."

Miss Black stomped toward her car parked in the street. "Well, tell her she can go away now and leave me alone."

"Don't let her leave. She'll do something sneaky like she always does," Georgia shrieked.

It was hard to understand Alden because he was laughing so hard in my head. *Are we having fun yet, Lenzi?*

"It's not funny, Alden. What do I do to get a resolution out of this?"

Well, you'd better learn to drive a little faster, because she's almost out of sight.

I sprinted to the car. "Stop laughing, Alden. Come on, Georgia, we're going to follow her."

As if driving while listening to Georgia rant about every crappy thing her sister had done since birth wasn't stressful enough, Alden decided to use the high-speed pursuit as a teaching tool for my continued driver's education. The old woman drove like a NASCAR racer in her tank of a Cadillac, and by the time she came to a screeching halt in front of a one-story brick house with colorful flowers in planters on either side of the door, I was ready to scream.

Stay in the car for a moment, Lenzi.

"But Georgia can't hear her. I need to speak for them."

Georgia can see her. Just relax for a moment and see what happens. It's better if the daughter isn't clued in to what's happening. If it goes bad, we'll act.

Miss Black tromped up the sidewalk and rang the doorbell. A woman in her thirties opened the door.

"That's my daughter, Cindy! Isn't she beautiful? She looks just like our mama," Georgia said.

A little girl who was maybe three years old peeked around Cindy's legs to smile at Miss Black. While the women talked, the child picked a flower from the planter on the porch and gave it to Miss Black. After leaning down to hug the child, Miss Black handed the necklace to Cindy. Cindy gestured to the open door and Miss Black followed her into the house after turning around to smile and wave at me.

"Well, I'll be darned," Georgia whispered from somewhere in the backseat. *"I guess that's it. If anyone can turn that mean old hag around, it's Cindy. I guess I'm done, huh?"*

"Yeah, I guess so," I said. "Is there anything else you need, Georgia?"

"Will you tell Karen thank you?"

"You bet."

Georgia became visible in the backseat. She was a small woman with huge glasses perched on her narrow nose, wearing a velour pantsuit. She had the same weird bluish luminescence

Suzanne had. *"Thank you, Lenzi,"* she said before she closed her eyes and disappeared in a shaft of white light, leaving behind the faint scent of floral perfume.

It was over. Almost. I placed a note on Miss Black's windshield that said, "Thank you, sister. Love, Georgia."

This resolution was every bit as gratifying as Suzanne's, and I enjoyed a heady rush the entire way to Alden's house.

Alden remained silent until I pulled the car into his driveway. *Great job, Lenzi. You were amazing.*

I was amazing. The same word he used to describe Rose. *Amazing.*

His words made me feel like I could fly. Unfortunately I couldn't, which meant another climb on the trellis. After struggling up the side of Alden's house, I practically fell into the room through the window. I stumbled to his bed and sat next to his empty body. Climbing through windows and ninja stuff was not my forte. Relief washed over me as I wiped the sticky vine sap on my jeans. I hadn't been arrested, I hadn't wrecked his car, I hadn't screwed up the entire resolution, and Alden said I was amazing. Now I just needed him to listen to me.

Well done, Lenzi. Grab my hand so I can exit.

I folded my arms across my chest. "No way. I want you to stay where you are so that I can talk to you without being distracted. It's easier if I can't see you." I glanced at the handsome seventeen-year-old boy lying peacefully on the bed next to me. Sheesh. He could even distract me when he was unconscious.

I turned my back to him and stared at Joe Bear instead. "You and I need to talk about Rose."

This isn't fair, Lenzi. We should talk face-to-face, Alden complained. *I'm at a disadvantage.*

"Well, Protector 438, according to you, *you're* the one with the unfair advantage. I'm simply, to use your own words, 'leveling the playing field.' Listen to what I have to say, then you can get out."

He didn't respond.

"Okay, Alden. We need to get something straight here. You showed me images of some woman from your past—a woman I don't know. You're holding her words against me. I'm not Rose, Alden. I'm Lenzi. The fact she didn't want anything outside of the Speaker-Protector relationship doesn't mean I shouldn't. I've wanted to kiss you from the minute I met you. If that makes me weak, ineffective, or less productive, then so be it. Quit holding her words against me. I'm not Rose."

I stifled a scream as Alden's soul left my body and entered his own against my will. Before I could catch my breath, he pulled me to him and kissed me so passionately, I was certain I'd be joining the ranks of the Hindered any minute.

TWENTY

"This is wrong," Alden said as he sat up. "I'm so sorry, Lenzi. It's wrong."

I lay on his bed, trying to catch my breath, waiting for the punch line. "What are you talking about?"

He walked over to the window, leaned against the sill, and brushed the hair out of his eyes. "Lenzi, we can't do this."

I laughed. "Wait a minute. You started it!"

"I know. That's why it's wrong."

I joined him at the window and put my arms around his neck. "Okay, then, *I'll* start it this time."

He grabbed my wrists from behind his neck and held me at arm's length. "No. Stop. We can't do this. It's not fair."

"Fair!" I jerked my wrists away. "Since when is kissing someone not fair? What rule book are you playing by?"

"The IC Rule Book. Life's rule book."

He had to be kidding. No way could he get me all hot and bothered and then pull this. I walked back to him and hooked my finger through his belt loop. "The IC Rule Book says that I have to lead, so follow me!" I stood on my tiptoes to kiss him. He ducked and retreated to the other side of the room.

"I can't let you do this. You don't know what you're doing."

"You're absolutely right, Alden, but I bet I'll figure it out."

"Enough!" He grabbed me by the shoulders and forced me into his desk chair. "I'm supposed to protect you. We can't do this. I'm so sorry, Lenzi. Forgive me."

I gripped the arms of the chair. "Forgive what, Alden? Kissing me? That's what I want you to do."

He slumped into a chair in the corner. "You have no idea what you want."

"I know that I want you."

He leaned forward in his chair. "You met me what? Five days ago? Lenzi, I've known you for lifetimes. This isn't right." He ran his hands through his hair. "You've always forbidden a sexual relationship. You made it clear it was absolutely off-limits. If you get your past-life memory back, I'm toast for what I've done already. Any further and you'll probably have me discontinued."

I turned my head so he wouldn't see that I was crying.

He walked over and knelt next to my chair. "Lenzi. Wait until you know what you want."

This was totally unfair. I was being held back by someone else's wishes. "I'm. Not. Rose! When will you hear me?"

He pulled me off the chair and into his arms. "I hear you all the time. I listen to your soul every minute. I love you. I always have."

"You love *Rose,* Alden, not me."

"I love *you.* Whatever you choose to call yourself. Despite your desperate attempt to deny who and what you are, your soul remains intact. Timeless and perfect."

I pulled away enough to look in his eyes. I could hardly see him through the blur of my tears. "Fine. Whatever."

"In past cycles you were very clear. I'm just asking for time until this all sorts out."

I wiped my tears away with the sleeve of my sweater. He was right . . . again. "Okay."

He kissed my forehead and then stood. "We need to get you home. We're almost an hour late."

I jumped to my feet. "Mom's going to be so mad!"

Alden slipped on his shoes. "Not as mad as she would have been if she'd seen you in handcuffs an hour ago."

Mom met us at the door and decided not to ground me after Alden took all of the blame for bringing me home past my curfew.

She almost changed her mind, though, when I broke out in uncontrollable giggles after she told me that she was so worried, she had almost called the police.

Right after Alden drove off, Zak pulled into the driveway. My stomach sank when I realized I had forgotten to call him. I hadn't even turned my phone back on after the cops returned it. This was going to be bad. I slipped out the door and ran down the steps to the lawn.

"I'm so sorry, Zak," I said as he jumped out of his car.

"Save it, Lenzi!" he said, storming toward me.

I took a couple of steps back.

"You lied to me," he shouted.

I shuffled back even further. "Zak, I—"

He stopped a couple of feet from me, and I moved out of arm's reach. "I saw him. He dropped you off. You told me you were studying. What were you studying, Lenzi? Human anatomy?"

I looked at the door and moved closer to the porch. "You're scaring me, Zak."

Grabbing my shoulders, he lowered his face even with mine. I could smell alcohol on his breath. "Do you think I'm gonna hurt you? I'd never hurt you, Lenzi. But you hurt *me*."

I stood still, not wanting to provoke him. "I didn't mean to."

He loosened his grip a little. "You didn't call like you said you would. You didn't answer when I called you. You didn't return my texts."

"My phone was off."

He shoved me away. "Not good enough."

I caught my balance and ran to the porch, grabbing the doorknob when I got there. "This isn't going to work, Zak." My voice was barely above a whisper.

"Damn right it's not. He's gone. Tell me he's gone." He stomped up the steps to the porch.

I held my hand up. "Stop!" He froze on the top step. "We're in different places right now. This isn't working for me. We—"

Before I could finish my sentence, he stormed down the stairs. "No!" he shouted. "You're not breaking up with me. I won't let you do this."

Mom pulled the door open and stepped outside. "What's happening out here?"

"It's okay, Mom. He's leaving."

"Nothing's happening," Zak yelled, slamming his fist on the hood of his car. "Nothing's happening. You're mine, and he's gone. Right, Lenzi?"

"You and I are finished. It's over, Zak," I called, but he'd slammed the door and revved his engine before I could get the words out.

TWENTY-ONE

The next day, Alden picked me up at school for my ten o'clock "doctor's appointment."

I slid into the passenger seat and patted my thighs to invite Spook onto my lap. "Thanks, Alden. You saved me from a trig quiz." Spook gave up her perch between Alden and the steering wheel and leapt across the console to me.

"At least one good thing will come out of it." Alden sighed. He seemed uneasy about this meeting, which worried me. "It'll be okay, Lenzi. I don't mean to be negative. I'm just tired. I didn't get much sleep. I had to close Georgia's file so that we would have the points before today's meeting."

"I could have snuck out and helped you," I said, stroking Spook under her chin.

"Speakers don't do paperwork."

"Oh, that's right. Our subordinates do the mundane tasks. We're above all that," I said.

"You didn't get much sleep either, did you, Lenzi?"

It was impossible to fall asleep. I kept alternating between hearing Zak's angry words in my head and the memory of Alden's kisses playing over and over like a continuous video loop. "I'm fine, Alden. I just hate you bearing the burden of everything. You took the blame for keeping me out late last night. You're taking the blame for the fact I haven't resolved enough cases. It's unfair."

"It's my job."

"You have a crappy job." I leaned the seat further back and Spook stretched out across my lap.

"I happen to think my job is marvelous." He cleared his throat and turned his attention to the road when I caught him sneaking a look at my legs.

Not changing out of my school uniform had been a good choice.

He pulled onto the freeway access road. "Any word from Zak today? He was pretty mad last night."

"How did you know that?"

He opened a compartment of his console and pulled out an iPod. "I was there. Your soul was practically screaming. I wanted to intervene, but I'm not supposed to interfere with your outside relationships."

I shifted Spook so her toenails didn't dig into my leg. "There is no relationship."

"You might want to tell Zak that, because he thinks otherwise." He plugged his iPod into a port on the dash. "Pick the tunes, Lenzi."

His face revealed nothing, but there was a jealous tinge to his voice. I smiled and selected an album by Coldplay. When I shifted in my seat so that I was angled toward Alden, Spook grumbled.

I didn't want to think or talk about Zak anymore. "Tell me about Maddi and Race," I said, previewing his playlists on the screen.

"What do you want to know?"

"How long have you known them?"

He switched lanes to get around a truck. "I have no idea. Past life memories are like childhood memories—the older they are, the less clear and abundant they are. There are lots of things I don't remember."

"Where are Maddi and Race's Speakers?"

"Race has a female Speaker who's always decades older than he is. They don't get along at all. They liked each other at first, I guess. Maybe too much. They made some bad choices and have suffered the consequences for generations. She works in the IC statistics department. She's some kind of math whiz. They're still paired by the IC each cycle, but haven't worked together for a long time. Not sure why the IC doesn't reassign them, but it frees her up to crunch numbers and makes Race a substitute Protector, which is an important job. He fills in for Protectors who are sick or injured and helps with resolutions that require more than one Protector."

"More than one Protector?"

He glanced over at me. "Yeah. Exorcisms take two. Someone has to enter the body of the Speaker and another the body of the possessed when the demon makes his move."

I gasped in horror.

"Don't worry. You won't be dealing with one for a long time. The IC assigns exorcisms. We can pass until you feel ready. Besides, they're very rare."

"Whew. What about Maddi?"

He smiled. "Maddi is another story altogether. Her Speaker is a female, which is unusual. Somehow, their souls are strongly linked. They get along very well, despite the obstacles. Her relationship with Race has helped defuse some of the social tension."

I set the iPod down on the console. "What tension?"

"Not everyone is so accepting of two women who are together all the time. Race hanging out with them makes it a little better. Some people still lift eyebrows."

"Oh, come on, Alden. We live in a pretty liberal society. People don't pay attention to that kind of thing." I rubbed Spook's ear and she turned her head so I'd rub the other.

"Wanna bet?"

I turned the volume on the stereo down a little. "Why haven't I met Maddi's Speaker?"

Alden passed another truck and pulled back into the outside lane. "She hasn't emerged yet. Race and Maddi usually hang out together until she arrives, which could be any day now."

Spook lifted her head and I scratched under her chin while she made happy grunts. "Do Speakers and Protectors always come back paired with the same person?"

"Yes. Our souls are branded when we're indoctrinated. The soul brand enables the IC to track us once we emerge."

"Oh, my God. My soul is branded? Like tattooed or something?"

He smiled. "Something like that. You and I have the same mark."

"I don't have any tattoos or marks on me."

He pointed at his neck. I reached over and moved his hair aside revealing a discoloration just under his ear similar to one I was born with. My mom called it a café au lait spot because it was the color of coffee and cream. "That's a birthmark."

"It's a soul brand. You have one exactly like mine."

I moved his hair again, and he tilted his head to give me a better look. It was in the same place as mine, but it looked different. Mine was a nondescript blotch, while his was a distinct crescent shape. "Mine doesn't look like this. It's an amoeba-shaped blob."

He winked at me. "Have you looked at it since your birthday?"

"No." I pulled down the sun visor and opened the mirror. I craned my neck to get a look at it. "Whoa! It changed shape." I ran my fingers over the perfect crescent just like his.

"It did that when your soul matured enough for you to begin speaking for the Hindered. That's when you began transmitting. That's how I found you and how the IC knew you were emergent."

"Man. Talk about Big Brother. How do they brand souls?"

"It's a closely guarded secret passed through oral tradition and performed in a closed ritual. Only the oldest of our kind participate. Imagine what would happen if immortality fell into the hands of the wrong people."

"So, it's like magic?"

"Magic or miracle, I suppose. As long as the mark is whole and you keep your soul in your body at the time of death, you'll recycle."

I patted Spook's shoulders. "Do you remember your soul being branded?"

He shook his head. "No. The oldest memories fade."

"I think I liked it better when I thought I was crazy."

He chuckled.

The stitches had become itchy and had been bothering me since my shower that morning. I shifted again, and Spook made a grumpy grunting sound. "Are Maddi and Race together?"

"They're just really close friends—like brother and sister. It's odd for Protectors to pair up. It's discouraged by the Speakers."

"Why?"

"It distracts them and makes them less effective," he replied pointedly.

"Ouch. I fell right into that one, huh?"

He smiled. "Yes, you did."

Wow, the stitches were bugging me. I scratched under my sternum. "So are they in school or anything?"

He nodded. "This is the first cycle I've been younger than them. They're freshmen in college this year. They both finished Protector training and wanted to keep up appearances. Maddi's living with her folks, and Race is in a dorm."

He reached over and stopped me from scratching my abdomen again. "I need to see that."

"It's fine. It's just itchy."

He pulled off at a gas station. "Let me see it, please."

I lifted the bottom of my shirt enough to expose the stitches.

"You're all healed. I need to take them out before you irritate the area. It won't be as itchy if I remove them."

"Inside the car?"

"Would you prefer to do it on the hood?"

"No."

Spook growled low in her throat. She stood up and raised her hackles.

I sat upright, trying not to gag. "Do you smell that, Alden?

There's a horrible odor. It smells like . . . death." I twisted to look into the backseat. Nothing, of course. "Who's here? What do you want?"

"Welcome back, my love." The voice was a soft whisper. I could hardly make out the words.

The odor was so bad it burned my nose, and I had to hold my breath. It smelled like rotten meat. Alden sat still, not taking his eyes off me. When I finally took a breath, the stench was too much. I threw open the car door and vomited on the pavement.

Alden ran around to my side of the car and helped me out. Spook jumped into the backseat and barked ferociously. Alden opened the back door and yanked her out by the collar. "Stop it, Spook. It will hurt you. Quiet."

The little dog fell silent at Alden's command.

I began retching again. Alden pulled my hair back and rubbed my shoulders. After I'd finished, he led me, along with Spook, away from the car. My stomach was cramping so hard, I couldn't stand up straight. I leaned over with my hands on my knees. "I'm so sorry, Alden. I don't know what happened. What was that smell?"

"It's a Malevolent, Lenzi. They sometimes put off foul odors to frighten people."

"It worked. Did you smell it?"

"No. Protectors are immune." He picked Spook up.

"You're lucky." I stood up straight and took a couple of deep breaths. Whew. "Do regular people smell it?"

"Sometimes. Some people are more sensitive to the paranormal than others. Children in particular are receptive to them. You are far more sensitive to them than any regular person. Do you still sense it?"

I shook my head. "No. I think it's gone." I looked down at my blouse. "Yuck. I'm glad I brought a change of clothes."

"In your backpack?" he asked as he passed Spook to me. I nodded. He walked to the car and pulled the pack out of the backseat. "We caught a break this time," he said. "Sometimes they tear up everything in sight. It didn't do a thing to my car."

He lifted Spook out of my arms and escorted me to the bathroom inside the gas station convenience store, which was a private, one-person affair with a plastic, fold-down baby-changing table. He placed Spook on the floor and commanded her to stay. He told me to go ahead and change while he moved the car to a parking place, instructing me to lock the door and verify who was outside before opening it.

After rinsing out my mouth, I pulled off my clothes, grateful the mess wasn't worse. I slipped into tan slacks and a dark brown sweater from my backpack. I had picked the outfit hoping it would make me look sort of professional for the IC representative.

Three sharp knocks on the door were followed by three more. I slid the lock over and opened the door. Alden glared at me from the threshold, gray eyes like storm clouds.

"What?"

"You didn't identify who was knocking," he admonished me.

"Sorry. I'm new at this. Is there a code word or something?"

He pulled the baby-changing table down to horizontal and set his medical bag and a brown paper grocery sack on it. "No. If we agree on a code, the Malevolent could hear it. You need to ask questions no one else could answer."

"Can't bogeymen just walk through walls?"

"Yes, but if they want to hurt you badly or kill you, they'll possess another person to do it. That's why Protectors are trained in physical combat. When demons get vengeful, it gets ugly."

"Sorry. I'll be more careful."

He smiled and brushed my hair behind my shoulders. "Are you feeling better? Do you need anything?"

"No. I'm fine now. Thanks."

"How about this?" He reached into the brown paper bag and pulled out a toothbrush and toothpaste.

"You're my hero!" I ripped the toothbrush out of the plastic wrapping and unboxed the tube of toothpaste. While I brushed, he picked up my discarded uniform and sealed it in a plastic bag he had removed from his medical bag. This guy was too much. He treated me like I was valuable. Like I mattered. My heart did a fluttery little dance that made me want to dance too.

"It's my job," he said with a wink.

When we returned to the car after Alden had removed my stitches with a funny-looking pair of scissors, there was no trace of the odor. Spook watched me protectively from Alden's lap while I sipped ginger ale. Alden had purchased it in the convenience store when he bought the toothbrush and toothpaste. He was right: the ginger ale settled my stomach.

As we reached the causeway bridge to Galveston Island, the terrain turned into coastal wetlands. The Texas City refineries puffed clouds like stalled steam engines off to the east. Building the huge expanse of bridge to get from the mainland to the island must have been a giant undertaking. I closed my eyes and ran Alden's memory of the storm through my brain. The bridge washed out and all those people died because they were trapped. *Poor Alden.* The survivors probably had it worse than those who perished.

"What did the Malevolent say?" Alden asked as we entered Galveston.

I shuddered when I remembered the ominous whisper. "It welcomed me back. Mainly, it just stank."

His brow furrowed. "What were its exact words? This is really important Lenzi."

I reached across to stroke Spook's head. "He didn't really say much. He just whispered, 'Welcome back, my love.'"

"Damn!" He whacked the steering wheel with his palm.

Spook startled and crossed over to my lap. "What?"

He shook his head. "It's just bad timing, that's all." He took a deep breath through his nose and loosened his grip on the wheel. "We need to be careful. I have no idea what he'll do. You can't leave my sight, not even for a second, until he makes his intentions clear. You can't even go to the bathroom without me. Do you understand?"

"That's pretty dramatic, Alden."

"My job is to keep you alive. You talk about how oppressed and subjugated I am. This is where the tables turn, Lenzi. In order for me to serve you, you have to do what I say."

I could tell by his tone of voice he wasn't kidding. Maybe the stinky thing was really dangerous. "Okay."

He glanced at the clock on his dash. "Even with the pit stop, we made good time. We have almost half an hour before we meet with the ICDC rep. How about a walk along the beach?"

"No!" My volume surprised me.

"You don't like the beach, do you, Lenzi?" he asked as he turned onto Seawall Boulevard.

"No. I can't stand it. I've never liked it." I peered with dread out my window at the rolling surf.

He glanced at me briefly. "That makes sense, I suppose."

"Why?"

He pulled into a parallel parking place at the seawall. "Because you died here."

TWENTY-TWO

Alden snapped a leash onto Spook's collar, led her around the front of the parked car, and opened my door. No way. I was not getting out of the car. He evidently picked up on that because he leaned against the car and stared out at the surf.

It was a clear, sunny day. The waves were tiny—less than two feet tall—rolling in even, benign bands to the shoreline. We were parked at the seawall over fifteen feet above the beach, and still I was frightened.

"You know this seawall didn't used to be here," Alden said. "Before it was built, the whole island was at sea level."

"Yeah, you told me about it when we met. Hobbit mausoleums, remember?"

He chuckled. "I remember that conversation well. They started building this seawall two years after the Great Storm. It took that long to clean the place up and settle on a construction strategy."

I stared down at the wall. It had a curved face on the Gulf side similar to the concrete barriers on a freeway, only huge. Behind it, the land was the same level as the top of the wall.

I crossed my arms over my chest. "Is there a point to this history lesson?"

I knew what he was trying to do. He'd said once that knowledge alleviated fear. Well, it wasn't working.

He smiled and held up a finger. "Did you know that Galveston was the first city in Texas to have electricity and telephones?"

"No, and I'm not sure I really care."

"It was also one of the busiest ports in Texas. It was a really big deal compared to Houston back then."

I reclined my seat back and closed my eyes. "You sound like Ms. Mueller, Alden."

Spook gave up pulling on her leash and sat at his feet.

"Why don't you come out here, and I can tell you about it on the beach."

I opened my eyes when I heard him pull on the latch. "Not a chance. I'll listen to your historical fun facts from the safety and comfort of the car, thank you." I pulled the door closed again.

He leaned down and looked into the car. "Come on, Lenzi. The beach is fun."

I shook my head. "Nope."

Alden stared out over the placid Gulf waters and leaned back against the car again. "Happy things happened here too," he said.

"I'm not staying in here because I'm Rose, Alden. I just don't like the beach, that's all," I said, putting the seat back up.

"I didn't say anything about Rose. Let me show you a memory. It's a pleasant one. You'll like it." He leaned down and looked in at me. "Come on, Lenzi. It'll only take a moment."

He knew I couldn't resist seeing memories of the past. I held out my hand and he took it.

"I can't leave my body out here on the Seawall. Scoot over." I shifted over toward the center of the car and he opened the door. He sat on the seat with me and pulled me up onto his lap. Spook leapt onto the floorboard at our feet. Alden shut the door.

My body thrummed with the energy he was transmitting. What had happened to "this is wrong" from last night?

"This is a little too cozy, don't you think?" I remarked.

"You're absolutely right." He patted the driver's seat. "Come on, Spook. Three's a crowd." The dog jumped up onto the driver's seat. "Better?" he asked with a grin.

"Um, you said—"

"Shhh," he interrupted. "I'm only going to give you a memory. Contact helps. Ready?"

I nodded.

"Out," he whispered. I braced for the pain that always followed. It wasn't bad this time. Not bad at all. Since he wasn't in his body, I relaxed against it, enjoying the contact.

Okay?

"Yeah. I'm fine. Let's see it."

Rose was walking down the beach with Alden. She wore a long, brown dress with a high lace collar and a funny-looking hat with a purple ostrich feather. Her hair was pulled up under it. Alden had short hair. He wore a suit and held a hat. Her arm was linked through his.

"We look weird." I giggled.

Yes, we do. Watch.

"Well, not 'we.' I mean you and Rose."

Right. Just watch.

Rose grabbed Alden's hat and took off running, which must have been difficult in the sand in that long dress and uncomfortable-looking pointy shoes. He laughed for a moment before chasing her. Her hat flew off, and he grabbed it up easily from the sand as he closed the distance between them. She ran a few feet out into the water before Alden caught her, and they both fell into the surf. Alden held her hat out of the water as they continued to laugh at each other. He placed it gingerly on her wet head. Giggling, she pulled his hat out of the water and put it on his head, dumping water on him.

The memory stopped.

"Wait a minute. I want to see more," I whined. I loved this

memory. Seeing the playful side of Rose almost made me like her.

Nope. I have to retain some of my mystique. I just wanted you to see that at one time, you loved the beach. It's one of the reasons you asked to be assigned to the Texas Coastal Region.

"C'mon, Alden. Let me see more."

We're out of time. I'm exiting now, okay?

Almost painlessly, he exited and came to life. Contact really did help. He squeezed me before he opened the door, gesturing for me to get out.

He called Spook out and locked the car. "I want to be sure we don't make the rep wait."

"What will he be looking for?" I asked, turning to face the Gulf so that the wind didn't blow my hair across my face.

"Anything odd about you—or me for that matter—that would keep you from doing your job. I guess for now, until we are caught up on points, you might want to not reveal the amnesia. We don't want them to think you might not be able to keep up. It would help if you acted a little more confident. Rose was very self-assured."

"Oh, great. He'll see right through me."

He looped Spook's leash over his arm and took my face in his hands. "You are powerful, Lenzi. You are the Speaker. He'll only see who you are." He gently pressed his warm lips to mine.

"Wait a minute! You said we couldn't do that!"

"No. That was nothing like what was going on last night. I kissed Rose like this all the time."

"No way. A kiss is a kiss, Alden," I said, frustrated he was breaking his own rule.

He laughed. "Lenzi. If you think that was anything like last night, then we weren't in the same room."

I glared. "Cheater."

He chuckled.

For a moment, an image flickered through my mind. I closed my eyes and concentrated on recapturing it. The perspective was as if I were standing on the beach below us. The Seawall wasn't there and loads of long, skinny bathhouses on stilts littered the beach. To the left, where the Hotel Galvez currently stood, there were only wooden buildings. This had to be how Rose remembered this spot trying to push its way into my conscious mind.

I opened my eyes with a jolt to current-day Galveston.

Alden touched my shoulder. "What is it?"

Before I could answer, he closed his eyes. "A Speaker is getting close. Maybe the rep is a Speaker instead of a Protector. That would be a lucky break. He won't feel your nervousness. Oh, yeah . . . he's real close. This is good, Lenzi."

"How do you know it's a he?"

"His soul doesn't feel like a girl's."

A handsome African American man in his early thirties was approaching us from the west. He looked out of place on the seawall in his suit.

"Four thirty-eight?" he called as he came near.

"Yes, sir," Alden responded, holding my hand. He had amped up the sedative effect of his touch, thank goodness. I needed it.

"Thanks for meeting with me." He shook Alden's hand, then turned to me. "I finally get to meet the famous Rose, Speaker 102."

No doubt, Alden felt my fear skyrocket. He increased the current and gave my fingers a squeeze before letting go.

"It's nice to meet you," I said, shaking the man's hand. "And you are?"

He smiled. "I apologize. I'm Speaker 956. You can call me Phillip."

"Nine fifty-six," Alden repeated. "You're a pretty young soul to abandon the role of Speaker for a job like this."

Phillip shrugged. "This is only temporary. My Protector was lost last year. I'll go back next cycle when she returns."

Alden shook his head. "Sorry, man. Exorcism?"

"No. Vehicular homicide. It happened in this region, actually. We came down because we were assigned a case by the IC. The Malevolent hangs out at some cemetery around here, swearing vengeance on the South. Calls himself Smith. Bad dude. Killed her by possessing a truck driver, who ran her down. He has a thing against women, I guess. Kept raging about some lover who double-crossed him. But then, this is your region. You probably know more about him than I do."

Alden took my hand again. "Yeah. He's been around awhile. We'll get him, eventually."

Phillip returned his attention to me. "So, Rose. You were gone a long time, huh? What happened?"

Alden responded to my jolt of fear with a squeeze and more

calming current. Thank goodness the IC didn't send a Protector. The charade would have ended right here.

"I have no idea what happened. It's irrelevant, I guess, because I'm back in action."

He tilted his head. Obviously, he wasn't convinced. "So, you're a bit behind in the numbers. You're barely over ten points a day. Is something going on?"

It took everything in me to fake a smile. "You'll have to ask Alden about that. I thought he was on top of things."

"It's totally my fault," Alden confirmed. "I've bogged us down. I've got a little sister this time, and I'm still living with my parents. I'm only seventeen and quite restricted. I'll overcome it."

I could tell by Phillip's demeanor and facial expression, he wasn't buying it.

"Rose, you have no theory as to why you didn't return for a century?" Phillip asked.

On the brink of panicking, I stood up straighter and tried to make myself into the picture of confidence. Like Rose in the wedding memory. "I don't have a clue what happened. The last thing I remember was climbing up onto the roof of our house with Alden and somehow ending up in the water. Nothing after that."

Thank God Alden had shown me that memory.

"You're not living on the coast right now. That's out of character for you," Phillip asserted.

"I have no control over where my mother in this cycle lives.

Alden and I plan to move here once we are no longer considered juveniles. We'll present ourselves as a married couple again. That was always the most convenient arrangement. I love it here. That's the reason I requested the Texas Coastal Region cycles ago." I smiled at Alden, feeling a bit more natural in my role. "I appreciate your concern. The numbers won't be a problem."

Phillip studied me for a moment. "They asked me to evaluate your Protector for reassignment if he's holding you back."

"If he doesn't get his act together, I'll take you up on that. But, really, Phillip, I've invested too many years in him to train another one. Plus, Alden and I work well together. We both know our limitations and avoid situations that would reduce our productivity. We always have. That's why we had the top score three cycles in a row."

Phillip lifted his eyebrows. "Okay, then. I'll suggest that the reassignment not be initiated. I think it would be detrimental to split up a partnership with a track record like yours. Obviously, you're just off to a slow start." Phillip shook our hands. "Best of luck to you both."

We stood still, not talking, while he crossed the street to the Hotel Galvez.

Once he was out of sight and the charade was over, I slumped down onto the top step of the stairs that led to the beach. Maintaining that kind of stoic confidence when I was terrified was one of the hardest things I'd ever done. Spook licked my face and wagged her short tail.

A blue four-door Dodge Ram pickup parked behind Alden's Audi. "It was a Speaker!" Race shouted as he got out of the passenger side. "He took the bait. I felt him change from doubt to admiration. Whatever you guys did worked."

"Lenzi did it. You should have seen her. She was fantastic!" Alden announced as he hugged Maddi, who had come around the front of the truck. I sat up straighter. Alden's approval was as calming as his touch.

Maddi laughed. "Well, I wish I *had* seen it, because I felt it. She was totally freaked out. It made it hard to concentrate on the other one. She was so panicked, I thought for sure she was blowing it. God, Alden, I was certain you guys were dead."

Alden put his arm around my shoulders. "No. She was brilliant. Sounded just like my Rose."

TWENTY-THREE

I stared over the railing of the patio at the surf. This restaurant on Seawall Boulevard was made of several old houses that had been smushed together to form one large structure. Below the patio was a row of sparkling motorcycles, all parked perfectly parallel to one another on a diagonal. It looked like a Harley ad.

Spook barked at a seagull and trotted back and forth across the deck, enjoying her freedom from the leash. Dogs weren't officially permitted in the restaurant, but the manager of the Spot would look the other way if the dog stayed on the patio and was well behaved. Alden snapped his fingers and pointed to the floor. Spook fell silent mid-bark and lay at his feet.

Maddi and Race sat together on the bench across the table

from us. Their western garb was so flamboyant they might as well have been in costume. Maddi was wearing another cowboy shirt with mother-of-pearl snaps down the front, and she had a rust-colored suede jacket with long fringe dangling from the arms and across the back. Race wore a matching shirt and jacket, minus the fringe. He had on a large turquoise bolo. Both wore black felt cowboy hats. Alden's gray pullover was invisible by comparison, but his looks made him stand out every bit as much. I found it hard to keep my eyes, or hands for that matter, off of him.

"How did you find us, Maddi?" I asked.

"We knew the meeting was on the seawall at noon near the historical marker. Your transmissions were so intense, though, we probably could have found you even if we hadn't had the exact location."

I wasn't sure if this was reassuring or troubling.

The pager the girl at the counter downstairs had given us when we ordered went off, letting us know our food was ready. Maddi stood.

"Helena will run you around enough when she emerges. Let me and Alden get this," Race suggested.

Maddi smiled and sat back down.

"I guess Helena is your Speaker," I said after the boys left.

"Yes. I expect to be called into duty any day now. She always emerges when I'm barely eighteen. I hope she turns up soon. It gets boring just being a regular person." She leaned closer. "So, you and Alden. Are you like . . . ?" She winked.

"No."

"But you're into him. I feel it."

I stared out at the Gulf. "He's into Rose."

"You *are* Rose. You talk like you're two separate people."

"We are. I'm nothing like her, or at least so I'm told," I said, staring down at the names customers had carved into the wooden picnic table.

Alden backed through the door with two plates of food and held it open for Race with his foot.

"If you gentlemen will excuse us for a minute," Maddi said as they set the plates on the table. "Lenzi and I are going to the restroom." Maddi grabbed my arm and dragged me through the door. We passed through a little dining room—a converted attic of one of the houses—and went down the stairs to the bathroom. She pulled me into the first stall, which was enormous, with a wooden double door.

Stunned by Maddi's forcefulness, I stood against the wall waiting for her next move. Her face was red. It looked like she was going to beat me up or something. Built like she was, my prospects were grim.

She shook her finger right in my face. "I can't believe you're doing this again!"

I shook my head. "Really, Maddi. I don't understand."

"You've jerked him around for centuries. I thought maybe you'd be different this time. You got your wish. Don't you see? You got your wish, and now you're going to blow it again."

I tugged at the bottom of my sweater. "What wish?"

"You really don't remember anything." Maddi held out her hand. "Give me your hand. I'll show you."

I put my hand in Maddi's.

"Out," she said.

I knew what was coming next. I braced myself against the wall as Maddi's soul ripped into my body.

I'm going to give you a memory, Maddi said. *I could tell you about it, but it'll have more impact if you see it.*

Images of Maddi and Rose sitting on a green velvet settee in a room that had dark wood paneling and a piano played through my head. Every inch of the place was decorated with pictures, paintings, and enormous potted palms. Ornate origami figures decorated every nook and cranny. Both women were wearing long, white linen dresses, and Rose had her hair loosely piled up on her head. Maddi's hair was bobbed short. She was less muscular than in this current cycle. Rose was doing needlepoint. *Needlepoint? Ugh.* I didn't have the patience to do needlepoint. One more reason to hate Rose.

"If a man like Alden expressed that level of interest in me, he would not have to ask twice," Maddi said.

Rose set the needlepoint down, walked over to the piano, and ran her fingers over the keys. "Oh, Maude, you simply don't understand. It is not like that between us. It never has been, nor will it be."

"Why not?"

Rose fidgeted with the black pendant she wore at her neck. "It would not be prudent."

Maddi looked angry. "Prudent or *convenient,* Rose? It's easier for you this way, cleaner. No one gets hurt if no one takes a risk. Alden has loved you forever."

Tears filled Rose's eyes. "And I have loved him, as well. There has been too much history between us, Maude. Alden and I have too much knowledge of each other to change now. It would ruin us." I was surprised when Rose began to cry. Evidently, she had a heart after all. "Oh, Maude. What a mess I have made of things! I wish I could just begin again. Start over fresh with no preconceived notions or mandates. I wish that I could forget everything about my past and just live again, seeing Alden for the first time through tender, open eyes. To love him the way he deserves to be loved. I'm going to approach the elders and see if such a thing is possible."

The memory stopped. *I'm exiting, Rose,* Maddi said.

"Ow!" I groaned as Maddi's brown eyes sparked with life and she gasped for breath.

"You got your wish, Rose, don't you see? You must have gotten to one of the old fogies, and they must have delayed your recycling so you'd lose your memory or something. Whoever did it must have done it on the sly because it wasn't documented, and believe me, the IC documents everything. I don't know how it happened, but this is your chance. When I felt what your soul was transmitting for Alden at the coffee shop, I thought maybe you were faking the amnesia so you could get a fresh start. Now, I know it's real. This is your chance to get it right."

I unlocked the door and walked to the sink. "Alden is the one who says we need to have a business-only relationship."

"Because he's as scared as you are. You're the Speaker. You have to lead. Get your act together." Maddi left the bathroom without a backward glance.

When I joined the others, they had moved to the small attic dining room located at the top of the stairs just inside the patio. We were the only ones in this section of the restaurant.

"It was too cold outside," Alden said as he pulled the chair out for me. "I thought Race was going to cry like a baby."

Race laughed. "You're the one who was whining about the wind," he teased.

"Being male, I'm surprised cither one of you had the good sense to come in out of the cold," Maddi said, pouring a tiny paper cup of ketchup on her hamburger.

I stared at my hamburger, appetite completely gone. The memory from Maddi had thrown me off balance. Did Alden know about Rose's wish? Had she really gone to the Council elders? I studied the black and white checkered vinyl tablecloth. "She was just like my Rose," Alden had said out on the seawall after the ICDC rep had left. It was Rose he really wanted, not me.

"Are you okay, Lenzi?" Alden whispered.

Stupid soul-feeling crap. I nodded and took a bite of my

burger to ease his mind. The room made me uncomfortable. Because it was the attic of a house, the ceiling was triangular. The space was dark and tight. Graffiti drawn by restaurant patrons covered the exposed wood of the walls and rafters. There were names and dates written all over the place in Sharpie marker. "Kiely was here," "George and Samantha, Spring Break 2011."

"Are you going to eat those?" Race asked, indicating my fries.

"No, you can have them."

Race grabbed several fries from across the table. Maddi glared at him. "That's why you're not built like Alden. French fries."

Race laughed. "I'd love to look like Alden. Hot female Speakers would be falling all over themselves to be paired up with me, just like they did with Alden, when Rose . . . Lenzi was gone. You should've seen it, Lenzi. It was hilarious."

My insides gave a jealous churn.

"Ha!" Race grinned. "I can feel that things have changed between you two!"

"Stay out of it," Alden admonished him.

Race clapped Alden on the shoulder. "Hey, man, I'm happy for you. It's about time you got a little action."

Alden's eyes narrowed. His voice was almost a growl. "I said, stay out of it!"

"Whoa, Alden. If this is about three cycles ago, I only did what any normal guy would have done—"

Alden slammed his fist on the table. "That's enough!"

Spook jumped up from her spot under the table and growled. Alden immediately turned to me. Spook became so agitated, Alden had to put her out on the porch. He returned to his seat facing me.

"What's going on?" I asked.

"Nothing yet, evidently, if you don't hear anything," Alden said, studying my face. "But Spook felt something."

Out of the corner of my eye, I sensed movement across the room. "There!" I pointed at the wall. The three Protectors turned in unison. Words appeared on the wall in red.

You have returned.

"What does that mean?" I asked, gripping the edge of the table.

Alden put his arm around me and transferred some of that calming energy, but it didn't work. My terror made it hard to even breathe. He gave my trembling shoulder a squeeze. "Shhh. I'm here. Ask what it wants."

I managed to gulp enough air to speak. "What do you want?"

Blood-red letters appeared on the rafter over my head.

Revenge.

This whole thing had a bizarre déjà-vu feeling to it. Struggling to not scream, I stared at the letters, fighting to access the memories just out of my reach. Dammit! If I only knew what Rose knew.

"Do you think it's Smith?" Race asked.

"Undoubtedly," Maddi said.

I scanned the room for movement. "Who is Smith?"

"You didn't tell her about Smith?" Maddi asked.

I will have vengeance appeared on the rafter.

Alden tightened his grip on me. "No, I didn't tell her. I didn't want to scare her off. She can't possibly resolve him."

He knew this thing was out there, and he didn't tell me? My breathing came in rapid gulps of air. He would never had done this to Rose. "Way to believe in me, Alden."

He leaned close to my ear. "You need to drive him off, Lenzi. He's too strong for you right now. Send him away."

I stood and shouted at the rafter. "I do not deal in vengeance. I deal in resolution. Demon, begone!"

Maddi gasped.

History repeats itself appeared on the tablecloth.

"Demon, begone!" I shouted.

Excruciating pain shot down my arm. I screamed and pulled back my sleeve. **I will kill you again** was carved across the flesh on the inside of my forearm. The terror left a copper taste on my tongue. "Out with you! Begone!"

Alden pressed a napkin to my arm to stop the bleeding. He nodded to Race.

"We can't let him have you. Lenzi, may I come in?" Race asked, grabbing my shoulders from across the table.

"Yes," I managed to say.

I clenched my teeth as Race entered. The scorching pain was horrible this time.

You're safe, now, Lenzi. I'll keep him out. Alden is going to get you out of here, okay? Just hang in there.

I screamed as my body was lifted from the chair by an invisible force. It didn't feel like hands held me. It was as if I were on top of a wave of energy. The energy snapped off, and I was dropped to the floor with a thud. Alden immediately picked me up and ran down the stairs. He bolted out the door and sprinted to his car. He set me down just long enough to pull out his keys, never letting go of me. He locked me in the car with Race still sharing the vessel.

"What now? What's going on?" I asked. The feeling of helplessness was maddening.

It's okay, Lenzi. Smith was trying to enter the vessel, Race explained. *I was keeping him out. That's why he threw you. I've never seen one quite this strong. He's been trying to kill you since the 1860s. The IC tried to resolve him several times in your absence. They should have known that if you couldn't do it, no one could.*

"Oh, God. It's trying to kill me? Why?"

You should really ask Alden that.

I wanted to pound my fists on the dash. "Clearly, he doesn't think I can handle it. I'm asking you, Race. I just need to know what I'm up against. Who is Smith?"

A bad, bad guy, he told me.

In the rearview mirror, I watched Alden stuff Race's body in Maddi's truck. "That's super helpful, Race. How about some details now?"

Let's wait for Alden, he said.

This was so irritating. "Let's not. I need information, or I can't do my job. Tell me everything you know about Smith." In the mirror, I watched Alden help Maddi buckle Race into the passenger seat. "Now, Race."

He sighed. *In 1863, Nicaragua Smith was court-martialed by the Confederate Army stationed on Galveston Island. They loaded him on a wagon with his coffin and took him to the cemetery for his execution. He stood next to his pre-dug grave and tapped his foot on his coffin, grinning like it was a party while he waited to be shot by a firing squad. He vowed revenge from the grave and refused a blindfold, saying he wanted to look at his killers' faces as he died.*

I shuddered. "That's creepy."

He asked to be buried facedown, facing Hell. They granted his wish. Evidently he hasn't made it there yet.

I jumped when the door locks popped open. To my relief, it wasn't Smith messing with us, but Alden, who had unlocked the doors with his key chain remote.

Spook jumped onto my lap when Alden opened the driver's door.

He looked into my eyes for a moment before starting the car.

My hands balled into fists in my lap. "You knew that this thing was hunting me! You *knew* and you didn't tell me! You broke the rules, Alden."

Hey, let's calm down kids, okay? Race chimed in.

"Be quiet, Race. Stay out of it. Mr. Rule Follower broke the rules! That's a bit hypocritical, Alden, don't you think? You can't kiss me, but you can neglect to tell me about a big, badass bogeyman who's been trying to kill me since . . . oh, yeah! The Civil War! Just a minor detail that slipped your mind. Huh, Alden?"

Um, maybe you guys could take this up later, when you have more privacy.

Alden gripped the wheel so tightly his knuckles were white. "The reason we can't have a physical relationship and the reason I didn't tell you about Smith are completely unrelated."

Okay, you two should really discuss physical relationship stuff when you're alone.

"Shut up!" I yelled.

"That was entirely uncalled for, Lenzi," Alden shouted.

"Not you. I was talking to Race."

"Oh." Alden exhaled through his clenched teeth. "Please, Lenzi, just wait for a moment and collect your thoughts. We're both too agitated to talk rationally. We need time to reflect."

Good boy, Alden, that's right from page eighty-two of the rule book.

"Good boy, Alden, that's right from page eighty-two of the rule book," I parroted.

"Shut up, Race!" Alden admonished.

Race laughed. *You guys are great together.*

"Keep your opinions to yourself," I grumbled.

Alden's phone rang. He pulled it out of his pocket. "Hey, Maddi . . . yeah, Clear Lake will work. He's never gone further north than Dickinson. He's probably too weak after that stunt to even make it off of the island. . . . Mm-hm, it was very impressive. Tremendous power. I bet we could take him with another team in the mix. Kind of like soul tag or something. We'll propose it to the Council. . . ." He looked over at me. "Yeah, they seem to be getting along fine. Race still hasn't learned to keep his big mouth shut, though. See you in a few minutes. Bye."

You need to talk to Alden about your feelings for him, Race said.

"You don't know anything about it. Mind your own business, Race."

You love him. I know. I'm in here. I feel your soul, Rose.

I was going to protest being called Rose, but didn't. Somehow the lines were getting blurry—either that, or it just didn't matter anymore. What did matter was what Race had said. Bogeymen or not, I was in love with Alden Thomas, regardless of what name I went by or what demon wanted me dead.

TWENTY-FOUR

"Did you hear her?" Maddi asked Alden as she met up with us in the gas station parking lot. "She said the same words and everything!"

I stepped out when Alden opened my door. "What words?"

"The stuff you said to Smith. You repeated yourself from over a hundred years ago," Maddi said.

"Weird coincidence," I muttered as I followed Spook to a patch of grass near the station store. Spook sniffed around in the unmowed weeds. Why had I said that? The words were odd, but somehow I knew what to say.

It's not coincidental, Race remarked from inside my head.

I jumped. I'd forgotten he was still there. "Stay out of it, Racc," I said while Spook finished her business.

Let me show you. I was there.

Spook sat in the grass and sniffed the air.

Seeing Rose again was too tempting to resist. "Okay, go ahead."

Images flooded my brain. Race was with Rose in the same room I'd seen in Maddi's memory. There were people talking in a room behind them,

"The meal was perfect, Rose. You outdid yourself," Race said, standing close to Rose, who was pinching the brown tips off of the slender leaves of a parlor palm. He was wearing a suit and was slim. The shoes Rose had on made her taller than Race. I couldn't see the shoes, though, because Rose's indigo dress almost touched the floor. I wondered how she could breathe with her waist drawn in that tight.

"Flattery is nothing but attention without intention," Rose replied without looking at him.

"I have made my intentions perfectly clear, Rose. My Speaker has given me liberty. There is no obstacle to our relationship progressing to something more . . . familiar." He ran his fingers down her bare arms. She moved away, gown rustling as she crossed to the window.

"I am married to Alden, Horace." She fiddled with the black medallion tied around her neck with a black velvet ribbon.

He laughed. "It is a charade, and we both know it."

"My answer is no. It always shall be. I cannot allow myself to be distracted."

Race's response was interrupted by the entrance of Alden and Maddi, who were dressed similarly to Rose and Race.

Alden looked from Rose to Race and back again. He shut his eyes. After a moment, he laughed. "She refused you again, Horace! Ah, well. Perseverance may pay off one day, old friend." He clapped Race on the back.

Rose flattened against the window. She appeared shaken. "Begone," she whispered. All three Protectors moved closer to her. She was listening to someone.

"I do not deal in vengeance. I deal in resolution. Demon, begone!" Rose shouted. "Alden, now!"

The memory stopped.

See? Exactly the same words.

"Yeah, weird."

Hey, Lenzi . . . my offer from a century ago still stands. If Alden doesn't treat you right, I'm here for you in any capacity, if you know what I mean.

Surely he was kidding. "Very funny, Race. Come on, Spook, let's go back." Knowing Race could feel my soul, I tried to suppress any and all emotion as I tromped back to the car.

"Let me see your arm, please, Lenzi," Alden requested after Spook leapt onto the front passenger seat.

I held it out, and he pushed up the sleeve of my sweater. He winced. "That's a lot of threat to fit on one tiny arm. Good thing Smith writes small."

"If that's a joke, it's not funny. Tell me it doesn't need stitches." I groaned.

"Nope. Just antiseptic, holy water, and time to heal."

Maddi looked over Alden's shoulder. "Aw, that's nothing. Remember the time he—"

Alden cut her off with a glare.

"Nice weather we're having," Maddi said as she strode to her truck.

After Race had returned to his body and my arm had been treated, there was debate over whether or not Race should ride with us in case someone needed to enter the vessel. Alden couldn't drive and protect me at the same time, but they decided that the danger had passed for now and Race could ride with Maddi. Smith had used up a lot of energy communicating, so he shouldn't resurface for weeks, even if he had expanded his territory.

Once we were on the highway, I turned Alden's iPod off. We needed to talk and clear some of this up. "Why did you have Race soul-share instead of doing it yourself?"

"It was the best tactic. There are several reasons; none of them are your concern."

"Oh, right. I thought we were a team."

He glanced at me and shook his head. "You're safe. It was the best way."

"Reasons?"

Alden sighed and switched lanes to get around a tanker truck.

"Lenzi, if I had been in the vessel, he would've had to drive my car. This was easier."

He was hiding something. "That's not it. You let me drive your car, and I don't even know how to drive."

Alden accelerated and turned the iPod back on. I switched it off the moment he set it down.

"You've been keeping things from me, Alden. You say we're a team, but you only tell me what you want me to know. You show me bits and pieces of memories and give me half-truths. You wouldn't do that if I were Rose, would you?"

A muscle twitched in his jaw. "Can we talk about it later?"

"No."

He took a deep breath through his nose. "Okay. I don't want Horace touching you. I would rather have him soul-share than have to watch him touch you. I trust him with your life—not your body."

"I thought you guys were friends."

"We are friends. There's no one I trust in a dangerous situation more than Race. He and I are in agreement on this. It's best I be the external Protector if both of us are needed."

"Well, I'll tell you, Alden, I wish you'd change your mind on that. It really hurt when he entered and exited."

He almost smiled. "Some souls are more compatible than others. I'm sorry it hurt."

I decided not to tell him about Race's offer at the gas station. I patted Spook, who grunted and shifted positions on my legs.

"I need you to tell me about Smith. If I'm going to be haunted by this ghoul, I want to know what he is and why he's out to get me."

He brushed the hair out of his eyes. "I'm sorry I didn't tell you about him. In retrospect, it was a mistake."

I examined the threat carved into my arm. "So, why does he hate me so much? I didn't execute him."

"No, you didn't." Alden reached over and brushed my hair behind my shoulder. "Smith is out to get you because he believes Rose betrayed him. My experience with him in life was very limited, and unfortunately, my memory about it isn't reliable because I was in jail when most of it was going on. Plus, I've been through two cycles of memories since then. I know that Smith set me up for a crime he committed. I know Rose got me out of jail by leading him on until he confided in her, which exonerated me. Basically, Rose set him up by seducing him, and he fell for it . . . and her."

"Ew. She had an affair with a demon?" I shuddered. "She must have really wanted you cleared of that crime. What was the crime?"

"Stealing a Confederate boat in Galveston Harbor. He wasn't a demon at the time, just a despicable crook. He was totally in love with her and didn't see her betrayal coming. Then, after he was executed, he approached her as a Malevolent, and she wouldn't let him use her body to exact revenge on the members of the firing squad. Insult to injury, I guess. He lay low until the next cycle, which was the one in which you . . . she was killed in the storm."

I did the math in my head. "If Rose was nineteen when she died in 1900, how could she have been around when he was executed in 1863?"

"That was the previous cycle. Rose was born for that cycle in 1831. She was thirty-two when she had the affair with Smith that led to his execution. She died from a fever in 1875 and returned for the next cycle in 1881."

Alden's description of Smith didn't make the ghoul any less creepy or dangerous, but at least I knew why he wanted me dead. I stared at the message carved into my flesh. *I will kill you again.* "Alden, what does this mean, 'kill me again'?"

"I have no idea. Smith just wants to scare you, I guess."

It was working. At least I knew what to be scared of now.

"You're not going to keep stuff from me from now on, right? We're partners, just like you and Rose were."

He reached over and squeezed my hand. "Yes. Partners."

I selected some upbeat music on the iPod and leaned my seat back and closed my eyes.

Soon after we reached the Houston city limits, Alden received a call from his mom's office manager asking him to go pick his sister up early from school. The teacher wanted to meet with a family member as soon as possible regarding Charlotte, Elizabeth's imaginary friend.

We drove straight to the posh learning center and were

ushered into a bright white room just off the lobby, decorated with framed artwork drawn by children. Alden drummed his fingers on the glass table while we waited for the teacher to arrive.

"This thing with Charlotte feels wrong," he said.

When Miss Mason walked in, I recognized her as the same teacher who had met Alden at the car when he picked Izzy up last time. She fiddled with the top button on her blouse as she sat. Her blond hair was pulled into a twist at the base of her neck, which made her look older than she probably was.

"Mr. Thomas, I appreciate your willingness to meet with me on such short notice. I tried to reach your parents, but they are both evidently in surgery today and sent word for me to speak with you in their place." She began fiddling with her button again. "I hate that it has come to this, but I need you to tell your parents that if they cannot end Elizabeth's obsession with her imaginary friend, we will need them to enroll her in counseling."

"Oh, come on, it can't be that bad," Alden said. "It's just a phase. Lots of little girls have imaginary friends."

"No, Mr. Thomas, this is not a phase." She wrung her hands in her lap. "It isn't normal. She expounds on women's rights and the Suffrage Movement. Little girls have princesses, ponies, bunnies, and unicorns as imaginary friends, not feminists. She says that Charlotte is very old, which is unusual for an imaginary friend as well. Mr. Thomas, I received my degree in child psychology. Honestly, I'm worried about Elizabeth."

"Seriously? You've got to be kidding me."

"Wait a minute," I interrupted. "Let me talk to her. If she agrees to not talk about Charlotte at school, will you allow her to stay without counseling?"

"Well, I suppose so, but she would need to stop completely. She becomes very animated and intense when she talks about Charlotte. It troubles the other children."

I stood. "Deal. She'll be Charlotte-free tomorrow."

Miss Mason seemed skeptical, but agreed and asked us to wait until she could retrieve Elizabeth.

"What are you thinking?" Alden whispered.

"I'm thinking it's time for a tea party with Charlotte," I said with a smile. I couldn't believe he hadn't figured this out.

"How is that going to help Izzy?"

It felt good to know more than Alden, for once. "I believe that it will help *Charlotte*."

He appeared mystified.

"Come on, Alden. Put two and two together. Charlotte is an old woman who lives in your little sister's room. Spook growled at Izzy's door the first time I was at your house. Izzy insists Charlotte is real. Izzy is picking up historical information that's not typical for a little girl. You said that kids are more sensitive to the paranormal than adults. Don't you think that sounds like a job I can handle?"

"No way! You think Charlotte is a Hindered?"

"Yep. Almost positive."

"I've never even considered that. Izzy's always had a great imagination. I would never have thought of . . ." A grin swept across his face. "That's brilliant! I hope you're right. Getting rid of a Hindered is a lot easier than getting rid of a figment of a little girl's imagination."

TWENTY-FIVE

Elizabeth loaded up a tray with a pile of Oreos to take upstairs, nibbling as she stacked. She said she needed to eat the broken ones because they were ugly and Charlotte should only have pretty ones.

"Are we going to take her some juice?" Izzy asked, standing on her tiptoes to see over the counter. She had black crumbs at both corners of her mouth.

"Does Charlotte drink juice?" I asked.

"She used to."

"Mm-hm." I pushed the refrigerator door closed with my foot and arranged juice boxes on the tray. "Before we go up, can we talk about Charlotte?"

Izzy tossed her gold curls and put her hands on her hips. "She's not 'maginary!"

"I know. I just don't want to ask questions in front of her. Okay?"

"'Kay." She climbed up onto a stool at the kitchen counter next to Alden, who was doing his part to make sure Charlotte wasn't exposed to offensive broken cookies.

"Are you able to see Charlotte, Izzy?" I asked.

"No. She just talks to me. But she's real!"

"I believe you. There are lots of real things we can't see. Does she go places with you?"

"No. She's scared to leave my room."

I nodded. "Why do you think she's in your room?"

Izzy stuffed another cookie piece in her mouth. "'Cause she's 'fraid of being alone. She said so. I tell my dollies to keep her company." She pushed Alden's hand away to keep him from wiping her mouth with a napkin.

"I see," I said.

Izzy finished off her cookie.

"Come on," I said, picking up the tray. "Let's go have a tea party."

We stopped outside the room. "Maybe you should tell Charlotte that she has company," I suggested.

Izzy disappeared into her room, shutting the door behind her. I put my ear to the door and motioned for Alden to do the same. "Do you hear that, Alden?"

"I hear Izzy having a one-sided conversation."

I grinned. "I hear two distinct voices, plain as day."

The resolution with Charlotte was simple. She was a charming lady of around eighty years old. She was thrilled with the news that the Twentieth Amendment had been ratified in 1920, giving women the right to vote. Charlotte had devoted a large part of her adult life to the Woman Suffrage Movement, trying to secure that right. She was even happier that women were serving in both houses of Congress, the presidential cabinet, and had even run for president of the United States. She didn't believe it until Alden produced a current newspaper.

"I have completed my job, then," Charlotte said.

"You did a good job," I said. "Is there anything else you need to finish before you go?"

"I wish I could hug Elizabeth."

"Elizabeth, is it okay if Charlotte gives you a hug through me?"

The little girl nodded and clapped in delight.

I invited Charlotte to use my body to complete this last task. She must have been a proud woman. She had me stand very straight when she entered. Before speaking, she cleared my throat. The voice was rich and much lower than mine. "Do not allow yourself to be denied, Elizabeth. You must make yourself heard, no matter the cost." She took Elizabeth in my arms. "Thank you for keeping me company."

"Are you ready to go now, Charlotte? I'll help you out," Alden said from his perch on Izzy's bed.

"Yes, young man, I am ready now."

Alden touched my shoulder and entered to dislodge Charlotte. She appeared, dressed in a long skirt and pleated striped blouse. She closed her eyes and smiled as she was engulfed in a shaft of white light.

Charlotte was a Hindered, Alden marveled. *I can't believe I missed that.*

"Why did she hang out with Izzy? Is Izzy a Speaker?" I asked.

No. Speakers are very rare. Charlotte was probably just drawn here because of me. Sometimes Hindered hang out where a Protector lives because they know the Speaker will turn up. Most kids can hear Hindered if they concentrate, but never get the chance.

Izzy walked over to where Alden's empty body stood. She took his lifeless hand and, after a moment, raised her frightened eyes to his face.

Time to go. She can't handle the whole story. Brace yourself.

I nodded.

Out, he ordered his soul. Immediately, the body that had been lifeless a moment before took a deep breath and looked lovingly down at his little sister. He got on his knees and hugged her to him. "I love you, Izzy. I know you'll miss Charlotte."

"Alden, what happened?" she asked.

"Magic. A secret that only the three of us share, okay? You can't tell anybody."

"Okay. Pinky promise." She held her tiny hand up and Alden linked his pinky finger through hers.

After having what Izzy deemed "the bestest tea party ever,"

Alden and I retreated to his room so he could close Charlotte's file and rack us up some more points.

I sat on the edge of the bed and watched him log on to his computer. I stared down at my arm and read Smith's words, "I will kill you again." The letters were raised and stung when I brushed my fingertips over them. Alden had said Rose drowned, but he had only shown me the memory up to the part where they kissed on the roof.

"Are you sure Smith didn't have something to do with Rose's death in 1900?"

He stopped typing, but didn't turn around. His shoulders rose and fell as he took a deep breath. "Positive."

I rolled my sleeve back over my forearm. "How do you know?"

Still facing away, he answered, "There's something you need to know about Rose's death. Something you deserve to know." He turned in the desk chair to face me. I'd never seen him like this—so troubled. "I should have told you right away, but I was so grateful you came back, I didn't want to ruin it."

I stood. "Oh, come on. It can't be that bad. You said I've died lots of times. I was a little late to the party, but so what?"

He put his face in his hands.

I ran my fingers through his silky hair. "Alden, what is it?"

He remained motionless with his head down and his hands over his face. What on earth could it be? He was unraveling before my eyes. I felt helpless . . . and responsible somehow.

"Look, Alden, if you don't want to talk about it—"

"I have to talk about it." His stormy eyes met mine. "I *need* to talk about it. I haven't told a soul for over a hundred years, and it's killing me. For three lifetimes, people have told me how sorry they were that you were taken from me in that tragic accident."

"Well, I'm sure they were trying to make you feel better, Alden."

"They shouldn't have." He pulled away and strode to the window, staring out with his back to me "I'm sick of pretending, Lenzi. I've planned for over a century how I was going to apologize if I were ever fortunate enough to see you again." He turned to face me. "Well, here you are, and what do I do? I take advantage of the fact you don't remember, and I act like it didn't happen. Instead of telling you the truth, I kissed you, for God's sake! I got so wrapped up in the fact that I turned you on for the first time ever, I became a selfish ass." He turned away and placed his hands on the window casing.

It made my heart ache to see him in so much pain. "It's okay, Alden."

He spun around. "It's not okay. It will never be okay. It wasn't an accident, Lenzi. It was my fault you died. I killed you!"

It was like the earth had stopped. I couldn't breathe. "That's impossible," I whispered.

"It's not impossible. I've played the memory over in my head a million times. It's irrefutable. Everyone was mystified that you didn't recycle. I wasn't. I knew why you stayed away. I broke the rules, and you died because of it."

I knew there was no way he would have intentionally killed Rose. "What rules? How did you kill me? I drowned. How is that your fault? Did you throw me off the roof or something?"

"No."

"Then how is it your fault?"

He sat down on the bed, appearing emotionally drained, staring straight ahead.

He'd never shown me what happened after the kiss. "Show me, Alden."

"It wasn't an accident."

I remained silent. It was frightening to see him teetering on the edge of control.

He ran his hands through his hair. "You may not remember, but your soul does. When I showed you the cause, you became very angry."

"I don't have a clue what you're talking about, Alden."

"The kiss, Lenzi. The kiss on the roof is why you died."

"Oh, you've gotta be kidding me! You're talking about the memory you showed me from the storm?"

"Yes. Your soul became turbulent when you saw it."

"I didn't get mad because of some cosmic past-life suppressed memory, for crying out loud!" I took his face in my hands and met his eyes. "Alden, you're right; I did get mad. I was watching you kiss someone else. I was jealous. I wasn't mad because you kissed me in some past life I don't remember. I was mad because you won't kiss me in *this* lifetime."

I let his face go. He groaned and shook his head. "You don't understand."

"Make me understand, Alden. Show me. If you killed Rose, show me, but let me tell you something—I know that you loved Rose and would never have hurt her. Any more than you would hurt me." I sat down next to him on the bed and took his hands. "Show me, Alden."

He closed his eyes. "Out," he whispered almost too quietly to hear.

I didn't make a sound as he entered. The memory started right away. Alden and Rose were huddled together on the roof. Debris slammed all around them. She pulled him to her, and they kissed.

"She started it, Alden," I said.

He remained silent as the memory ran through my mind. I started it over from the beginning again.

"See? She started it, and she's totally into it."

The kiss deepened, and Rose pulled away screaming, "No, Alden. No." She scooted down the roof away from him shouting for him to stay away. She screamed something else as lightning ripped through the sky and thunder drowned out her words.

"She's not mad, Alden, she's scared. Totally freaked out by something. Look at her. It isn't you."

He remained silent.

In my mind, Rose stood on the edge of the roof, paused long enough to meet Alden's eyes, and jumped backward into the water. Was that the look my dad had on his face before he killed himself too?

Alden stopped the memory before she went under.

I'm sorry. I can't watch you die again.

I sat motionless on the bed. "Please return to your body, Alden."

Out.

He poured his soul back into his body and we sat side by side, hands clasped. After a while, I let his hands go and walked over to the window. He had it all wrong.

"What am I supposed to do with that information, Alden?" I waited for an answer that didn't come. "Am I supposed to rant at you for kissing Rose back when it's obvious she jumped you first? Am I supposed to kick you out of my life or report you to the big bad IC meanies because she freaked out and committed suicide?"

He shrugged.

"There's more to this. We can't hear everything she said because of the thunder. She didn't do this because you kissed her. I mean, I'm sure it was good. You're a great kisser, but come on. You've told me over and over how in control she was. No way she'd lose it over a kiss."

"You saw it yourself, Lenzi. There's no other explanation."

Spook began to growl and bark fiercely from downstairs. Time felt suspended as we stared at each other, waiting. Then it hit. "Oh, God, Alden. It's that smell! The one from the car." I covered my mouth and held my breath. Terror grabbed my insides so hard I felt numb. This time I knew who it was, and I knew what he wanted.

Alden took me in his arms. "Remember to call me when it's time, Lenzi."

"No!" I screamed at the demon. "Begone!"

Smith's voice was close, and when he spoke, his clipped consonants echoed in my head. *"Ah, so brave, my love. Will he be too late again?"*

"Now, Alden!"

Alden entered before I finished saying his name.

I'm here, Lenzi, you're safe.

"That was a tragic mistake," Smith growled. *"If I cannot have you, I will have one you love!"*

Alden's empty body fell as if it had been knocked over. Oh, God! The thing was hurting Alden. I had to do something, but what? A cut streamed across on his cheek as his body was lifted over my head and dropped to the floor. Smith's terrible, menacing laughter rang out as I threw myself over Alden's body.

"No! You can't have him," I screamed.

"A little too attached this time, perhaps? That's what happened last time," Smith taunted. *"But you can't save everyone!"*

His laughter faded into empty air.

I remained draped across Alden's empty body. I had never felt rage like this. It made me shake from head to toe. I wanted nothing more than to send Smith from this world permanently.

I feel your anger. Let it go. It's okay. My body isn't damaged. Focus, Lenzi. He's not finished yet, Alden warned.

I sat up and listened. Spook ran by the door, growling. She began barking like crazy from somewhere down the hallway.

Alden and I reached the same horrifying conclusion simultaneously.

"Izzy!"

TWENTY-SIX

S*top, Lenzi,* Alden said before I'd made it to his bedroom door. *We can't act without a plan.*

I didn't want to wait long enough to make a plan. "We have to stop Smith, Alden. He'll hurt Izzy."

You can't take him on alone, Lenzi. We need help.

"I have you to help. Go back into your body."

Spook was still barking from the hallway.

No. That would leave the vessel open for him, and you aren't ready to take on a demon this powerful yet. That's what he wants. We can't leave you unprotected. Use my phone to call Horace.

"No, Alden. I think—"

Stop thinking, Lenzi, and please do as I say! Call Horace!

Knowing he could feel my soul, I swallowed my hurt. I found

Race's number, called him, and told him what had happened. Race said that he and Maddi would pick us up as soon as possible.

Alden was convinced Smith wouldn't hurt Izzy unless I was there to see him do it, so I didn't push to go to her room again. I needed to trust his experience and judgment. I was clueless about these things.

I retrieved Alden's medical kit from his car when he asked me to. Following his instructions, I cleaned the cut on his face and applied butterfly closures.

Go get three belts from my closet, Alden instructed. I didn't ask why.

Spook stopped barking.

The doorbell rang.

Alden's cell phone rang.

My heart stopped.

Phone first, then door, Alden instructed.

It was Maddi on the phone. She and Race were right outside. I ran down the stairs and let them in.

"Where's Alden's body?" Race asked as Maddi took the belts from me.

"Upstairs, in his bedroom."

"That figures," Race said as he took the stairs two at a time. "Sleeping on the job. Stay here, Lenzi. I'll be right back."

He returned carrying Alden's empty body. Maddi and I followed him out the front door to Maddi's truck. She opened the driver's door and Race dumped Alden's body behind the steering wheel.

"Stay with Alden's body, Lenzi," Race instructed as he ran around to the passenger side. He sat in the seat and put on the seat belt. "Now, lean across him and take my hand. Keep contact with both of us."

I stepped up onto the running board of Maddi's truck and grabbed Race's hand. It was a tight squeeze because of the steering wheel. I pressed my side against Alden's chest.

"Tag, you're it, Alden," Race said. "Time to give up the home base. On three: one, two, three!"

I held my breath as Alden exited and Race entered, but it didn't help, I screamed in pain anyway.

"Let's go, Alden," Maddi said, pulling me away from him. "We've got a date with the devil."

Alden stepped out of the truck. "Please wait here, Lenzi, while we go get Izzy."

"But I could help."

"No. You wouldn't be helpful. Quite the opposite." He ran up the sidewalk to the house.

I sat on the curb, determined not to cry. There was a lot more at stake here than my ego.

Hey. Whoa there. What's wrong, sugar? Race asked.

I'd forgotten he was there.

What happened? Was Alden mean to you? I can straighten him out, you know.

"No, Race. I'm just a screwup, and he knows it. Rose would've been helpful. I'm 'quite the opposite.'"

He didn't want you to go in because Smith would go nuts and hurt his baby sister. It's you Smith wants. Alden was right to keep you out here. He wasn't being mean.

"He told me not to think and ordered me to do as he said."

What was it he told you to do?

"Call you. I wanted to have him go in with me so that we could help Izzy."

There was a considerable pause. *Lenzi. You had no choice but to call me. Exorcisms take at least two Protectors.*

"Exorcism!" I leaned against the truck. "No, it can't be. Alden told me they were very rare and that the IC assigned them."

That's correct unless the person possessed is your little sister. Then you don't wait around to untangle the bureaucratic red tape.

My heart hammered, and my skin was clammy. I fought the urge to vomit. "I don't know how to do an exorcism. Surely he's calling in someone from the IC to help us, right?"

Calm down. It takes a Speaker. You are the Speaker, Rose.

"I'm not Rose! That's the problem, don't you see? All of you think I'm Rose, including the creepy ghoul in Izzy's room, but you're wrong. I'm not anything like her. I don't have a clue what I'm doing."

If you don't get it together, Elizabeth and Alden are dead.

"Get in the back of the truck, Lenzi!" Alden shouted as he

ran down the sidewalk carrying what I assumed was Izzy rolled up in a blanket. Maddi rushed past him and opened the back door of the four-door pickup cab. Alden shoved the bundle into the backseat and climbed in, laying his body across the full length of it. Maddi pitched Boo Bear and Alden's medical kit to me and jumped into the driver's seat.

Go ahead, Lenzi. Get in the back bed of the truck. You can't be inside with them. Smith will go crazy, Race instructed me. I put my foot on the tire and hoisted myself into the bed of the truck. I was thrown backward as Maddi took off down the street like a maniac. I stared down at Boo Bear. He certainly hadn't kept the ghosts away this time.

The wind ripping through the back of the truck bed caused my teeth to chatter—or maybe it was fear. I hugged my legs and put my head down on my knees.

My phone buzzed. Alden had texted me.

I had to keep you away from Smith.

I looked at him through the window in the back of the cab and nodded. My hair whipped into my eyes. I held it out of my face and read his next message.

Sorry I upset you. Are you okay?

I nodded.

We can't talk in front of Smith. He is listening through Izzy. Dangerous. She could die.

I bit my lip and nodded.

I believe in you, Lenzi.

It was hard to read his next message through my tears.

Promise him your body if he will release Izzy. Maddi will protect her. I'll beat him into the vessel.

I nodded.

Only you can hear him when he gives up possession and is noncorporeal. Tell me when to enter. Don't talk to me before then.

I nodded again. He smiled back. I turned around and curled up, pulling my knees to my chest. Trembling. Terrified.

Maddi parked her truck sideways, so that she blocked the ramp to the roof of the parking garage. There was only one other car. I could see Transco Tower and the Galleria shopping mall as I climbed out of the truck bed. *Why would they come to the top of a parking garage for this?* I wondered. Race had been silent the entire trip.

Maddi helped Alden pull the squirming, screaming, blanket-covered bundle out of the truck. It sounded like Izzy was screaming through her nose. I watched in horror as Alden removed the blanket. Izzy had a piece of duct tape over her mouth. Her wrists and ankles were bound with belts and her arms were pinned to her sides with a third one around her torso.

I realized now why we were on the top of an empty parking garage: no one could hear the screams.

Don't let Smith know you're freaked out. Stay cool, Race urged. *Alden isn't hurting the little girl. He bound her to keep Smith from hurting her. If he can't talk, run, or fight, he'll give her up more easily. The trick is to wear him down and reduce his power. It'll weaken him to share a body and not be able to use it. If we get him out of the little girl by baiting him with your body and Alden beats him in, he'll have nowhere to go because Maddi will enter the little girl to prevent repossession. And he can't use one of our bodies because we're closed vessels.*

"Will that resolve this? Will that be the end?"

No, but it'll buy us more time so you can get stronger and learn the ropes again.

"How do we get rid of him for good?"

We can't do that. It would require you to take him on one-on-one and wear him down enough for one of us to push him out, which you aren't ready to do. He has to be weakened to the point he doesn't have the power or will to stay Earth-bound. Right now, the most important thing is to get him out of Elizabeth's body before he forces her soul out.

"Okay."

I'll exit on your cue, so he sees you're open and unprotected. Alden won't be able to touch you for this one, so it'll hurt like hell. Be prepared. You might want to sit down before it happens.

I sat on the concrete in the middle of the lot. I met Alden's eyes and nodded. He gently removed the tape from Izzy's mouth. She spat on him. He didn't react.

The voice that came from her tiny body sounded nothing like a child's. "You fools. Do you think you can outsmart me?" Izzy's body sat up and glared at me.

My heart pounded.

Smith couldn't win. I couldn't let him hurt this child. I clenched my jaw and stared right into Izzy's eyes, only it wasn't Izzy who looked back. It was evil embodied.

"Welcome back, my love," the foreign voice growled from her mouth. "I'm so glad you deemed me worthy of your presence. I thought I had killed you for good last time when I pushed you off the roof and drowned you. I thought perhaps you were too frightened to come back."

So Rose hadn't killed herself. Alden closed his eyes for a moment, and his shoulders rose and fell as he took a deep breath. His eyes were shining with unshed tears when he met my gaze briefly.

I got to my knees. "I'm not afraid of you, coward."

"Coward?"

The Protectors exchanged glances. Maddi, who was holding Boo Bear, moved closer to Izzy. Alden remained crouched next to her.

"Only a coward would attack a four-year-old child," I said.

He strained against the belts. "Only a coward would fear one. Untie me."

"No. I'll do better than that. I'll give you what you want. You can come on into the vessel and talk to me."

His laugh crackled though the air like static. "Right. But before I get there, your lover will block me. We've been through this before."

"Are you okay, Izzy?" Alden called.

Izzy's head turned to him, but Smith answered. "You want to talk to little Elizabeth? Here she is!" Izzy flung herself onto her back so quickly Alden didn't have time to react. Her head hit the pavement with a sickening crack, followed by the shrill scream of a little girl.

"Make it stop, Alden!" the tiny voice cried.

Alden took Boo Bear from Maddi and put him in Izzy's lap. "Focus on Boo Bear, Izzy. Stay strong in there and think about Boo. If you stay on the surface, you won't be hurt."

"Oh, Boo," she wailed in her sweet voice.

Alden took her in his arms. She relaxed against him and wept. Then, without warning, she stiffened and bit him on the neck. Alden didn't yell, but I did. The blood flowing down his neck saturated his shirt, causing my stomach to flip over. I closed my eyes and fought the waves of nausea coursing through me.

Flickers of Alden in a jail cell ran through my mind. Images of Smith in a white shirt sipping wine with me. A look so hateful, *evil* was too weak a word to describe it, as he was hauled away by soldiers. Rose's memories.

"Enough!" I screamed. "That's enough. You want me? Come on, then, Smith. Get out, Race."

Lenzi. Wait. Give Alden time to get ready, Race said.

"No. Change of plans. It's me he wants, not any of you. I won't let Smith hurt anyone else because of some event from a past lifetime I don't remember. Let's make some new history, Smith." I stood up. "I mean it, Race. Get out. Alden, stay where you are!"

Alden was holding his neck, shaking his head, blood seeping through his fingers.

"I'm serious, Alden. I know the rule. You're not allowed to enter the vessel without the permission of the Speaker. This is between me and Smith."

You don't want to do this, Lenzi, Race warned. *He's too strong. You can't handle it.*

My rage bubbled over. I was sick of everyone protecting me and covering for my inadequacies. "Out, Race!"

The ripping sensation of Race's exit sent my head reeling. Before I could catch my breath, another soul entered my body with a scorching worse than any I'd ever felt. I took a breath. It was a familiar soul, one I'd housed before. I waited for the pain to stop, glad Alden had ignored my order and beaten Smith in.

"Now what?" I whispered.

What indeed? Smith replied.

TWENTY-SEVEN

"Get Elizabeth out of here, Race," Alden shouted.

Race picked up Maddi's empty body and carried it to the truck, where Alden was buckling Izzy into the reclined passenger seat. He placed Boo Bear in his sister's lap.

"Thanks, Maddi. I'll call when it's over," he said to his friend inside the body of his four-year-old sister. Izzy looked so helpless. As helpless as I felt.

I was crumpled into a fetal position on the concrete roof of the parking garage. My whole body shook because of the evil bulldozing through me. Smith's presence was powerful. The first Malevolent had been a picnic compared to this. I was in way over my head, but I had no choice. It was me he wanted. They needed to get Elizabeth away safely before I dared move.

Horrible laughter rang in my head.

"No!" I screamed, writhing in pain. "Demon, begone!"

The truck finally took off, and Alden moved closer, still applying pressure to his neck. He crouched next to me, his brow furrowed and his lips tight.

"I'm sorry, Alden," I whispered.

"Why did you do it, Lenzi?"

"I wanted to keep—"

My body jerked to a sitting position. My mouth involuntarily spread into a grin, then I laughed. It was a deep, eerie, guttural laugh that coursed through my body from deep inside. The laugh of the devil himself.

Isn't this amusing, my love? Smith asked. *We continue this dance lifetime after lifetime. Eventually, you'll grow weary of it and will not return. Why continue fighting me? Make it easy on yourself and just give in. I'm far more powerful.*

"You have no power over me."

He laughed again. *I have no power over you?*

Against my will, I stood and sprinted toward the edge of the parking garage. I fought, but couldn't gain control of my own muscles.

Alden caught up just as I reached the railing. Smith was trying to kill me—again.

"No, Lenzi! Fight!" Alden yelled as he grabbed me around the middle. I felt my body struggle against Alden and heard myself growl like an animal as Smith continued to control me. Oh, God! He was trying to make me jump.

It will only hurt for a moment as you hit the ground, love, Smith said. *Tell him to let you go and I won't kill him too.*

I wouldn't allow Smith to hurt Alden. The separation of my soul and body was pronounced, but it wasn't complete—I knew it wasn't over yet. I struggled to regain control over my body, but couldn't.

"Release me," Smith said to Alden through me. "Don't make me hurt her more than is necessary. I can make it painful for her, you know."

"No, Alden. Don't listen to him," I managed to yell despite the resistance from my own body.

Ah, naughty girl. You shouldn't push me like that, Smith said. *Now you've angered me.*

Smith forced me to raise my arm to my mouth. As if in a surreal nightmare, I fought, but was unable to stop myself from biting my own arm just below the shoulder. The pain was excruciating.

"Now, Lenzi?" Alden yelled over my screams, still struggling to keep me from leaping over the railing of the garage.

Oh, yes. Bring him in here so the three of us can hit the pavement together. Pity only you will feel the pain.

"No, Alden, no!" Smith was right: in the amount of time it would take Alden to force him out, Smith could throw me off the garage. Besides, there was no way I was letting Alden in until Smith was so weak he had to move on. This was going to end today.

Alden gave a hard tug and wrenched me from the railing just as I threw my leg over it. He forced me to the ground, facedown, and lay on top of me. He pinned my arms under my chest and held them in place, effectively immobilizing me. This infuriated Smith, who began cursing and shouting through me.

"Keep fighting, Lenzi. Tell me when you need me," Alden said.

"It's too late," Smith growled. "She doesn't need you anymore. She has me."

"You're temporary, Smith. I'm permanent," Alden said.

I gained some control over my body for a moment before Smith overpowered me again, slipping an arm out from under my chest.

"I'm here. Just say the word," Alden whispered in my ear, adjusting to pin my arm back under me again. "You have to be strong enough to hang on when I enter. Stronger than he is."

The blood from the bite on Alden's neck dripped in my hair. I was able to move my legs slightly. Maybe Smith was beginning to weaken.

Look at him bleed. He'll die, you know. You should give up so he can get some medical attention, Speaker. I'm the stronger soul, and I'm not leaving, but you can.

I couldn't give in. "Alden," I said. "Alden . . ."

"Fight, Lenzi!"

Fight me? You don't stand a chance. You are just a weak, confused little girl.

I knew Smith's taunting was an effort to weaken my resolve. I had to be strong—strong like Rose. "I'll never give in to you."

Oh, come now. Is that the best you can do? I'm doing you a favor by ending your pathetic life. You are no more qualified to resist me than the child I inhabited before you. If you choose to return again, try to come back with a little of the conviction you used to have. You were a magnificent woman. What a disappointment you must be to your Protector this time around.

Smith was right. I didn't have a clue how to get him out. And I was sure that I *was* a disappointment to Alden, whose breathing had become ragged. He was probably weakened by the blood loss. If I gave up, he could get some help. The tiny bit of control I'd gained slipped away, and I could no longer move.

Now, that's better. Tell him I'm gone. He'll let you up, and we can end this. He's too weak to stop you from jumping now. It will be quick and easy. Tell him it is over.

"Alden," I said. Speaking was almost impossible. I was too weak to finish. "So sorry."

Alden buried his face in my hair. "Don't let him win, Lenzi. Stay at the surface and resist. He's a demon. He'll do anything to weaken you so he can succeed. Fight, so I can get him out."

Your Protector is dying. I am stronger than he is, and you know it. Tell him I am gone so he'll let you up, and we can end this. Do it.

Just ending it would be so easy. Being possessed felt like being boiled alive from the inside. If I jumped, my pain would end and Alden could get help. I'd recycle and we'd be together in the next lifetime. If I kept fighting, I might weaken Smith, but it might be too late for Alden.

"Please, Lenzi. Don't let him win. I need you. Fight back. You can do this."

Alden's words echoed in my head. "I need you," he had said. Did he?

Do it now, or I'll withdraw my offer and kill him too. He's so weak, it wouldn't even be sporting. Tell him to let you up. You don't want to force me to shove your soul out. If I do, it's over. If you want to be with him again, do as I say.

I took a deep breath. It would only hurt for a second, and Alden would be safe.

Alden shifted his weight and brushed my hair from my face. "Don't leave me again. Stay with me. I love you, Lenzi."

No. I was not going to let this demon win. I was stronger. Alden loved me. I wouldn't let Smith win.

There was a tingling in my extremities as I regained some muscle control. I wasn't the weak little girl Smith said I was. In my past lives, I had been Rose. I would fight Smith . . . for Alden.

This time it was easier for me to speak—as if my new resolve had weakened Smith and he could no longer keep me down. The burning sensation had also lessened. "You have no control over me. You never have. We're just soul-to-soul now, and without the opportunity to destroy the vessel, you have nothing. Begone."

Smith laughed, but it sounded forced. His voice was weaker in my head. *You'll have to do better than that.*

"So will you. You can't stay in here much longer. It weakens you. Evil can't win unless it's allowed entrance. I deny you any power over me. You say my Protector is weak; well, his body may be injured, but his soul is far stronger than yours will ever be. And so is mine. Love is stronger than hate. Just give up this vendetta and move on. Let go, Smith. This is over."

I felt my own power returning as if an electric current were being increased in my body. I could move my arms and legs and no longer felt under Smith's control. He was weakening. "You can never get what you want. My soul will continue to return because you can't force me out. This vendetta is pointless."

A heartbroken pain struck my chest. Smith's pain.

I loved you . . . trusted you and you betrayed me. He stopped speaking for a moment and his anger flared. *I'll kill you in each of your successive lifetimes so that you never even have a chance at love. I'm going to kill you, and I'll keep killing you until you stop coming back.*

"Then what?"

He didn't answer.

"What will you do then? Aren't you sick of this? I won't give up. I'll always come back because even though you can kill my body, I'll never let you evict my soul. My reason for returning is a lot stronger than your reason to kill me. End this. End it now."

Never.

His voice wasn't as loud or sharp. He was losing power. I had to act now, while I had the upper hand. If Alden became so weak from blood loss he couldn't dislodge his soul, or if he died, I didn't stand a chance. Smith would force me out, and I'd never see Alden again in this lifetime or any other.

"Now, Alden," I whispered. "Get him out."

The pain was excruciating, but I couldn't even muster enough energy to scream. I felt like my insides were fighting among themselves. Smith was no longer talking to me. He was yelling obscenities and threats at Alden. Every now and then, Smith would cry out as if he had received a physical blow. I focused entirely on keeping my soul in my body. If he forced me out, I'd die and wouldn't recycle. I'd never see Alden again. "I won't be evicted. I have too much to lose," I chanted.

The scorching sensation increased and Smith gave a series of unearthly howls. Just as I was certain I couldn't keep my soul intact, the pain stopped. Smith wasn't swearing. I could hear myself breathing. My heart pounding. When I opened my eyes, I was greeted by red pavement. Blood.

I felt weighted down, as if buried alive. I couldn't move with Alden on top of me.

"Game well played, my love." Smith's voice came from somewhere behind me. He was out! I turned my head in the direction of his voice, but he wasn't there. He laughed. His clipped voice seemed to bounce off the concrete. *"Next time we meet, you'll join me in Hell."*

"Not if I can help it," I shouted. Smith's laughter faded into silence.

I lay there for a moment and then it hit me. The blood was Alden's. There was too much of it. Oh, God. I'd killed him.

It took all the energy I had to turn over. Alden's body rolled off me onto its back.

This is what I'd most wanted to avoid. I'd thought that if I could distract Smith, Alden and Elizabeth would be spared. I was wrong. Elizabeth was safe, but I hadn't been quick enough to save Alden.

He hadn't been responsible for my death in my last lifetime, but I was certainly responsible for his in this one.

"Alden, no," I cried. "I'm so sorry."

I ran my hand through his hair. This was my fault.

You have no reason to apologize. You were amazing.

"Oh, my gosh. You're in my head. You're not dead!"

No. I'm not dead, but I might be soon if Maddi or Race doesn't sew me up. Please call them to come get us. Tell them to call the IC for medical backup. I might need some blood. My phone is in the back pocket of my pants.

I rolled his body enough to reach into his back pocket. Race's number only rang once before he picked up.

"Hey, man. Is it over?"

"Race. It's Lenzi. Alden's hurt. Come quick."

"Where's Smith?"

"Gone."

"No way. You're shittin' me. You did it? Wow, you won!"

As I looked at Alden's unconscious body, it didn't feel like I'd won anything. "Just hurry, Race. And bring help. He might need blood."

I heard the truck motor start on the other end of the line as Race answered. "Gotcha, sugar. I'll be right there. Congratulations on your first exorcism, which just happened to be the IC's most-wanted Malevolent. Way to go!"

Congratulations? I brushed a strand of blood-soaked hair out of Alden's face. I might have weakened Smith and forced him out, but he had weakened me too. My vulnerability was painfully clear. I loved this boy. Life with him, regardless of how weird or dangerous it was, was better than life without him. Maddi was right. It was time for me to get my act together.

Race arrived within ten minutes. He stitched Alden's neck right there in the parking lot. I didn't want to watch, but Alden did, so I accommodated his wishes and allowed him to watch through my eyes.

I was glad Alden decided to keep his soul in my body. His injuries looked painful. Mine, on the other hand, weren't that bad. My self-inflicted bite was going to leave a giant bruise, but it didn't need stitches.

Race started the truck and drove out of the parking garage. "Maddi stayed at your house with Elizabeth, Alden. Poor little kid won't turn loose of Boo Bear, but doesn't remember anything about the incident."

That's a relief, Alden said from inside my head.

I turned in the seat to angle more toward Race. "It would be a hard thing to explain to a four-year-old."

"It would be hard to explain to an adult," Race said, flipping on his blinker. "Maddi told her that she hit her head on the pavement by the pool when she was playing with Spook. That cute little dog hasn't left Elizabeth's side either." The light changed, and Race turned left, the opposite way from taking us home. "We kinda freaked out when your mom came home early from the hospital to work on some surgical dictations, Alden, but she bought the story, so we're cool. I told her you and Lenzi were out on a date and Maddi had been babysitting."

"Some date," I grumbled. "Where are we going?"

"Maddi's meeting us at a hotel. The medical team is already there. I told them you needed blood, Alden." Race looked over his shoulder into the backseat of the truck at Alden's body. "You look bad, man."

Guys in lab coats met us at the back loading dock of the hotel. They put Alden's soulless body on a stretcher and took it up to the seventh floor on the service elevator. In no time, they had him hooked up to a machine with two bags dripping into tubes. One bag contained clear fluid, and a smaller bag contained blood. The IC medical guys talked to Alden through me as if two souls in one body were as normal as Houston rush-hour traffic. Alden would be fine, they decided. They insisted he transfer his soul to his body so that they could see how much pain he was in before they administered a painkiller. Alden groaned as his soul rejoined his body. The guys in the lab coats nodded at one another and injected something into the tube of Alden's IV.

I called my mom and told her that I was with Alden and would be home late. She dished out the usual "it's a school night" lecture, but sounded relieved. She said Zak had come by several times, and she had threatened to call the police because he was acting crazy.

Zak. I needed to deal with him, but it was pretty low on my priority list right now.

Race flipped on the TV, and we talked about the exorcism and watched sitcoms until the bell went off on the machine regulating the IV. Race pulled the needle out of the top of Alden's hand and turned the machine off.

"I brought you a change of clothes and the thing you wanted from your desk drawer," Maddi said with a wink.

Race helped Alden to his feet. "You're lookin' pretty rough there, buddy."

Alden gave a half smile. "I'm feeling pretty rough."

He then went with Alden to the bathroom and stayed with him while he showered the blood off and changed into the clean clothes that Maddi had brought.

Alden seemed more himself when he lay back down on the bed.

After writing something on the hotel stationery on the desk, Maddi placed it in my hand and pulled Race to the door.

Race winked at me. "We'll just leave you two alone now. I hate to see a good hotel room go to waste, especially when the IC's paying for it."

Maddi shoved him out the door. "You are such a caveman."

I stared at the paper. On it was written one word: *Wish.* I placed the paper on my thigh and folded it in half.

"What does it say, Lenzi?" Alden asked.

"Nothing." I made diagonal folds from all four corners that touched in the center.

"Mmm. 'Nothing' was not what I felt when you read it."

The soul-reading thing was so irritating. I shrugged and folded it in half again, forming a triangle. "It's no big deal, Alden. Just a joke between girls."

He sighed dramatically. "Ah, well. I'm sure Horace will tell me about it in great detail. Grisly, painstaking detail." He reached for his phone.

My fingers froze mid-fold. "Wait. Okay. You play dirty." What could he make of one silly word anyway? I straightened out the paper and placed it in his hand.

"Wish." He raised an eyebrow. "What wish?"

I pulled my fingers across my lips as if zipping them closed.

He laughed, then winced. Poor Alden. It must have hurt a lot.

IC guys called to let us know that they were on the way up to get the medical equipment.

They were the same men who had been here earlier. One guy checked Alden's vital signs while the other one packed the machine into a big suitcase. They warned him to take it easy because of the painkillers. Drive safely, blah, blah, blah.

"How are we going to get home?" I asked after I closed the door.

"Maddi drove my car over. I'll be fine to drive in an hour or so. Do you need to go now? I can call Race to come get you."

I sat down next to him. "No. It's still early." My stomach rumbled. I was starving. Smith had interrupted lunch, and I hadn't eaten dinner.

Alden groaned as he stretched across the bed to reach the hotel phone. He dialed room service and ordered two steaks with baked potatoes. If the IC was picking up the tab, why not?

I felt much better after I'd eaten, and Alden looked better. There was some color returning to his face. I let myself relax for the first time all day. Alden lay back on the bed and closed his eyes. The vaguest hint of a smile brushed his lips.

It was hard to believe what had happened. I'd met with the IC representative, resolved Charlotte, and defeated Smith all in one day. That plus Georgia last night was worth more than one hundred points. Over five days' worth in twenty-four hours. Maybe I wasn't half bad at this after all.

Alden brushed my arm with the back of his hand, leaving a trail of tingles that caused my heart to kick into high gear. "Maddi brought me something along with my clothes, Lenzi—something that belongs to you. I was waiting for the right moment to give it to you. This seems like a good time." He shifted and pulled a tiny satin bag out of his front pocket and handed it to me.

Something that belongs to me? I ran my fingers over the silky purple satin pulled tight with a drawstring. "What is it?"

He rolled on his side to face me. "Open it and see."

The top pulled open easily. I tipped the bag over into my

palm. It was the pendant I'd seen Rose wear in the memories. I turned it over in my hand. The medallion was carved from some black material. It was oval with an intricate rose carved in relief on the surface. Instead of a velvet ribbon, like in the memories, it was attached to a gold chain.

Something about holding it made me feel a link to her.

Alden smiled. My soul's response must have pleased him. "I gave it to Rose in 1899, right after she emerged. It's a Whitby jet pendant. Very popular in Victorian times. Rose loved it."

"I do too. Thanks. It's beautiful."

"So are you, Lenzi. You were amazing today."

Chills ran through me. I'd almost lost him. I'd almost lost everything.

"Here," he said, gesturing for me to lean closer. He took the necklace from my trembling fingers and clasped it behind my neck. He smelled like soap, and his hair was still wet from his shower. "Congratulations on successfully battling Smith."

"Is he really gone?" I asked.

He removed his hands from behind my neck. "Well, he's gone for now."

"What does that mean?" My heart fell. I thought it was over.

"He left of his own will—sort of like running chicken from a fight. He wasn't weak enough for me to shove out, but honestly, I wasn't at my best."

"So he's still out there wanting me dead."

He laid his hand over mine. "You did a hell of a job. You

wore him way down. Hanging on to you took a lot of his energy. He'll be lying low for a very long time. You're safe, Lenzi. You did it. You won this round."

For some reason, I didn't feel the thrill I'd expect at one-upping my nemesis. Perhaps it was all my unanswered questions. While Alden was stuck here, maybe he'd answer some of them.

"Why did Spook stop barking outside Izzy's door?"

He shifted higher on his pillow. "Because Smith was no longer there. He had transferred his energy to Izzy's body."

"He had so much hate, Alden. I could feel it. He was in pain."

Alden closed his eyes. "He's pursued this vendetta for over a century. Hate has a long memory. His pain is self-inflicted."

Smith was much harder to handle than the first Malevolent. He was relentless. If it hadn't been for Alden, I'd have given up. He told me to keep fighting. He told me that he loved me. He asked me to stay with him—like it was more than just his job. Hate like Smith's had a long memory, but maybe love's memory was even longer. When I looked back down, he was staring at me.

"What's going on, Lenzi? Your soul is turbulent."

I fiddled with the black rose pendant. "Alden, when I was fighting Smith, you said things. . . ."

He pushed up to where he was sitting against the headboard. "I meant them."

"You said that—"

"I love you." He took my hand. "I said I love you, Lenzi, yes. And I do."

"But if you love me, why can't we—"

He squeezed my hand. "We've been through this. I can't run the risk of losing you. You're too important to me."

"So who I am now and what I want doesn't matter? Only what Rose wanted matters? Even if I do remember, it won't make a difference."

"Somewhere deep down you remember—I just know it. I was surprised when you repeated Rose's words from a century ago, but it verified what I've known all along: you might have no recollection of her, but it's the same soul, and deep down inside, perhaps in a recess you can't access consciously, you are Rose, only better."

My heart leapt. "Better?"

He shifted in the bed to his side so that he faced me and placed his other hand on mine.

"Yes, better. The gap in existence improved you somehow. Your emotions are genuine and real. You hold nothing back, and, well, you're funny. I like it."

My grin probably looked goofy, but I didn't care. I'd beat Smith *and* Rose. Ha!

I squeezed his hands. "I do have *some* recollection of her. Not memories, exactly—more like glimpses into her memories. It's happened a couple of times, and they get more detailed each time."

He sighed. "I don't think it matters. Until your memory is fully intact, we can't act on this."

My disappointment was probably evident—even if he hadn't been able to feel my soul.

He squeezed my hands. "Lenzi. This is so difficult for me. You're offering me what I've wanted for lifetimes, hell, probably forever." He tucked my hair behind my ear. "Don't think for one second I don't want to pursue that. I just know it's not what you really need from me. We need a stable working relationship. Doing what I want to do and doing the right thing are entirely different."

I jumped up. "No, they're not."

"Lenzi, I know what I'm talking about."

"Well, I know something you don't know, Alden." I bit my lip. "I know why my past-life memory is messed up."

He sat up.

I looked in his beautiful gray eyes. "Rose got her wish."

It was as if he were afraid to say anything for fear I'd stop.

I sat back down next to him and continued. "Maddi showed me a memory today. It was from before the storm. I told her . . . *Rose* told her that she wished she could start over with no history or preconceived notions. She wanted to forget her past lives and see you through new eyes. She said she was going to approach one of the elders about it. Evidently, she did. She got her wish."

He shook his head. "I find that hard to believe. It's forbidden to tamper with recycling."

I shrugged. "Rules are made to be broken."

"Not IC rules."

"Listen to me. Regardless of whether or not Rose got someone to help her, her wishes were clear in that memory. She wanted to change your relationship. And I'm going to do my best to carry out her wishes."

His eyes never left my face. It appeared he was holding his breath.

"I know who I am, Alden, and I know what I want. I'm your Speaker, and I'm supposed to lead in this relationship, so it's high time I did."

I pulled his hair aside and ran my lips over the crescent mark on his neck. "I love you. So did Rose. Rose didn't kill herself because of you; Smith killed her. Rose *wanted* you to kiss her." I brushed the hair out of his eyes. "So do I."

And so he did.

TWENTY-EIGHT

From the front window of my house, I watched Alden's car disappear around the corner at the end of my street. I ran up the stairs two at a time and unlocked my bedroom window so he could sneak in if Mom got home before he came back. I had just enough time to shower.

Before I could even kick off my shoes, the doorbell rang. Maybe he'd changed his mind about checking in with his parents and grabbing his laptop.

The doorbell rang again several times in a row as I bounded down the stairs. "I guess you decided to use my computer to file that exorcism report after all, huh, Ghost Boy?"

My grin dissolved when I pulled the door open to find Zak

on the stoop. He placed his hand on the door to keep me from closing it. "Expecting someone else, babe? Maybe the guy who just dropped you off?"

I fought my instinct to back up. "What do you want, Zak?"

He leaned down so his face was level with mine. The smell of whiskey was overpowering. "You, babe. The same thing *he* wants."

"Zak, I'm not going to talk to you right now. I told you—"

"Wait." He ran his hand through his hair, stepped back, and took a deep breath. "Just hear me out, okay?"

The headlights from Mom's minivan flashed across the porch and along the front hedge as she turned into the driveway.

"Please," he said. "Just listen to me before you blow me off."

His eyes flitted to the garage when the automatic opener chain rattled and the door squeaked on its way up. With Mom home, I had an excuse to keep it short. And I needed to put an end to this. I stepped out onto the porch and pulled the door closed behind me. "Okay, Zak."

The van door slammed shut, and the garage door groaned on the way down.

Zak shifted his weight foot to foot, swaying a little. "Let's go talk someplace else. Someplace more private."

"No. I'm not going anywhere with you. You're drunk."

He glanced over my shoulder as the lights in the kitchen flicked on.

"Lenzi?" Mom called from inside the house.

"Out here, Mom."

Zak pulled his shirt straight and ran both hands through his hair.

She cracked the front door open and peeked out. "Everything okay?"

I'd battled a Malevolent today. A drunk ex-boyfriend would be a piece of cake. "Yeah, we're cool," I said. "I'll be right in."

Zak stared at his boots while she studied him. "I'm right inside if you need anything," she said before closing the door.

It was a while before Zak looked me in the eye and broke the silence with slurred words. "Why him? Why not me?"

"I . . ." I couldn't answer that. Not really. Not without making it worse.

Cold mist had begun to fall, making everything look shiny and soft around the edges. I bit my lip and stared up at the cloud of moths circling and slamming into the streetlight next to his car. I pulled my sleeves over my cold fingers.

"Help me."

Perfect. A bogeyman. Just what I needed right now. "Go away!"

"No!" Zak shouted.

"Not you." A cold trail of water snaked down my spine.

He placed his hands on my shoulders. "Who, then?"

I closed my eyes and shivered as the mist saturated my clothes.

"You need a doctor, Lenzi. You're . . . not right."

I shook my head. Even if I told him the truth, he'd never believe it.

"Let me help you."

His grip on my shoulders tightened when I tried to turn away. "I don't need your help, Zak. Let me go."

He slid his hands down my arms and took my hands between his. The warmth caused the tips of my numb fingers to tingle. "You do. You're sick like your dad."

I jerked my hands away.

"Look, Lenzi. I really care about you." As drunk as he was and as slurred as his words sounded, I knew he meant it. "That Alden guy's gonna take off when it gets too weird. I'll stay with you no matter what."

The mist had totally soaked through my clothes, and my teeth chattered.

He stared at Mom's silhouette through the kitchen curtains as she unloaded the dishwasher. "You're freezing. How 'bout we get out of this rain and go sit in my car to talk. We don't have to go anywhere if you don't want to."

I shook my head.

He fished his keys out of his jeans and held them out to me. "You can have the keys. I just want to talk to you. You owe me that at least."

I glanced at the water bouncing off the hood of his car, wishing my porch were covered. "Okay." I took the keys. "But I need to go in soon."

He lost his balance when he turned to pull me by the hand,

but managed to stagger to the car. I got in the passenger side as he all but fell in behind the steering wheel.

"What can I do to prove I'm serious?" Zak asked, turning in the seat to angle toward me. The streetlight over his car made the water drops on the windshield sparkle golden against the dark blue night—like the flecks in his eyes.

"I know you're serious, Zak. It's not you, it's me." *I'm a freak who hears dead people.*

"At Last Concert, I thought things were really good between us. What happened after that?"

I found out who I really was. What I really was. I tucked my fingers between my knees. "Nothing. I just . . ." He'd never understand. I bit my lip.

He brushed my wet hair behind my shoulder. "You're still cold. Why don't I start the car and turn on the heat?" He pulled the keys from my lap, and after several tries, the motor turned over. Heat blew from the floor vent. I pushed my feet closer.

"You've gotta give me a chance, Lenzi." It was a demand, not a request. "I can make you happy."

"It's not that simple."

"Yes, it is," he said through gritted teeth. The hair on the back of my neck prickled as my fight-or-flight instinct kicked in. "You've gotta give me a chance to prove it. I'm right for you. He's not."

I should never have gotten in the car with him in this condition. "I've gotta go now."

He reached over and grabbed me before I could reach the

handle. Headlights flashed across the windshield as a car turned the corner onto my street.

"You can't do this. You and music are the only good things I've got." The acrid odor of alcohol mixed with his warm cologne. I squinted as the headlights of the approaching car got closer. It was Alden's Audi. "Give me a chance, Lenzi."

I heard Alden's car door slam. "Let me out," I said. Alden tugged on my door handle, but it was locked.

"I won't let him have you. He doesn't love you like I do." Zak jerked the car into gear, and Alden jumped back as we pulled away, barely missing Alden's bumper.

"Don't do this, Zak!" I screamed. He took the corner so fast the back end of his car fishtailed, barely missing a fire hydrant. "Let me out!"

He wiped a tear from his cheek with the back of his hand. "Nobody ever gives me a chance." The ancient engine of his Delta 88 sounded like it was going to rattle apart when he floorboarded it. "Not my old man . . ." He ran the red light at the entrance of my neighborhood. "Not my mom—"

"Zak! Stop! You're gonna kill us!" If he'd only slow down, I could jump out. At this speed, I'd never survive a jump.

"But you're going to give me a chance." He swerved and nicked the curb at the base of the freeway entrance ramp.

I tugged on the seat-belt buckle at my shoulder, but it was stuck and wouldn't pull out. If he wrecked, I was through the windshield. I had to calm him down. "We can fix this. Just pull over, and we'll work through it." A driver in the right lane slammed on his brakes as Zak forced his way onto the freeway. I gave the broken seat belt another futile tug.

I was going to die tonight. Even Alden couldn't help me.

The rain hammered down so hard as we crossed the bayou overpass, I couldn't make out the lane dividers. "Zak, please."

He slammed the palm of his hand into the steering wheel. "Why *that* guy? Why not me?" I looked over the backseat at the car following us off the freeway. If it was Alden, there was nothing he could do to help us unless he'd called 9-1-1. Maybe it was a cop and he'd pull us over before Zak killed us both.

We skidded through the U-turn and headed back toward the bayou. The rear wheel rubbed the curb, and I was thrown to the side, shoulder smacking the window.

"Zak, you're hurting me. Stop!"

"You hurt *me,*" he said, blowing through a stop sign. He took a hard right onto the road that followed the path of the bayou and I was thrown into him, causing the car to swerve. He overcorrected and slid back and forth until we sideswiped a streetlight. The car slowed enough for me to jump out without killing myself. I had to get out. *Now.*

I shot across the car, pulled up on the lock, and ripped up on the handle. The door swung open, but as I scrambled to escape, Zak screeched to a halt and yanked me back by the leg.

"No, babe. For the first time, I'm going to get a second chance."

Headlights sped toward us from behind.

"Damn!" Zak pinned my thigh under his palm as he stretched across me to slam the door shut. The smell of his warm cologne filled my nose. There was a time when I thought it was the most wonderful smell in the world. "He's not gonna win," he growled.

"Please," I said. "You're acting crazy. Let me go."

"No, babe. You're the one who's crazy. That's why you need me." He looked out the back window at the approaching car. "I can't let you go." He shifted into drive. "I won't."

I braced myself on the dash as he launched toward a two-lane bridge that crossed the bayou. "Zak! You're too far to the right. You're going to crash." If he didn't pull back onto the road, we were going to hit the metal bridge rails head-on.

I closed my eyes and braced myself for impact.

Zak yelled as if he were in pain. He slammed on the brakes and turned hard right, barely missing the bridge. I screamed as we slid sideways through the mud at the edge of the ravine sloping down to the bayou. The car slogged to a stop and stalled. He grabbed his head and yelled a string of profanities. Then, as if a switch had been thrown, he fell silent, breathing hard. Somehow, the silence was even more terrifying—like waiting for the eye of a storm to pass and the raging to begin again, not knowing if it'll be better or worse.

He looked around the back of the car, eyes wild. "What the hell?" he whispered. "Who are you?" Zak twisted to look around his car. "What do you want?"

It wasn't a Malevolent or Hindered because I'd have heard it. I didn't hear anything except Zak freaking out. He had to be hallucinating.

"Get out of my head!" He bumped his head on the ceiling of the car as he flung the door open. "Leave me alone! . . . Do what? . . . Hell, no!" Zak trembled all over and whimpered.

"Walk away," Zak whispered as he stared over his shoulder toward Alden's car. It was parked under the streetlight several blocks back, where I'd tried to jump out.

"Oh, God. Lenzi! Oh, God. I've screwed up. I've screwed up bad." His eyes were full of tears. He grabbed his head and groaned, then got out, staggering around the front of the car. "Shut up. I'm doin' it," he said to no one as he pulled my door open.

"Go," he said, pointing at Alden's car. "Go back to him."

I couldn't move—couldn't breathe—as if the fear had caused complete paralysis. Zak pulled me out of the car. He cradled me in his arms as if I were the most precious thing in the world to him and lowered me gently to my feet on the muddy bayou bank, whispering, "Don't hurt her, there's hope until the last second, walk away, don't hurt her, second chance, walk away. . . ."

Afraid he'd snap out of it and pull me back to the car again, I shook myself out of my stupor and bolted toward the road, cold air stinging my lungs.

"Leave me alone," Zak shouted in the direction of the bayou. "I pulled over and let her go like you said. Now leave me alone."

He staggered a few steps toward his car. "Like hell I'm going to call a cab. Screw you!"

I had no idea who or what he thought he was arguing with, but no way was I going to hang around so he could change his mind. Once on the paved road, I sprinted to Alden's car. He was belted in, staring straight ahead. When I banged on the window, he gasped a deep breath.

He flung open his door and took me in his arms, clinging to me like he'd never let me go. Zak's car roared to life and after spinning his back tires in the mud, he finally pulled back onto the road and drove over the bridge away from us.

I was safe.

"I tried," Alden whispered in my hair. "I really did."

"There's nothing you could have done. I'm just glad you're here," I said. "And really glad he decided to pull over and let me out."

I pulled away enough to look at his face. The rain had stopped, but he was drenched from trying to open my door before Zak took off—and pale. Almost ashen.

"You okay?" I asked.

He pulled me to him again. "I almost lost you. I couldn't bear that again."

"Hey." I ran my hands under his shirt and up the smooth skin of his back. "I'm okay. It's over now."

After a deep, shaky breath, he pulled away. "Yeah." He leaned down and showered light kisses all over my face and neck, as if memorizing the smell and feel of my skin. My knees became liquid, and I leaned into him, finally whole.

I was awakened by an unfamiliar, high-pitched beeping. My clock showed eight o'clock. *Dang.* I'd been having the best dream. *Dream. Wish. Oh, man.* I realized the beep was coming from Alden's watch, which was on his arm draped across my body. He had driven me home and dropped me off, saying he had to go take care of some things. He must have climbed in through my window during the night. I turned to face him. His unearthly gray eyes met mine.

"Hey, Lenzi. How are you feeling?" he murmured.

His neck was still bandaged, and he looked tired. "Probably better than you," I said.

He pulled me closer, so that the entire length of my body pressed against his.

"When did you get here?"

"I've been here all night."

I started to sit up. He tightened his grip and kept me close. "Alden, my mom—"

"Has gone to work. She decided you needed more sleep when you only rolled over when she flipped on the light. She called the school and told them you were sick. She left a note for you."

"Oh, my gosh! Does she know you're here?"

"No."

"Well, how—"

"You really need to clean out your closet, Lenzi."

I laughed. "I'm a slob."

"You always have been."

There was an intensity about him I hadn't experienced before. I stared into his eyes, and then it dawned on me. "Something happened, didn't it, Alden?"

"Shhh. Let's pretend for five minutes it didn't." He buried his face in my neck.

"Alden, what happened?"

"Please, Lenzi. Just let me hold you."

"What happened?"

He rolled me under him and kissed me. It wasn't a gentle kiss like at the beach, or a romantic, passionate kiss like the one that happened in his room. It was desperate. Desperate and hungry and sad.

A good-bye kiss.

He released me and sat on the side of the bed to put his shoes on, keeping his back to me.

"Lenzi, Zak was going to kill you last night. I couldn't let him do it. My job is to protect you, so I saved you the only way I knew how. I put my soul in his body and threatened him."

It made sense now. "That's the reason he pulled over. It's *you* he was talking to."

There were tears in his eyes when he turned to me. "You've come back this cycle fresh, with a new life and so much promise.

I couldn't watch you die again. Especially like that. I'd rather die myself."

The truth hit me like a head-on with a truck. He had broken one of the primary IC laws. He had entered the body of a human outside an exorcism. Breaking primary laws resulted in discontinuance. *Oh, no.* They were going to execute him.

"No. Alden." I climbed out of the bed and faced him. I took his beautiful face in my hands, avoiding the cut on his cheek and the bandage on his neck. "No, Alden. There has to be a way out."

He shook his head. "There's no way out. The rule is absolute. I knew what would happen when I broke it. It's just a matter of time, Lenzi."

"No, but if you—"

He stood. "Stop. It's over. Fighting it will only waste our remaining time together. I don't want to leave this earth scraping and clawing for life. I've had a good life—lots of them, actually. I'm grateful."

A glimmer of hope warmed my chest. "Lives. That's right. We'll be together again in the next cycle."

He flipped his hair out of his eyes. "No, Lenzi. I'll be discontinued, body *and* soul. They'll destroy my soul brand before I die. I won't come back. Ever."

Cold chills danced up and down my spine as I processed his words. Never come back . . . ever. I wouldn't even have the hope of being with him in the next cycle?

My legs shook as I paced the room, wishing I had more

knowledge. Wishing I could remember my past lives. Wishing I were Rose.

"Rose would know what to do," I said.

He faced me. "Rose would know that there is nothing she could do. It's over, Lenzi. The offices open at eight o'clock. I'm going to get the call any second. Nothing can stop it. It's just a matter of time. Please, let this be peaceful."

I ran to his arms and held him. This couldn't be happening. There had to be a way. I had to *find* a way.

"How did they find out?"

He stroked my back. "I reported it last night."

I pulled away. "Why would you do that? *Why?*"

"Because you would have figured it out and it would have put you in danger." He took my face in his hands, wiping away a tear with his thumb. "If I hadn't, they would have discontinued you for covering for me. I couldn't bear that."

"They would never have known!" I yelled.

He wrapped his arms around me again. "They know when I split my soul. I'd have to file a report if it were a resolution."

I twisted out of his arms. "You could have lied!"

"That's not how it works. My job is to protect you, not put you in danger."

His phone rang.

ICDC.

"This is Protector 438." Alden ran his fingers through my hair as he listened. "Yes, I know. . . . Yes, I am aware of that." He took me in his arms and kissed the top of my head. "I will be at the Galvez by noon. Yes, sir." He dropped his phone and squeezed me tighter.

"What did they say?" I buried my face in his shirt, trying to get closer to him.

"They told me to get my affairs in order."

I began to sob, my fingers digging into his back. "No, Alden. Tell them no."

He tilted my head up and kissed me. Soon, the desperation of the kiss lessened, and he let me go. I watched the fire leave his eyes as he pulled away from me emotionally.

"You don't tell the IC no," he whispered. "I'm not scared. It'll be painless, and they'll make it look like I had an accident to give my parents closure."

"I don't want closure—I want you with me," I cried as I twisted my fingers into his shirt, trying any way I could to keep him near me.

"They'll probably pair you with Horace. You'll work well together. I trust him with your life."

"My life. That's right, Alden. It's *my* life—not the IC's. If they discontinue you, I'm done. I'm finished with this crap. I'm quitting or retiring, or whatever Speakers do. They can take their brand and their rules and—" He stepped away and the loss of him left me as helpless as I'd been last night. Only this time, there were no comforting arms waiting, no rush of air back into my lungs.

There was only a life without Alden.

"Good-bye, Lenzi Rose." I hated his tone of voice. The calmness of it, the resignation. My hands tightened, refusing to let him take one step away from me. He couldn't do this, he couldn't leave me now. Not now.

"No! It's not good-bye. I'll tell them you had to do it. I'll tell them it's all my fault."

He pried my fingers from his shirt, curled them into my palms, and kissed the insides of my wrists. "I have to go now. I hope you'll change your mind about retirement. You are a brilliant Speaker. You can make the world better. You certainly made my world better." He kissed me lightly on the lips. The platonic Rose kiss.

He was out of the room before I could remember how to breathe.

Too late, I stumbled after him, more falling than running, and I slammed into the front door. From the narrow vertical window beside the door, I caught a glimpse of his car turning off my street.

"Alden! Don't leave me!" I sobbed, pounding my fists on the door, just like I wanted to pound the stupid IC and their inane rules.

My legs gave out, and I slid down to sit on the tile floor. I wrapped my arms around my legs, pressed my forehead against the cool glass, and stared out of the window long after he'd vanished.

"Alden," I whispered, closing my eyes, trying to feel some bit of him, but there was nothing, only pain, regret, and emptiness.

I had no idea how much time passed. I didn't care. I didn't care if I ever moved from this place, or ever helped another Hindered, or ever took another breath.

The hole in my heart was bigger and emptier than the one that had been there before Alden came along and blew my life apart at the seams.

Lenzi Rose Anderson would never be the same.

TWENTY-NINE

I sat inside my front door. There was no need to do anything. There was nothing I could do. My phone rang. It would hurt too much to hear Alden's voice again, and talking to my mom would be a nightmare, so without checking the number, I let it ring . . . and ring . . . and ring. . . .

There was nothing I could do.

Ding-dong.

Nothing.

Ring . . . ring . . . ring.

Nothing.

Knock, knock.

"Nothing can stop it. It's just a matter of time," Alden had said.

I couldn't help him, just like I couldn't help Dad.

"Lenzi. Open up!" It was Race outside my door. "Alden needs his phone, Lenzi. He left it here. He has to turn it in to the IC."

"Screw the IC. Tell them to come and get it themselves!"

"He has to turn it in. It's the honorable thing to do."

That's it. Enough. I stood up and shouted through the door. "Honorable? There is nothing honorable about any of this. The only honorable thing was what Alden did, and they're going to kill him for it. I hate this, Race. I hate the IC. I hate the entire system."

"Then you hate Alden. He typifies the system. Open the door, please, Lenzi. Let him do this with dignity. He needs to return their property. It's important to him."

The system. Dignity. The whole thing sucked, but I didn't want to make it any worse on Alden than it already was. I jerked the door open and climbed the stairs without greeting Race. Alden's phone was on my floor where he had dropped it.

A memory tugged at the back of my brain. I closed my eyes and focused. Alden was in jail. The shadows cast by the flickering gas lamp at the end of the row of cells made the walls seem alive with motion. "It's hopeless, Rose," he said. "Smith saw to it there is no evidence in my favor. I'll face a firing squad for this."

Rose placed her hands over his on the iron bars between them. "There must be a way. I will find a way."

"Nothing can stop it," Alden in the memory whispered. "It's just a matter of time."

I opened my eyes. Those were the same words he had just said to me.

And this memory was from the Civil War. He had been wrong back then. Rose found a way. She *did* stop it. And so would I.

"Thanks, Rose," I whispered.

I picked up Alden's phone and turned it over in my hand. "ICDC" was the last call received. I highlighted the number and hit Send.

The voice that answered was a deep baritone. "This is Protector 236."

"This is Speaker 102. You called my partner this morning and told him to get his affairs in order. Well, I'm one of the things he had to get in order, and I'm not very orderly, my friend. I'm going to testify at his hearing." I was surprised by the forcefulness in my voice.

"I'm sorry, but that is not appropriate. The facts are irrefutable."

"Wanna bet? I'm going to refute them. I'll be there at noon, and I will be heard. I expect you to pass that on for me. Do you understand, Protector 236?"

"I will convey your request to the Council. I will warn you, however. If your presence was not requested, you will not be heard."

I felt like my head was going to explode. "Like hell I won't!" I ended the call and stood in the center of the room gasping for air. I knew that Race was standing in the doorway, but I couldn't face him yet. I glanced at my watch. Ten twenty-one.

"Race, please take me with you to Galveston when you deliver Alden's phone," I said.

Race shifted in the doorway. "Lenzi, that's not a good idea. If you show up, it'll only make it worse for Alden. Surely you realize how hard this is for him. Let him do this gracefully."

"There's hope until the very last second. Alden said that to me."

Race rolled his eyes. "Of course he said that. It's on the cover page of the IC Rule Book. It's kind of our motto. Most certainly, he said it in relation to the Hindered. You can't just take a sentence out of context like that. It doesn't apply in this case."

"To me, it does." I held the phone up and wiggled it. "Take me, Race, or no phone. You'll have to tell him you failed him."

Race pursed his lips. "Fine. But I don't want you to make a scene. He's proud of his record and reputation."

"So am I. That's why I have to go. Please wait for me. I'll only be a minute."

I brushed my teeth and tried to comb my hair, but there was blood matted in it. Alden's blood. Ten twenty-eight. It took less than an hour to get there. I stepped in the shower to wash my hair. Alden's blood turned the water pink. There was no time to cry.

I put on a pair of tan slacks and a cream-colored turtleneck. I pulled the chain and rose pendant to the outside of the shirt. Seeing it in the mirror made me feel stronger.

After throwing some makeup and Alden's phone into my purse, I bolted down the stairs.

Race kept his eyes on the road and his thoughts to himself. I could tell he was unhappy with my decision to interfere, but at this point, I really didn't care.

I couldn't believe my bad luck. Construction on I-45 and a wreck on the mainland side of the causeway. Eleven fifty-five. I buried my face in my hands and prayed. No way I'd be on time.

A Protector named Paul met us in the opulent lobby of the Hotel Galvez and informed us that he'd been apprised of my arrival and that the hearing had already begun.

Paul was shorter than Race. He looked to be about seventeen or eighteen, tops. His brown hair was impeccably cut in a conservative style that matched his gray suit and blue tie. We followed Paul past the reservations desk, down a marble stairway to a dark hallway with a door at the end. There was a small desk outside the door with a security monitor on it.

"Please wait here while I tell them you have arrived," Paul said.

The minute the door closed behind him, Race and I scrambled to the security monitor. It showed a narrow conference room dominated by a long wooden table so shiny it reflected the lights above it like a mirror. Alden sat in a chair at the end of the table. There were three people seated at the other end. Two men and a woman. All three were dressed in somber gray suits.

The woman spoke first. "Thank you for being punctual, Protector 438. You know why we are here, of course."

"Of course," Alden replied.

Race turned up the volume on the monitor. "That woman is a real hard-ass. She's at all the hearings. She hasn't been doing it long, though. This is only her second cycle at this post."

The short balding man across from the woman cleared his throat before speaking. "Then I assume you have nothing to say in your defense."

"I've never seen that Speaker before," Race said.

"I did what I had to do," Alden responded.

"You knowingly broke the code by entering the body of a human?" he asked.

Alden looked right into his eyes. "Yes, I did."

The woman shifted in her chair. She looked uncomfortable. "Protector 438, did you know the penalty for breaking the code at the time of the infraction?"

"Of course I did."

An old man sitting at the head of the table drummed his fingers and looked at Alden for the first time. He looked familiar to me, but I wasn't sure why. I also wasn't sure why Alden wasn't defending himself. It was like he'd totally given up.

Well, *I* sure hadn't.

"Whoa," Race said. "That old dude is Speaker 14. I think he's the most senior Speaker in the U.S. He's in charge of the whole shebang down here in our region. The IC must think this is a really big deal for him to be here."

The balding man at the old man's right stopped making notes and addressed Alden. "Have you anything to say before we render judgment?"

Alden leaned forward. "I'd like it to go in the record that I took what I thought was the best course of action to protect the life of my Speaker. I do not regret my decision and would do it again if presented with the same set of circumstances."

The old man furrowed his brow and studied Alden. Paul stepped forward from his post just inside the door. "I'm sorry to interrupt, but Speaker 102 is in the hallway demanding to address the Panel. She is extraordinarily agitated. I've never felt anything quite like it."

Alden buried his face in his hands.

The old man spoke for the first time—his voice was familiar too. "How interesting. Please ask her to wait. We will hear her in fifteen minutes."

Paul nodded and closed the door behind him.

Race and I jerked away from the monitor, but it was obvious we'd been eavesdropping. Paul stared at us and then at the monitor.

He cleared his throat. "I think it's best we wait upstairs," he said.

• • •

I fidgeted in a wicker love seat on the terrace of the hotel. Soft tones of jazz floated in from where a pianist and guitarist entertained guests in the entry foyer. I couldn't find any paper, so I tried to finger the guitar chords along with the musicians. Paul paced up and down the corridor, which was lined with French windows. Light slanted through the glass, illuminating the pattern in the carpet, which resembled Persian rug inlays. Race had tossed back a few drinks at the bar and was leaning against the wall opposite me.

The hotel felt haunted. Race had told me it was built in defiance of the Great Storm of 1900. When another storm passed over the island in 1915, a huge party was thrown in the Hotel Galvez. People danced while the wind and rain howled. The citizens of Galveston had won, but the island never recovered completely from the Great Storm. Many of the shipping businesses moved inland to the Port of Houston, but Galveston stood. The Hotel Galvez stood to prove it.

"Can you feel anything, Race?" I asked.

He sat next to me. "No. Your fear is blocking everything else out. The Speakers on the panel are really old and have practiced hiding their transmissions. Your rebirth, or whatever you'd call it, makes your signal pretty intense. You're like a live wire. Keep cool, Lenzi. The young guy's a Protector and you're pretty transparent. Fear won't get you anywhere. Fear is too basic to warrant merit. And, Lenzi, if I were you, I wouldn't let on there is anything different about you. The shit's hitting the fan, and your amnesia might not help."

"Miss, they will see you now." Paul gestured for me to come with him.

Race followed, but remained outside the door. I stopped in the doorway. Alden's eyes met mine. There was no emotion in them, just hollow grayness. He stood and placed his USB drive on the table.

"I defer to the Speaker," Alden said as he brushed by me.

The bald man stood. "Protector 438, you have not been dismissed."

Alden took his cell phone from Race as he passed him outside the door of the conference room.

"We need to stop him," the woman said.

The old man held up his hand. "No. Let him go. He won't go far. He's not running away from us. He's running from her."

All eyes turned to me.

THIRTY

"Please be seated, Speaker 102," the old man said, gesturing to the place at the foot of the table, catching my eyes as if he were looking for something. Where did I know him from?

I slipped into the chair, running Race's words through my head like a mantra. *Fear is too basic to warrant merit.* I stared at the heading on the sheet of paper on the table in front of me.

Discontinuance Hearing: Protector 436
Unlawful entrance of human vessel—

"What can we do for you today?" the balding man asked, before I could read further.

His casual question caused my anger to flare, trumping my fear. "You can let my Protector go."

"You, of all people, know that is impossible," the woman responded.

I gripped the edge of the table. "I know nothing of the kind."

The old man sat forward in his chair and clasped his hands together on the table. "What is she transmitting, Paul?"

"She's angry, sir," the Protector said.

The old man tilted his head. "Isn't that interesting. Why are you mad, 102?"

I leaned forward. "Why would I *not* be?"

The balding man spoke. "Speaker 102, we understand that you are troubled by this. You have been in a partnership with Protector 438 for many cycles. Being as experienced as you are, you understand the necessity for justice."

"Justice? This isn't justice. This is murder!" I stared at their astonished faces. Faces with no names. People with no hearts. Only the older man at the head of the table seemed unsurprised by my outburst.

I continued. "You can't just take an act out of context like that, any more than you can take a sentence out of context. It loses its meaning entirely, just like this bogus hearing has."

The old man smiled at me, which threw me off balance. "What is the context, 102?"

"I have a name. Do you?"

"Of course I do. We all do. This is Ophelia, and on my right is Robert. My name is Charles. My last name is MacAllen this cycle. I am the elder of this Panel. In fact, I am the director for the IC Coastal Region. Why don't you tell us *your* name now?" His smile broadened.

He knew. Somehow this man named Charles knew about my memory loss. From the confused looks on Ophelia and Robert's faces, it was clear they didn't.

"What is she transmitting now, Paul?" Charles asked.

Paul was standing just inside the closed conference room door. "Fear, sir."

"Help me," the disembodied voice of a woman called to me. *"Help me, please."*

"Not now. Go away," I said.

A male voice came from over my shoulder. *"You must help us."*

"Beat it, bogeyman!"

Charles laughed. It was an amused laugh. No malice. "You have always had such a strong pull for the Hindered. It is your emotion that draws them. You and I have rarely had a conversation that was not interrupted by them, have we?"

He had me, and I knew it. Fine. I had nothing to lose anyway. "I wouldn't know," I said. "I have no recollection of my past lives."

Charles leaned back in his seat. "So what is it exactly you would have us do, Lenzi?"

He knew my name. I wanted to scream.

A chorus of Hindered voices began calling out to me.

"There you are." The deep, gravelly voice behind me was familiar.

I jumped to my feet so fast my chair fell over. I spun around to find no one.

"We've gotta talk, babe."

Just when I thought it couldn't get worse.

"Zak." I slumped against the wood-paneled wall.

Charles turned his chair to face me. "Is this Hindered the boy from last night? Is this the same Zak?"

I nodded and slid down the wall to sit on the floor, heart shattering into a million pieces. Zak was a Hindered—he was dead. Just like Dad. Just like Alden was going to be. It was too much. I closed my eyes, wishing I could just evaporate into nothingness and make all this madness stop. My body convulsed with sobs, but no cries came out—only gasps. Zak was dead.

"Would you like one of us to resolve it? Your emotion will make you less efficient," Ophelia said.

Her words were like a cup of ice water thrown in my face, wrenching me from my grief-induced stupor. "Less effective?" I pushed to my feet. "Well, maybe a little less efficiency is preferable to unfeeling rigidity. Come on, Zak. I'll help you. What do you need me to do?"

Zak's voice came from directly in front of me as if we were having a normal conversation. He sounded confused and agitated. *I just . . . hell, I guess I just wanted to see you again . . . you know?*

The members of the panel studied me, and I realized that being Speakers, they could hear Zak too. I wasn't quite sure what to say.

Zak was dead.

My chest ached so bad it was hard to concentrate. *Focus, Lenzi. You owe him this.* "So, is that why you're here? Why you haven't moved on?"

"I don't know why I'm here. I just felt like I was supposed to find you. To let you know I wasn't mad anymore, I think. But I am. I'm pissed. Am I supposed to tell you I'm sorry? 'Cause I'm not going to. Is that why I'm here?"

I closed my eyes in an effort to not cry. "I've no idea, Zak. All I know is it's my job to help you find resolution. Tell me how to do that."

"Let us take over from here," Ophelia said. "He is borderline Malevolent."

"Not a chance." I clenched my jaw so hard it hurt. Adrenaline raged through me like flames. They thought I couldn't handle it—that I was incompetent. Well, I'd prove them wrong. They planned to kill Alden; there was no way I'd let them screw Zak over too. He wasn't a Malevolent, and my last act as Speaker would be to prove it and get him to heaven. *It's never too late,* Alden had said.

I grabbed my overturned chair and placed it upright. "Zak, please let me help you. If you feel compelled to apologize, maybe that will make it right and you can move on."

"Why should I apologize? You cheated on me. You never even gave me a chance. You chose that punk from the cemetery over me."

"Zak, calm down." Maybe his agitation was because he didn't know what was going on. I sat in the chair. "You know you're dead, right?"

"Of course I know I'm dead! I wrapped my car around a tree last night. I didn't even make it back home."

My heart pinched painfully. "Do you remember what happened right before you . . . before you wrecked the car?"

"Yeah, I was partying at a friend's apartment."

I folded the paper in front of me into quarters. "Was that before or after you came to my house?"

There was a beat before he answered. *"I didn't go by your house."*

"You did." Maybe that was it. Maybe he didn't know what had happened and that was holding him back.

"Stop screwing with my head, Lenzi."

"I'm not, Zak. I'm trying to help you." If only I had Alden's ability to transfer memories, but I didn't. "I wish I could show you what happened."

"You're lying, just like you lied about the guy at the cemetery. I never went to your house."

"You did, Zak."

"Bullshit," Zak yelled. *"This is some mind game you're playing with me. Why am I here?"*

"You are losing him." Ophelia again.

"I can handle it."

What was I supposed to do? Zak was getting angrier. Ophelia was right—I was losing him. I could resolve Zak; I was certain of it. I folded the quartered paper into quarters again, feeling the tension ebb through my fingers.

That was it! Folding paper soothed me. If I could get Zak calm, I could pull him away from this Malevolent edge.

"Why the hell am I here, Lenzi?"

I had to resolve Zak successfully so that Alden's death wasn't for nothing. I turned to Charles, who was watching my hands with interest as I pressed the creases tighter on the paper. "I need something," I said to him. "I need a guitar. There was a guy playing one in the foyer upstairs." He lifted a white eyebrow. "Could Paul get it for me? It's really important."

He looked at the glass bubble on the ceiling that no doubt contained the camera feeding to the monitor in the hall and nodded.

"Zak, I want you to enter the vessel so I can help you. Do you know what I'm talking about? You can put your soul in with mine."

"Yeah, I know what to do. I don't know how I know, but whatever."

I suppressed a scream when Zak entered. It hurt, maybe because he was so close to being a Malevolent. I felt his emotions, which hadn't happened with the other souls I had allowed in other than Smith.

I dug my nails into the arm of the chair as I experienced a wave of darkness coursing through me. It was awful. Poor Zak. "Why can I feel his emotions, Charles?"

Charles's voice was calm. "Because you knew him in real life."

Zak was confused and angry. Really angry. Maybe I was too late to help him. I remembered the Malevolent from Kemah and how he had dissolved into a black cloud, still cursing.

No. I wouldn't let that happen to Zak. I had to make this work.

Paul entered with a guitar. Zak's soul shifted slightly away from anger when I placed it in my lap.

"Will you stay please, Paul?" Charles asked. "Speaker 102 is soul-sharing and will need your assistance."

Paul nodded and stood near my chair.

I strummed a few chords. "Want to play, Zak?"

Yeah, why not?

I relaxed and allowed him to gain control of my body. He shifted the guitar on my lap and changed the angle of it. When he began to play, his soul lightened again. It was going to work; I just knew it. If I could get him to relax, maybe he would remember what happened and would understand his compulsion to apologize.

He transitioned from simple chords into the classical piece he'd played for my birthday. I'd given him complete control of my body, and I was amazed how quickly he could make my fingers move over the strings. My vision blurred from the tears filling my eyes. Zak's tears.

I loved you, babe, he said.

The song reached a crescendo and his tears streamed freely down my face.

I had to keep my emotions out of it. I had to stay focused. "Think, Zak," I said. "You left your friend's apartment and you came by my house. You saw Alden drop me off. You wanted to talk. Remember?"

He loosened my grip on the guitar and the tempo slowed.

"I was cold, so we talked in your car. When you saw Alden, you freaked out and took off with me in the car. You almost hit the bridge guardrail. Do you remember?"

He stopped playing. The silence in the room was stifling and dragged on forever.

Yeah, that guy told me to turn right and miss the bridge railing. Oh, God. I remember now. I . . . That guy made me stop and take you out of the car.

I didn't say anything. I felt his soul shift to absolute remorse as he remembered.

If that guy's voice hadn't gotten in my head, I'd have . . . Really, I mean . . . I almost killed you. If he hadn't made me stop and let you go, you'd have been in the car when I crashed. Oh, babe, I'm so sorry.

"It's okay, Zak. I wish things had happened differently." I looked straight at the three Speakers. "I wish lots of things had happened differently."

That guy. Where is that guy from the cemetery? I need to talk to him. I think that's it.

"He's not here, Zak." I handed the guitar off to Paul, who leaned it against the wall.

I felt Zak's emotions shift to something that felt like desperation. I knew he was struggling to hang on to what was good in his soul and not give in to darkness. How could I help him? Rose would have known, dammit! What was I supposed to do? I didn't even try to stop the tears running down my face.

I need to talk to that guy, Lenzi. That's definitely it. I owe him one.

Because Zak was in the vessel, the other Speakers in the room couldn't hear him. "You can't speak to Alden directly, Zak, but you can pay him back another way." I felt his emotions spike to hope. This was the best his soul had felt—the first time he hadn't felt like a Malevolent. If I were lucky, this would work on two levels: resolve Zak's issue that was keeping him Earth-bound and, even though it might be too late to save him, I could clear Alden's name. "You can come on out and tell the people in this room what you were going to say to him." I looked over my shoulder at Paul. "He's ready," I said.

Zak's emotions surged to what felt like joy right before Paul entered and Zak's soul ripped out of my body. I covered my face and held my breath as Paul exited.

"Now, babe?" Zak asked from somewhere behind me near the door.

"Yeah, now." I glared at the three Speakers. I knew they could hear him because they were looking in the direction of his voice. "Go ahead, Zak."

"Um, cool. Okay. Yeah, so it kinda hurts to stay here, and Lenzi thinks telling you what I want to say to that guy who jumped into my head last night will help." He was silent for a moment.

"Please proceed," Ophelia said.

"I guess I was going to tell him thanks. Tell him that he was right about something. He said that there was hope until the last second, and yeah, I think he nailed that. I'm a screwup. Always have been, but he kept me from messing up bad. Real bad. If he hadn't convinced me to get Lenzi out of the car, I'd have killed her too. He knew that." He was silent for a moment before he began to speak again. *So, uh . . . wow, I feel weird. Like I need to go somewhere. It feels good, babe.*

I wiped my eyes with a Kleenex Paul handed me. "I'm glad, Zak. You deserve to feel good." He was such a cool guy. One of the best guitarists I'd ever heard. And a great friend when I needed one most. A sob escaped my lips.

Zak appeared by the door in the familiar blue luminescence of a Hindered, dressed in his tattered jeans and Metallica T-shirt.

"Bye, Zak," I whispered.

"Take care, babe." He flashed me the dimpled grin I loved so much and gave me a thumbs-up as he was absorbed in a white shaft of light.

Gone.

I folded my arms on the table and put my head down. First Dad, now Zak, and any minute, I'd lose Alden too. The pain in my chest was intense—unbearable.

Alden's words ran through my head. *Pain lets you know you're alive.*

No, thanks. I couldn't hurt like this for lifetimes. Not without Alden. "So, how do I get out of this Speaker gig?" I asked, crossing my arms over my chest. "What witches' brew do I drink or what incantation do I chant to end this?" I pulled my hair aside, exposing my soul brand. "Do you just cut this thing out or is it removed with some hocus-pocus?"

Robert cleared his throat. "Really, 102. This is unnecessary. You've had centuries of success. Why would you let something like—"

Charles cut him off with the wave of his hand. "Don't try to talk her out of it, Robert. You're wasting your time. I know her well. I was her mentor for her first three cycles. I've never met anyone quite like her." He'd been my teacher? He turned his wrinkled face to me. "You changed over the cycles, Rose. . . . I beg your pardon, *Lenzi*. And it appears the gap in cycling renewed you and made you more like your original self."

My wish. He was one of the elders. *Is he the one Rose approached? Is that how he knew about my amnesia?*

He scanned a sheet in front of him. "Your points are high too. In fact, with the exorcism from yesterday and the resolution just now, you and Alden are in first place for the region in daily averages."

I made no effort to hide the anger in my voice. "I'm sure Alden was thrilled to hear that."

"He doesn't know yet."

Does that mean they'll tell him? Does that mean there's still a chance?

Charles folded his hands in his lap and waited. "Tell me what's happening, Paul."

"Um, it's hard to say," Paul replied.

Charles swiveled to face him. "Now, Paul. You cannot be effective if you can't discern the condition of the Speaker."

"Why don't you ask the Speaker yourself, Charles? Stop using me as a teaching tool and take me seriously," I said.

"I take you very seriously. We are about to lose a fine Protector, and now one of our best Speakers is requesting to be removed from service. It could not be more serious."

I turned to Paul. "What is my condition now, Paul?"

"Um, I . . ."

I rose from my chair and began pacing. "I'll tell you my condition. I'm outraged! 'There's hope until the last second.' That's on the inside cover of the IC Rule Book, isn't it? You can stick to your immovable zero-tolerance rules, but I'm going to stick to the motto 'There's hope until the last second'!" I paced behind the head of the table so that they had to turn to watch me. "Why are you here if all you're going to do is follow an absolute rule? No gray scale. No way out. Is this hearing being held just to make you feel better?

"Alden is going to be killed because he did his job. He protected the Speaker. Without a doubt, I would be dead if he hadn't made the decision he did. You're Speakers, so you heard Zak. If Alden hadn't put his soul in Zak's body, Zak's resolution would have been much different. Would you destroy a soul for the crime of saving two others?" I circled back to my end of the table. "I was on a dead-end track before Alden came into my life. Without his influence, I could have ended up just like my dad.

Alden is the kind of person who makes things happen, a catalyst for positive change. His destruction would be unconscionable and detrimental to the purpose of this Council."

I grasped the back of my chair and caught my breath.

Charles folded his hands on the table. "You may not remember being Rose, but she is definitely in this room, my dear." He gestured to Paul. "If you would wait outside with Lenzi for a moment, I would like to confer with my colleagues."

Paul opened the door for me. Race was right outside the door, trying a little too hard to look nonchalant.

"You were eavesdropping on a private Council session," Paul said after he closed the door.

Race shrugged. "Not a chance. That would be reckless and dangerous. As Protectors, you and I both know that's just not in our nature. Didn't they teach you that at Wilkingham?"

Race and Paul looked at each other before breaking into smiles.

"How'd you get stuck with this duty?" Race asked Paul.

"I'm Charles's current prodigy. It's an honor."

Race stepped closer to him. "What's going to happen?"

Paul shrugged. "It's hard to say. These things never turn out well for Protectors, but she had them going in there."

"I couldn't feel any of them except Lenzi. Her soul drowned them out," Race said.

We heard footsteps coming toward the door. "You'd better get scarce before they find out you were here, man," Paul warned him. Race made it up the stairs just before Robert opened the door to call me back.

I resumed my seat at the foot of the table.

Charles shuffled the papers in front of him and tapped a stray paper into place. "Speaker 102, you asked if we held hearings to make ourselves feel better. The answer is no. We hold them because sometimes a miracle happens. Sometimes we need to be reminded that there are circumstances under which rules should be broken. Sometimes we need to show the same compassion to each other that we show to the Hindered."

My heart was hammering so hard, I was certain everyone in the room could hear it.

I held my breath as Charles continued. "You have delivered a miracle today. You put Alden's breach into context for us. We have decided unanimously that Alden's choice was justified and his soul should *not* be discontinued."

I inhaled through my nose. My lungs ached as if I'd been underwater too long.

"He will be on probation, however," Charles continued. "The two of you will check in with us one month from today for reevaluation. We will not allow you to step out of your role as Speaker until that time. You and Alden must perform your job as usual until we meet again. It is our sincere hope that you will change your mind during this month and decide to remain a Speaker."

Charles nodded to the others, and they exited, leaving me

alone at the opposite end of the long, shiny table from him. Paul stuck his head inside the room. "Ophelia said you wanted to speak with me, sir?"

Charles folded the top paper from the stack in front of him in quarters and then over several more times. "Yes. I would like to converse with Speaker 102 privately for a few minutes." He deftly folded the corners on a diagonal. "Do you understand what I'm asking of you, Paul?"

Paul glanced up at the camera bubble. "Yes, sir. I'll take care of it." He strode from the room, closing the door behind him.

I watched in silence as Charles placed the pinwheel of paper in his palm and began to twist it. He smiled at me, then pulled on the exposed edges.

"You said you had been my mentor in my early cycles." I nodded to the paper he was working on with amazing speed. "Did you teach me origami too?"

His fingers never stopped moving, even when he looked at me to answer. "I did."

I clasped my hands in my lap, resisting the urge to work on my own partially finished paper in front of me.

"Have you put the pieces together yet?" he asked, rotating the paper in his palm as he worked his way around, shaping the paper.

"You're the elder Rose went to with her request."

He answered with a smile, then placed his completed paper rose on the reflective tabletop. "Even Council elders aren't permitted to tamper with the recycling of souls. Not even if it is for the best of reasons." He stood and walked to the door. "Do you understand?"

I stood. "I do."

"I think it best that you convey the outcome of the hearing to your Protector yourself." Charles winked and handed me Alden's USB drive before opening the door. "Be careful, Speaker 102. We don't take second chances lightly, and neither should you."

He nodded to Paul, who escorted me back to the lobby, where Race was wringing his hands and pacing.

When I gave him the news, he whooped so loud, hotel patrons stared. After kissing me and hugging me to the point I thought my ribs would break, he invited Paul to the bar in the hotel lobby for drinks.

I watched as Paul slid on a stool next to Race. Paul presented ID and the bartender gave him a beer. The fake ID didn't surprise me. Nothing about the IC would surprise me. These guys lived in a world that would seem unreal to anyone who wasn't inside it. A world of ghosts. A world where Heaven and Hell could be confirmed. A world that made a difference. *My* world.

Squinting, I stepped out of the lobby into the sunshine. I knew exactly where Alden would be. I ran down the drive of the Hotel Galvez, across Seawall Boulevard, and down the stairs that led to the Gulf.

This was the beach where the happy memory Alden had

shown me took place. For the first time ever, the sound of the ocean brought peace instead of dread.

I paused when I stepped off the concrete step into the sand. I inhaled the salty sea air and faced into the wind, letting it blow through my hair. Dad's death would always sting, but because of Alden, I understood it was beyond my control—just like Zak's death was beyond my control. Alden had enabled me to help Zak find that shaft of white light he deserved. I could only hope another Speaker had done that for my dad if he needed help.

I brushed away my tears and struck out through the sand. The sun was brilliant, and even though it had been cool for several days, the temperature was in the seventies. I loved this place, and I loved Alden, who was leaning against the seawall staring at the surf. I knew he could feel the joy my soul was transmitting.

When I met Alden that first time at my dad's grave, I was certain he was a figment of my imagination. Nothing could be more real than this.

He didn't look at me as I approached; he continued staring out at the waves. This was the first time I'd ever seen him without a shirt. My throat tightened when I noticed a small tattoo of an origami rose on his upper arm. A smile pulled at the corners of his beautiful mouth as I placed the USB drive on his discarded shirt and brushed his hair away from his face.

"Hey, Lenzi," he whispered, barely louder than the surf.

"Rose," I said as our lips met. "My name is Rose."